For my dear friend Mary Vacher.
Thank you so much for all your brilliant
professional support –
and all your loving care and kindness.

★★HETTY★★
FEATHER

Jacqueline Wilson

HETTY FEATHER

ILLUSTRATED BY
NICK SHARRATT

CORGI YEARLING

Hetty Feather was partly inspired by Jacqueline Wilson's role as the inaugural Thomas Coram Fellow of the Foundling Museum. To find out more about the Foundling Museum which tells the story of the Foundling Hospital, please visit **www.foundlingmuseum.org.uk**

CORGI YEARLING

UK | USA | Canada | Ireland | Australia
India | New Zealand | South Africa

Corgi Yearling is part of the Penguin Random House group of companies whose addresses can be found at global.penguinrandomhouse.com.

www.penguin.co.uk
www.puffin.co.uk
www.ladybird.co.uk

Penguin
Random House
UK

Doubleday edition published 2009
Corgi Yearling edition published 2010

022

Printed and bound in Great Britain by Clays Ltd, Elcograf S.p.A.

The authorized representative in the EEA is Penguin Random House Ireland, Morrison Chambers, 32 Nassau Street, Dublin D02 YH68

A CIP catalogue record for this book is available from the British Library

ISBN: 978-0-440-86835-4

All correspondence to:
Corgi Yearling
Penguin Random House Children's
One Embassy Gardens, 8 Viaduct Gardens
London SW11 7BW

1

My name is Hetty Feather. Don't mock. It's not my *real* name. I'm absolutely certain my mother would have picked a beautiful romantic name for me – though sadly I have not turned out beautiful or romantic.

I shall picture her:

'My little darling,' my mother whispered, wrapping me up tightly in a shawl. She held me close close close to her chest, as if she could never bear to let me go.

'My little . . .' Rosamund? Seraphina? Christobel? My eyes are my best feature, as blue as the summer sky. Did she perhaps call me Sapphire? Azure? Bluebell?

I like to think my baby hair had not yet sprouted from my little pink head. A bald baby can still just about be beautiful. An infant with hair as scarlet as sin is an abomination, spawn of the Devil. So says Matron Bottomly, and she pulls my hair hard. Once when I cheeked her really wondrously, calling her

1

Matron Stinking Bottomly, she pulled so fiercely, a whole hank of my hair came away in her hand. She would have been in trouble if anyone had spotted my poor bald patch, but she crammed my cap down hard and no one saw. Well, two hundred foundling girls witnessed her assault on me, but Matron Bottomly didn't give a fig about them.

It took an entire year for my hair to grow back properly, but it was worth it because from that day onwards we *all* referred to her as Matron Stinking Bottomly – though not out loud. No other girl is as bold as me. I have a nature as fiery as my wretched hair.

I do so *hope* I was bald when I was newly born in 1876. Suppose I came into the world with little red tufts. Oh dearie, what a shock for my poor mother. Maybe she was tempted to call me Carrot or Goldfish or Marmalade.

No, I am absolutely certain my mother would not mock me. She held me close, she rubbed her cheek over my flaming head, she gently wound a little lock around her finger. She loved my red hair because it was mine. She cut off one tiny tuft to plait with pins and keep within a locket. That way she kept a small part of me for ever.

She didn't *want* to give me away. She loved me with all her heart. I know I was a poor, puny little thing, hardly weighing so much as a twist of sugar.

I'm sure my mother nursed me night and day, trying her hardest to build me up and make me strong. If I close my eyes now and hunch up small, I can almost feel her arms around me, hear her humming a lullaby, smell her sweet perfume, clasp her white hand with my tiny fingers. I cannot focus properly, but if I try really hard I can see her pale face, the tears in her own blue eyes.

Everyone says you can't remember back to babyhood. I've asked the nurses and the teachers and they all say the same. Even Jem insisted this is true, and he is the wisest boy ever. However, I'm absolutely certain they are all wrong on this point. I *can* remember.

I remember the worst day ever, when my mother bathed me and dressed me in my napkin and my petticoats and a little white gown she had stitched herself. She wrapped me up in a crocheted shawl and then carried me outside. She took me on a long, long journey. I'm sure I remember the roar and whistle of a train. Then I think we took a cab because I cried at the strange bumping and the clack of the horses' hooves. She held me tighter, rocking me in her arms, crying too.

Then the bump-clack stopped and my mother stayed crouching inside, shaking, so that I shook too. The cabman shouted at her and she gave me one last desperate kiss.

'I will always love you,' she whispered right into my ear.

Then she clambered out of the cab, clutching me close. She said a few words to the cabman and then walked over to a tall gateway. She murmured to the gatekeeper, so softly that she had to repeat herself. Then the gate creaked open and we stepped inside. There must have been other mothers, other infants, because I heard wailing all around us.

My mother and I stood in front of a long polished table where a line of solemn men sat and asked questions. My mother answered, while I whimpered dolefully. Then we were led to a little room with a bright gaslight overhead. I blinked and tried to burrow into my mother's breast, but large cold hands snatched me away from her.

I was laid on my back on a hard table. My shawl was tugged away. My beautiful white dress was unbuttoned and taken from me. Both my petticoats were pulled over my head. They even removed my napkin so I was lying there stark naked. The hard hands turned my head from side to side, prodded my belly, moved my arms and legs about while I protested vigorously, screaming my head off.

Then the hands wrapped me in strange coarse clothing, not mine at all! They picked me up and carried me away. My arms and legs were too small and weak to punch and kick. All I could do was scream. I screamed and screamed for my mother, but she wasn't there any more. I was being carried down endless corridors in this vast building, away from my mother for ever.

I was bound so tightly within the scratchy woollen shawl that I couldn't move. I was laid on my back in an iron cot, still screaming. I cried for my mother, but she didn't come to rescue me. I cried for my own soft familiar clothes, but I stayed stuck in these harsh, worn garments reeking of carbolic. I cried for the comfort of my thumb, trapped inside the shawl. I cried for gentle arms and warm sweet milk.

'Now now, what a terrible noise! You're disturbing all the other babies. What are you crying for, hm?' said one of the nurses, picking me up.

What did she *think* I was crying for? I was only a few days old and I'd lost everything I loved. No wonder I howled. But she meant it kindly enough. She held me against her flat starched chest and patted my back as if my problem was just a little trapped wind.

'There, there, nearly time for your feed,' she said.

She put me down again and I cried harder. I only quietened for a few seconds when someone plucked me once more from my cot. I desperately hoped they were about to return me to my mother, but the hands that held me were coldly capable, not tender and stroking. A bottle was thrust into my mouth. My lips puckered and would not suck. It tasted wrong. It wasn't my mother. I choked and tried to spit it out.

'This one's a hopeless feeder – and she's tiny as it is. I don't know why they accepted her. She's not long for this world.'

'They'll have to christen her quick or she'll be off to Limbo-land,' said another. 'Let me try. I'll make her feed.'

I was passed over promptly and the bottle poked hard against my mouth. I kept my lips pressed together. She pinched my nose so I had to open my mouth to breathe. I yelled furiously at this mean trick.

'Temper, temper! Never mind Limbo-land, she's like a little imp from H-e-l-l,' she said, giving me a shake. 'Take the bottle like a good girl! You don't want to starve, do you?'

I did not care whether I lived or died if I could not be with my mother. I cried all day, until my throat was raw and I shook all over, but it was no use. She still didn't come.

There were other babies crying too, though not as loudly and insistently as me. I couldn't see them as I was stuck on my back, but I could hear them.

I heard their sucking and sighing after the hateful hands had lifted them from their cots.

'Won't you feed too, poor little lamb?' This was a gentler voice, with smaller, softer hands. She wasn't my mother but she cradled me almost as carefully. She didn't ram the choking bottle into my mouth straight away. She shook a few drops of milk onto her finger and stroked it against my lips. I opened my mouth and sucked.

'Ah, it's good, isn't it? Some more?'

She gave me more drops on her finger and I sucked it dry. She did this again and again. When I opened my mouth eagerly for more, she edged the bottle very cautiously against my lips. I could not resist sucking – and felt the sweet milk splashing down my sore throat. I still did not like the feel of the bottle, but I ached with hunger and thirst so I sucked and sucked.

'My, look at Winnie with 25629! She's got her sucking away a treat now.'

So the kind nurse was called Winnie. And 25629 seemed to be *my* name now. I was not old enough to understand numbers, but the long sound was harsh and I hated it. However, before long I was given yet another name. I was dressed in a gown so stiff with starch I was stretched out rigidly, scarcely able to draw breath. I was carried to a new place, vast and echoing, with strange windows that played patterns of red and blue on the stone floor. There was solemn talk and then a voice addressed me.

'I christen you Hetty Feather,' he said, and sprinkled icy water on my forehead.

I cried, trying to tell him that I didn't *wish* to be called Hetty Feather, that wasn't my real name at all, my real name was . . .

But I couldn't speak yet so I simply screamed, and someone tutted and scolded, whispering that I was a bad example to the other babies. I paused for breath and heard thin copycat wails. I took satisfaction in the fact that no one else could achieve anywhere near my volume, for all that I was so small.

I was carted back to the sleeping room in disgrace. Gentle Winnie was there and rocked me gently.

'Hello, little Hetty! No need to cry so. There now. I'll take the christening robe off and fix a bottle for you.'

I was soon soothed, though I hiccuped a little as I gulped my milk. Winnie laughed and hiccuped too, teasing me. I peered up at her, trying hard to focus. She had a round rosy face with fair hair escaping from her cap. She wasn't special like my mother – but perhaps Winnie could be a second mother to me now? I was too small even to smile, but I fixed my blue eyes on her. She looked back, doing all the smiling for both of us.

Other babies were wailing now, demanding attention, but Winnie still held me, whispering my new name. 'Little Hetty Feather! Well, you're light as a feather and no mistake.' She whirled round and round so that I whirled too. We danced in and out of all the iron cots. It felt as if I was flying. I willed Winnie to whirl us right out of the door, away from this chill, puzzling prison, but another nurse spoke to her sharply and she put me back in my little bed, both of us breathless.

I did not cry for my mother that night. I still thought of her longingly, but I consoled myself with the thought that I'd see Winnie in the morning – and every morning after that.

I couldn't have been more wrong. The next day new hands fed me, bathed me, and then dressed me in my uncomfortable clothes. The shawl was wound extra tightly and knotted at the ends, so that I resembled a small woollen parcel – and like a parcel, I was picked up, carried along corridors, taken outside the huge door and posted into a waiting cab.

I was stuffed into a large basket padded with rags. I lay there, too stunned even to scream. What was happening to me now? I wanted Winnie. I wanted my mother. My heart started beating so fast it nearly burst through my shawl. *Were they taking me back to my mother?*

The cab door opened again. I heard an infant wail, so sad, so scared. My mouth was shut so it couldn't be me. The cries grew frantic as another child was crammed into the basket beside me. I let out a little wail myself and the other crying stopped in surprise. Then it started up again and I started too. We drew breath at the same time so we were crying in unison. Then I stopped and the other babe stopped too. It was as if we were talking to each other.

Hello! I'm here too. I'm just as anxious as you are.

Where are they taking us?

I don't know. I want them to take me back to my mother.

I want mine too!

Well, at least we have each other.

Our hands were trapped in our woollen shawls, but it was as if we were reaching out and clasping each other.

The cab jerked and the horses' hooves clacked and I remembered my own mother so painfully. Then we stopped and the door opened, and my fellow basket baby and I blinked in the sudden light. Someone took us up out of the cab, swinging us along into a vast, roaring, smoky hall. This brought back memories too. I now know that we were at a vast London station. Soon we were stowed in our basket upon a seat and the train jerked into motion. The other baby and I cried lustily, but the steady chug and whir of the wheels beneath us grew soothing and soon we both slept.

I dreamed that I was back in my mother's arms, but when I woke I was still trussed up in the shawl and stuffed in the basket, and the baby next to me was wailing forlornly. I cried too because I was hungry and thirsty, my stomach empty and aching. The baby beside me set up a mournful descant.

When we lived in the huge bleak building we had always been fed every few hours and our napkins changed. I was now wet and sore, my shawl damp and reeking. So we cried and cried, and then slept some more out of sheer exhaustion – and then the train slowed and stopped. The door opened and we were swung out into the fresh air. Our carrier stamped his feet and marched forwards. There was a clamour of voices with a softer country burr. The basket rocked as hands reached in, lifting out my baby neighbour.

'This here is Master Gideon Smeed, fresh from the Foundling Hospital!'

I heard laughing and cooing and clapping. I was left in the basket by myself! I screamed – and more hands came back for me.

'No chance of forgetting this one. Miss Hetty Feather. I'm not sure you'll want her, missus. She might be little but she's a shocker for screaming. She's been squealing like a pig ever since we left London.'

'Oh well, it shows she's got spirit,' said a voice. 'Let's have a squint at her then.'

I was placed in strong arms, my face pressed against a very large soft chest. I snuffled against her. She smelled of strange new things, lard and cabbage and potatoes, but she also smelled of sweet milk. I opened my lips eagerly and I heard laughter all around.

'There! She's smiling at you, Mother! She's taken to you already!'

I was stunned. This was not my real mother. Was she a *new* mother? She held me in one arm, my basket baby brother in the other. Her large hands held us safe as she walked out of the station, children clamouring about her.

'I dare say you'll do a good job with them, missus. You bring on the scrawny ones something wonderful,' said the basket-carrier.

'It's a bit of challenge, two little ones together, but I dare say I'll manage,' she said. 'Let's take you home and get you fed, my poor little lambs,' she murmured in our ears.

We had a home. We had a mother. We were safe.

We never had to go back to the great chill baby hospital again.

Don't mock, I say! I was only a few weeks old. I didn't know any better.

2

My new home was a small thatched cottage with whitewashed walls, and roses and honeysuckle hanging around the front door. It was small and dark and crowded inside. It smelled of cooking all the time, plus strong yellow soap on a Monday, washday. That was *our* washday too. When the sheets and all our shirts and frocks and underwear were flapping on the line, our mother, Peg, popped all us children in the clothes tub. Gideon and I were tossed in first. Gideon always cried, but I bobbed up and down like a duckling and only wailed if Mother rubbed soap in my eyes.

Gideon was my foundling brother, my baby travelling companion in the basket. He was not much bigger than me, a pale, spindly baby with a thatch of black hair and large eyes that fixed you with a mournful stare.

'There's not enough meat on these two together to bake into a pie,' said our new father, John.

He poked both of us in our belly buttons. It was

15

a playful poke but we both shrieked. We weren't used to big, loud father people. All men were big and loud to us babies, but when we were older we saw that John was the tallest man in the village, with arms like tree trunks and a belly like a barrel. His voice was so loud his holler could carry clear across five acres. He was as strong as the huge shire horses he used to plough the land. No man dared argue with him because it was clear who would win – but Peg wasn't the slightest bit frightened of him.

'Get away from my new babies, you great fat lummox,' she said, slapping his hands away. 'You're scaring them silly. Don't cry, my lambkins, this is just your father, he don't mean you no harm.'

'Chickee-chickee-chickee, coochie-coochie-coochie,' said Father, tickling under our chins with his big blunt fingers. We screamed as if he was a storybook ogre about to snap our heads off our necks.

'Get out of it,' said Peg, flapping at him with a towel. She gathered Gideon and me up out of our improvised bathtub and wrapped us together in the towel, warm from the hearthside. She held us close against the vast pillow of her bosom and we stopped crying and snuffled close to our new mother.

'*My* muvver!' said Saul, swotting at us with his hard little fists.

He was just starting to walk, though he had a withered leg so that he limped. Father had fashioned him a little wooden crutch. Saul used it to prod Gideon and me. He hated us because he wanted Mother all to himself.

'There now, my little hoppy sparrow. You come and have a cuddle too,' said Peg, hauling him up into her arms alongside us.

'And me, and me!' said three-year-old Martha, burrowing in. Her eyes were weak, and one of them squinted sideways.

Jem held back, his chin held high.

'Don't you want to come and join in the cuddle, Jem dearie?' said Mother.

'Yes, but I'm not one of the babies,' said Jem stoutly. 'I'm five. Nearly.'

'Yes, my pet, you're my big boy – but you're not too big to say no to a cuddle with your old mum. Come here and meet your new brother and sister.'

I was wriggling and squirming, squashed by Saul.

'Here, Jem, you take little Hetty for me,' said Peg. 'Ain't she tiny? You were twice her size as a baby. She's had a bad start in life – both the babies have, bless them. Still, we'll soon fatten them up, just you wait and see.'

I nestled in Jem's arms. He might still be a little boy not yet five but he seemed as strong as our father to me – but nowhere near as frightening. Jem's hands cupped me gently.

'Hello, little Hetty. I'm your brother Jem,' he said softly, rubbing his face against mine.

I couldn't speak but my lips puckered and I gave him my first real smile.

Jem wasn't the eldest. He was the youngest child who really belonged to Peg and John. They also had Rosie and Nat and Eliza, and there were more still – Marcus, who'd gone off to be a soldier, and Bess and Nora, who were away in service.

All these children – so many that your head must be reeling trying to keep count of them all! *I* find it hard enough to sort them all out in my head. The older ones kept themselves separate from us younger fostered foundlings, though Eliza sometimes liked to play schools with us.

She lined us all up in a row by the front step and asked us to add two and two and recite the alphabet. At first Gideon and I couldn't even sit up by ourselves, so we clearly had no chance of coming top in Eliza's school. She lisped our answers for us, and answered for Saul and Martha too. She didn't have to invent replies for Jem. He knew simple sums and could read out of *The Good Child's ABC*.

'A is for Apple. B is for Bear. C is for Chair. D is for Daisy. E is for Elephant.'

I could chant my own way through by the time I was two. Eliza fancied herself a teacher and sat us in the corner if she felt we were stupid and caned us with a twig if we protested.

Jem was the true teacher. He showed me how to eat up my porridge and my mash-and-gravy and my tea-time slices of bread and jam. 'That's right, you're a baby bird. Open your beak,' he said.

I opened my mouth wide and then smacked my lips together, swallowing every morsel, though I was a picky eater and fussed and turned my head away when Mother tried to feed me.

We didn't have any toys. Mother would have thought them a waste of money. She didn't *have* any money anyway. However, Jem found a red rubber ball in a rubbish heap. He washed it well and polished it so it shone like an apple. He flung it high into the air and caught it nine times out of ten, and then kicked it from one end of the village to the other.

'Me, me, me!' I said, on my feet now, but still so little that I toppled over when I tried to kick too.

The others laughed at me, especially Saul, but Jem held me under my arms and aimed me at the ball until one of my flailing feet connected and gave it a feeble little kick.

'There, Hetty, you can kick the ball, just like me!' he said, hugging me.

He sat beside me on the front step and drew me pictures in the dust with his finger. His men and women were round blobs with stick arms and legs, his babies were little lozenges, his animals barely distinguishable one from the other, but I saw them through Jem's eyes and clapped and crowed delightedly.

He helped me toddle down the road to the stream and then held me tight while I splashed and squealed in the cold water. If I kept my legs still while he dangled me, the minnows would come and tickle my toes.

'Fishy fishy!' I'd shriek.

Sometimes Jem turned his hand into a fish and made it swim along beside me and nibble titbits while I laughed.

When I grew bigger, he pushed me in a little cart all the way to the woods and showed me red squirrels darting up the tree trunks.

'That's where they've got their houses, right up in the trees,' said Jem. 'Shall *we* have a squirrel house, Hetty?'

He knew an old oak that was completely hollow inside. He stood on one of the great spreading roots, lifted me up, deposited me inside the tree and squeezed in after me. There! We were in our very own squirrel house. We were only a foot or so from the ground but it felt as if we were right up in the treetops.

'There, little Miss Squirrel. Are you happy in your new house?' Jem asked, poking me gently on my button nose.

'Yes, Mr Squirrel, yes yes yes!' I said happily.

I loved our little treehouse so much I didn't want to go home for tea. I shook my head and protested, clinging to the bark with my fingertips. Jem had to carry me home kicking and screaming. I wouldn't be quiet until he promised we'd play there the very next day.

I went leaping onto the boys' bed at five o'clock in the morning, before Father and Mother were stirring, demanding that Jem keep his promise.

He stayed true to his word, even though I was behaving like an almighty pest. He carted me back to our house in the woods straight after breakfast. He patiently ate another pretend breakfast of acorns and grass, and he helped me care for my squirrel babies (lumps of mud wrapped in dock leaves). He even lined the floor of our house with moss and sprinkled it with wild flowers to make a pattern on our green carpet.

I stupidly babbled about our wondrous squirrel house that bedtime, and of course all the other children wanted to come and see it too, even

Rosie and Eliza. Nat sneered at Jem for playing a girly game of house with a baby, but Jem was unruffled.

'I *like* playing with Hetty, it's fun,' he said, and my heart thumped with love for him.

I wanted to keep the squirrel house just for us, but Jem was far too good-natured. 'Of course you can all come a-visiting,' he told everyone. But then he added, 'But you must remember, it's *Hetty's* house.'

I didn't mind Gideon coming. He was my special little basket brother and I loved him second best to Jem. I was a few days older than Gideon but he was a half a head taller than me now, though still ultra-spindly, his neck and wrists and ankles so thin they looked in danger of snapping. Mother took it to heart that he looked so frail and sneaked him extra strips of bacon and a bite of Father's chop, but the ribs still stuck out on his chest and his shoulder blades seemed about to slice straight through his skin.

Mother tried to encourage him to run about and play in the sunshine with us, but he preferred to cling to her skirts and climb on her lap whenever she sat down to shell peas or darn stockings.

I could sometimes tempt Gideon away to play, though he was incredibly tiresome when it came to my special picturing games.

'Listen, Gideon. Let's picture we're in the woods. We're lost and a huge huge huge howling wolf is going to eat us all up,' I'd say.

Gideon would start and tremble, and when I growled he ran screaming for Mother. She'd scoop him up in her arms and aim a swipe at me.

'Stop scaring the poor little mite senseless, Hetty. I'll paddle you with my ladle if you don't watch out.'

I'd been well and truly paddled several times and I didn't enjoy the experience. I didn't mean Gideon any *harm*. It wasn't *my* fault he was such a little milksop. But I smiled at him even so, and said he could come and visit my squirrel house. I let him squeeze into the cart with me while poor Jem puffed along pushing the two of us.

Gideon squirmed uneasily as I chatted about my house. 'Squirrels might bite,' he said fearfully.

'Oh, Gideon, *squirrels* don't bite! We'll bite *them*,' I said, giggling.

'Can't climb up the tree, Hetty,' Gideon wailed.

'It's easy, Gideon. I can climb. Jem can too,' I said.

'I might fall!' said Gideon, nearly in tears.

'Don't cry, Gideon. You won't fall. Just think, you're getting to see my squirrel house and Saul *isn't*.'

'Saul can come too,' said Jem quickly. 'And Martha.'

'No they can't – too much of a squash,' I said, wishing Jem wasn't always so kind. I just wanted him to be kind to *me*.

It was a waste of our kindness inviting Gideon. To help him appreciate the charm of the squirrel house I made us 'climb' in the air for several seconds before we hopped up into the hole in the tree. This was fatal. He clung to me desperately.

'*Whee* – we're right up in the treetops! See the birds flying!' I said.

'Have to get down! It's too high, too high!' Gideon said, peering down fearfully, though if he reached right out he could put his hand on the ground.

'It's not *really* high, Gideon, look,' said Jem, dangling his leg down.

'Hetty makes it high!' said Gideon.

Jem laughed. 'That's what she's best at, picturing. She's grand at it.'

'I wish she wasn't,' said Gideon, and he closed his eyes tight, as if he could shut out my picturing that way.

Gideon stayed in the cottage with Mother when Jem made me take Saul and Martha to the squirrel house. That was a waste of time too. I didn't mind Martha, but she was so near-sighted she had no idea what a squirrel *was*. She sat in the tree and blinked solemnly, waiting for something to happen. I served her tea in an acorn cup and gave her a slice of fairy bread on a leaf, and she tried to eat and drink politely, but she looked puzzled when there was nothing in her mouth. She started to eat the leaf itself and Jem had to prise it out quickly lest she was sick.

I'd have happily stuffed a whole *tree* of leaves down Saul's throat.

'This is a stupid place. It's not a *real* squirrel house. That's not a fine green rug, that's moss. That's not china, it's leaves. They're not babies. They look like pig poo. *Dirty* Hetty, playing with pig poo.'

I pushed him hard in the chest, because no mother can stand to have her babies insulted. I pushed a little too hard. Jem tried to catch him but he wasn't quite quick enough. Saul fell right out of my squirrel house. It truly wasn't far, and any other child would have jumped up again and laughed – but not Saul.

His eyes slid into slits and his mouth went square. 'You've hurt my poorly leg!' he bawled. 'I'm telling Mother!'

Oh dear. Gideon was clearly Mother's favourite, but she had a particular soft spot for Saul, Lord knows why. She fussed over his leg, rubbing it with different remedies – goose grease and witch hazel – and knitted him a special soft pair of stockings because his boot rubbed his twisted foot. Saul enjoyed this attention and exaggerated his limp in front of Mother for all he was worth.

She was outraged when Saul told tales on me. 'You pushed our Saul out of a *tree*, Hetty?' she said, horrified. She reached for her paddling ladle and I ran to hide behind Jem.

'It wasn't high up in the tree, Mother, and she didn't *mean* to,' said Jem, doing his best to defend me.

Oh, I did so love Jem. But it was no use: I was well and truly paddled, and Mother forbade all of us to play in the squirrel house.

Gideon looked mightily relieved, Martha was indifferent, Jem was clearly sad for me – but I was so aggravated I stamped and shouted and screamed at Mother. You can guess the result. I got paddled all over again, and sent to bed without any supper.

Mother came and sat beside me as I snuffled in the dark. 'Now, Hetty, are you sorry for being such a bad girl?'

'No, I am not sorry. *You* should be sorry for being a bad mother,' I mumbled beneath my blanket.

Mother had sharper ears than I'd reckoned. '*What* did you say, Hetty?' she said.

Oh no, was I about to get *another* paddling? My bed started shaking. Mother was making odd gasping sounds. Had I shocked her so much she was having a fit, like Ruben in the village after drinking too much ale?

I peeped above the blanket in terror. Mother was sitting on the edge of the bed, her hands over her mouth, splitting her sides with laughter. Oh, the relief!

'Don't you grin at me, girl!' she spluttered. 'I've never known such an imp as you. What am I going to do with you?'

'Paddle me and paddle me, even when I'm a big girl like Rosie,' I said, laughing too.

But Mother suddenly stopped. She put her arms round me and hugged me tight. 'Oh, I'm going to miss you so, little Hetty, even though you're such a bad, bad girl.'

I am absolutely certain that is what she whispered into my red hair. I didn't understand. I thought she meant when I had to attend the village school like Jem. I didn't dream I was only a temporary member of Mother's family.

Martha

3

I found it sorely trying when the blissful summer holidays ended and Jem had to spend all day long at his lessons. I didn't miss Rosie and Nat and Eliza one jot, but I missed Jem horrendously. I was left at home with Martha, who was no fun, and Saul, who was a sneaking toad, and Gideon, who was a milksop. They wouldn't play lovely games with me like my dear Jem. Mother didn't want us under her feet in the cottage, but neither did she want us toddling down the village lane and into the woods without Jem to keep an eye on us, so we were confined to the front step and our little patch of garden.

If I suggested spitting in the earth and making mud pies or drawing in the dust with a stick, then Martha would hang her head dejectedly because she couldn't see well enough. If I organized a game of Chase and held Martha's hand, she could run as fast as me – but then Saul would whine, because he always came last with his limpy leg. If I tried a picturing game and pretended a tall oak was a warty ogre and the grunting pig in the back yard a mythical monster, Gideon would play on gamely, but he'd wake screaming in the night. He'd refuse point blank when told to feed the pig our potato parings, and whimper to be held whenever Mother took us for a walk past the oak tree.

I'd hold my breath when Mother comforted then questioned him. Gideon did not wish to tell tales on me and get me into trouble. He would press his lips together when she asked what was ailing him – but Saul *delighted* in getting me into trouble and told all sorts of stories to Mother about me, and then of course I'd get paddled.

Sometimes I decided it was *worth* being paddled to plague sly Saul. I'd see him lick the jam from Martha's bread or drop a spider in Gideon's special mug of milk. I didn't tell stories on him – where was the fun in that? – but I'd creep up on him unawares and punish him. Once I spotted him leaning right over the gate to poke the poor pig with his wooden crutch, laughing when she squealed. I darted forward and gave him a shove. Oh, how *he* squealed when he fell face down in the pigsty. It was so soft with smelly mud he didn't hurt his poorly leg or his other leg either. He just hurt his dignity, lying there bawling, covered in potato peelings and pig poo.

I laughed and laughed and laughed. I even laughed while I was being paddled.

Jem laughed too when I told him, but he said I must take care not to be so bad when I went to school.

'Teacher has a big cane, Hetty, and she swishes it all day,' he said. 'She hurts much more than Mother.'

'She swishes *you*, Jem?'

'She swished my friend Janet for chalking her *b*s and *d*s the wrong way round, and when I said it wasn't fair, Janet had tried and tried to learn, she's just not very quick, Teacher swished me too and told me not to answer back.'

'I don't like Teacher,' I said.

I knew my *b*s from my *d*s already because Jem had taught me. But then I thought of Martha.

'Martha can't write any of her letters,' I said. 'Will Teacher swish *her*?'

'I won't let her,' said Jem stoutly.

But Martha didn't go to the village school when she was five. Mother boiled up a tub of water one evening and gave Martha her own special scrub, even though she'd had a washday bath on Monday. Mother gave her a special creamy mug of milk for her supper and held her on her lap while she drank it.

Father gave Martha a ride on his knees. '*This is the way the ladies ride*,' he sang, jiggling her up and down while she giggled.

Saul whined that it wasn't fair, *he* wanted a ride. Gideon said nothing, but he sucked his thumb and stared while Martha drank *his* milk. For once I didn't complain. I was too little to understand, but I saw the tears in Mother's eyes, heard the crack in Father's voice as he sang. I knew something was wrong – though Martha herself stayed blissfully unaware.

She went to sleep that night as soon as her head hit the pillow. I stayed awake, cuddling up to her, winding a lock of her brown hair round and round my finger as if I was binding us together.

Mother came and woke us very early.

'Is it time to get up?' I asked sleepily.

'Not for you, Hetty,' said Mother. 'Go back to sleep.'

It was still so dark I couldn't see her, but I could tell that she'd been crying again. She gently coaxed Martha up and led her out of the room. I turned over into Martha's warm patch and breathed in her faint bread-and-butter smell, wondering why Mother had woken her so early. I decided I should creep out of bed and go and see, but it still seemed like the middle of the night and I was so tired . . .

When I woke up again, the sun was shining through the window. I ran downstairs, calling out for Martha. She wasn't there. Mother wasn't there either. Rosie and Eliza were brewing the tea and stirring porridge.

'Where's Mother? Where's Martha?'

'They've had to go out,' said Rosie. 'Come and sit down like a good girl, Hetty.'

I didn't want to be a good girl. I wanted Mother and Martha. My heart was beating hard inside my chest. I was very frightened, though I didn't quite know why. I started screaming and couldn't stop, not even when Eliza bribed me with a dab of butter and sugar, not even when Rosie slapped my kicking legs. Jem eventually quietened me, lugging me up onto his lap and rocking me like a newborn baby, but he seemed almost as anxious as I was.

Rosie and Nat and Eliza knew something we didn't. They nudged each other and wouldn't look us in the eye over our breakfast. Jem questioned them persistently, I cried, Saul snivelled, and Gideon didn't get out to the privy in time and wet all down his legs. We couldn't manage without Mother. She was always there, as much a part of the cottage as the roof and the four walls. We were lost without her. And why had she taken Martha with her?

'You know where Mother's taken her,' said Jem, standing on the bench so he was eye to eye with Rosie. 'Tell us!'

'Stop pestering me, Jem. I've got more than enough to do without you and the babies fuss fuss fussing. Hetty, if you start that screaming again, I'll paddle you with Mother's ladle.'

'Don't you dare paddle Hetty,' said Jem. 'She's not being bad, she's just fearful. She wants Mother.'

'Well, Mother will be back presently,' said Rosie evasively.

'Why did she go off without saying goodbye? Why did she take Martha with her?'

'Poor little Martha,' said Rosie, suddenly softening. Her lip puckered as if she was about to cry.

'Is Martha poorly?' Jem persisted, but Rosie wouldn't answer.

When Gideon had been poorly with the croup last winter, Mother had called in the doctor. He had looked grave and said Gideon might have to be sent to hospital.

'Is Martha so poorly she's had to go to *hospital*?' Jem asked.

He lowered his voice when he said the word. We'd heard the villagers talking. Hospitals were terrifying places where doctors cut you open and took out all your insides.

'She's had to go to the hospital, that's right,' said Rosie.

Nat sniggered, though even he looked troubled, his eyes watering as if he was near tears.

Perhaps Martha was very ill, about to die?

But this was all such nonsense. I had cuddled up to Martha all night long and she hadn't been poorly at all.

I clung to Jem and he rocked me again. He didn't go to school that day. He told Rosie he was staying home to look after us little ones. Rosie tried to make him go but she sounded half-hearted. She was glad enough to have him in charge while she scrubbed the cottage and set the cooking pot bubbling on the hearth.

Jem played patiently with Saul and Gideon and me. When the two little boys had a nap after their soup, Jem took me to the forbidden squirrel house, trying his best to distract me. I was deeply touched but it didn't work. No matter how hard I tried to picture, it stayed a grubby hole in a tree. My mind was too full picturing Mother and Martha.

Rosie had once won a Sunday school prize, a book called *Little Elsa's Last Good Deed*. It was a pretty book, bright blue with gold lettering, and I'd begged Jem to read it to me. He'd stumbled through the first few pages until we both got tired. It was a dull story and Little Elsa was tiresomely *good*. She didn't seem real at all. I leafed through the whole book, looking for pictures, but they weren't exciting like the Elephant and the Mandarin and the Pirate and the Zebra, my favourite pictures in *The Good Child's ABC*. I only liked the last picture, with Little Elsa lying in bed looking very pale and poorly, and an angel with curly hair and a shiny hat flying straight through the window to carry her up to Heaven.

But now I kept picturing Martha as the ailing child in some grim hospital, a doctor sawing at her stomach, an angel at one end, intent on stealing her away up to Heaven, and Mother down the other end, hanging onto Martha's ankles.

I sobbed this scenario to Jem and he did his best to reassure me.

'Mother and Martha will come home safe and sound, you'll see,' he said. 'In fact I reckon they're home already, and when Mother finds I've stayed off school she'll be right angry with me. And if you pipe up we've been to the squirrel house, we'll both get a paddling.'

We trailed back home. When we ran into the kitchen, there was Mother at the table, still stiff in her Sunday best, bolt upright because she was wearing her stays, though her head was bent. Martha was nowhere to be seen.

'Where's Martha, Mother?' Jem asked.

'Martha?' I echoed.

'Martha's . . . gone,' Mother said.

'The angels got her!' I said, starting to cry again.

'What? No, no, she's not dead, Hetty,' said Mother.

She took a deep breath. 'Where are the others, Saul and Gideon? Having a nap? Go and get them, Jem. I might as well tell all of you together. But Jem, wait – what are you doing at home, young man? Rosie, why didn't you make him go to school? Oh, never mind, make me a cup of tea, I'm parched.'

We gathered around Mother, staring at her. I nudged up close to Jem. Gideon clasped my hand tight. Saul started snivelling.

'There now, you needn't look so tragic,' said Mother, sipping her tea. 'Martha's very well. She's just not going to live with us any more.'

We stared at her, baffled.

'Where *is* she going to live, Mother?' Jem asked.

'She's gone back to the Foundling Hospital, dearie,' said Mother. 'You were too little to remember when she came to the family.'

'The hospital! They'll cut her into bits!' I wailed.

'No, Hetty. It's not that sort of hospital, my lamb. It's a . . . lovely big home for lots of children who don't have mothers,' said Mother.

'I remember you telling us about the hospital,' said Jem. 'That's how we got Martha, then Saul, and now Gideon and Hetty.' He put his arms round me, hugging me tightly. 'But why did Martha have to go back there? You're her mother now.'

Mother's face crumpled. 'I know, my dear. But

I was only her foster mother. I was simply looking after Martha until she was a big enough girl to go back to the Foundling Hospital.'

'So when will she come home to us?' Jem asked.

'The Foundling Hospital is her home now, my dear.'

'But Martha won't be able to manage without us! She can't see properly, and she's a little slow. She needs us to help her!' Jem cried.

'She will find some other good kind big child to help her,' said Mother. 'Now do stop your questioning, Jem. You're upsetting the little ones.'

She entreated him with her eyes, while Saul and Gideon and I sniffled by her side. We were too little and stupid and stunned to work out the obvious just yet.

4

We all mourned Martha – but within a few weeks we had almost forgotten her. I sometimes dreamed about her and reached out in my sleep for her hand or her hair, and then felt a pang. But Martha's place was soon taken by another little girl, a baby called Eliza.

'That's *my* name!' said our Eliza. 'Oh, let me hold her. She's such a little darling.'

Eliza and Mother fussed excessively over the baby. I thought her a plain, puny little thing, with a mewling wail that was most aggravating.

'Oh, Hetty, you should have heard yourself when you were a baby! You shrieked like a banshee,' said Jem, chuckling.

I was so relieved to see that Jem showed only a mild interest in my new little sister. He was fonder than ever of me, taking me everywhere with him. Father wanted Jem to help out on the farm when he wasn't at school, so Jem took me along too.

41

I helped with the harvest, I dug for potatoes, I milked the cows.

I thought at first that they were *our* crops, *our* cattle, and all the land was *ours*. It certainly felt that way, for all the other men treated our big father with respect. Some of the young lads even doffed their caps to him. But when Jem took me to the harvest supper in the barn beside the big farmhouse, I saw our father doff *his* cap to Farmer Woodrow.

His wife, Mrs Woodrow, was pouring cider and serving great plates of meat to everyone. She laughingly gave Jem half a tankard and said, 'Only give your sister a sip, young Jem.'

She was peering at me curiously. I stared back at her, and she laughed and pulled one of my red plaits. 'She looks a fiery one!' she said. 'So she's one of your mother's foundling children?'

Jem pulled me onto his lap protectively. 'Yes, ma'am. This is our Hetty.'

'Well, it looks as if your mother's doing a good job with her. How much does she get paid for looking after her?'

I craned round. Jem was red in the face.

'I don't rightly know, ma'am,' he said. 'But our Hetty's worth her weight in gold.'

'What did that lady say?' I asked when Mrs

Woodrow had passed along the bench to patronize another village child.

'Oh, take no notice,' said Jem, which of course made me notice more.

'Does Mother get paid for looking after us?' I asked.

'I'm big, not little like you. I don't *need* looking after,' said Jem, not really answering my question.

That Christmas Mother made me a doll – a rag baby with a sacking dress and a scrap of white muslin for a bonnet. She had little button eyes and a mouth that smiled. I thought her the most beautiful doll in the world and cradled her in my arms all the time, even while I ate my roast chicken. Gideon looked longingly at my soft, pretty rag baby, and begged to hold her just for a moment. Mine was the *only* doll. The new baby, Eliza, was too little for dolls, and big Eliza and Rosie great girls long past the doll stage.

Gideon's own present was a little horse carved out of wood by Father. It was an excellent horse with its own brown leather saddle. Saul had a horse with a saddle too, and made it gallop across the floor. Jem and Nat got pocket knives, and Rosie and Eliza bead necklaces, one blue and one green.

Marcus and Bess and Nora, the grown-up children, were not given leave to come home, but

Mother had sent them parcels. She said she'd sent another parcel too, a twin rag baby to mine, specially for Martha.

'Will Martha have a lovely Christmas day like us?' I asked.

'Oh yes, Hetty, she'll have a wonderful time with all her new sisters. I dare say they'll all get lots of presents and fancy food and they'll play games and have such larks,' said Mother. 'Don't you worry your little head about Martha, Hetty.'

I did still worry. Mother did too. When I trailed downstairs that night to trek out to the privy (I'd had two helpings of figgy pudding and had bad stomach ache), I found Mother weeping in a corner, holding Martha's old checked pinafore, clutching it to her chest as if it was her own rag baby.

Mother took me out to the privy and held my hand while I groaned – and then, when I was better, she carried me back indoors. It was chilly downstairs without a fire, but Mother wrapped me up tight in Father's huge smock and cradled me in her arms.

'There now, my lambkin,' she said. 'I have you safe. Don't fret.'

Her voice was hoarse and I felt a tear drop on my face. I wrenched a hand free from my tight wrappings and reached up and stroked her damp cheek.

'There now, Mother,' I said. 'Don't *you* fret.'

She laughed at that, but she was still crying too. She murmured something. I didn't quite catch what she said, but now I am absolutely certain it was: 'I shall miss you so, Hetty Feather.'

The enormity of what was to happen to me didn't dawn until late spring, when Saul went. For days Mother had been favouring him, pretending not to see when he poked me with his crutch, when he tripped Gideon, when he pinched Eliza in her cradle. Mother rubbed his poorly leg and encouraged him to stand up straight when he walked.

'That's it, my little man. Step out like a soldier – left, right, left, right.'

'Yes, I'm a soldier, like my brother Nat. I'm a soldier and I shoot people with my gun,' said Saul, aiming his crutch at me. 'Bang bang, you're dead, Hetty!'

He banged so enthusiastically he struck me sorely in the chest.

'No, *you're* dead, Saul,' I said, seizing the broomstick. 'I'm a soldier and I'm on my horse, gallopy gallopy, and I'm going to whack whack whack you!'

'Hetty, Hetty, stop that now! Stop plaguing us! I need a little time with your brother,' said Mother, pushing me away.

I flounced off in a temper. Jem was at school so I played with Gideon instead.

'We'll play whacking, Gideon,' I said.

'No! Don't want to!' Gideon whimpered.

'I'm not going to whack *you*, Gid. We'll whack Saul. Whack whack whack.'

'Not really?' said Gideon, looking horrified.

'Yes, really. We'll whack him and bash him and stamp on him,' I said.

'We'll hurt him!' said Gideon.

'He hurts us,' I said, pulling up my dress and examining the angry red mark where Saul had prodded me with his crutch.

'We must turn the other cheek.' Gideon was parroting the Bible in a sickening fashion. He always listened hard at Sunday school and absorbed the moral lesson. I listened when there were tales of lions and whales and animals walking two by two into a great ark, but I didn't pay attention otherwise.

I didn't feel like turning my other cheek to Saul, especially when Jem came home from school and *he* started making a fuss of Saul too. He gave him a piggyback ride all around the house and then let him play soldiers, taking pains to fall down dead every time Saul potted a shot at him.

When I tried to join in too, Saul screamed, 'No no no, this is *boys'* play, Hetty,' and Jem didn't dispute this.

46

I stomped off and murmured darkly to my rag baby, hating them all, even my Jem. I especially hated Saul. When Mother bade us kiss goodnight, I sucked my lips in tight and wouldn't kiss Saul. I did not relent, even when Mother shook me.

'You will be sorry, Hetty,' she said ominously.

'No I won't,' I said, but it came out 'Mm mi mn't' because my mouth was still shut into a slit.

'Please, Hetty, there's a dear,' Jem whispered into my ear, but I took no notice.

Saul didn't care in the slightest. He laughed at me triumphantly, eyes bright, cheeks scarlet with excitement, the centre of everyone's attention. He didn't have any idea what was going to happen either, not till Mother woke him at dawn.

I heard him getting cross, then crying . . . then screaming. I sat up, my heart thudding. I ran to him. Mother had him half dressed in his best Sunday clothes, but he was kicking hard with his good leg and pummelling with his arms. All the while he screamed, 'No, Mother, no, I won't, I won't, I *won't* go.'

Rosie and big Eliza were trying to help Mother get him dressed, while baby Eliza wailed miserably in her cradle.

'What are you doing? Why are you dressing Saul in his Sundays?' I asked.

'For pity's sake, Hetty, I can't be doing with your

47

questions, not now,' Mother gasped. 'Oh, Saul, my sweetheart, try to be a big brave boy.'

But Saul scrunched himself up small and sobbed. I stared at him. Suddenly I didn't care about all his proddings and pinchings. He was Saul, my brother, and I couldn't stand to see him so scared.

I plunged forward and threw myself at him, planting eager wet kisses on his cheek and neck and curly hair. Saul clung to me.

'Oh, Hetty, Mother's taking me away to the hospital and I can't never never come back!' he sobbed.

'No, you can't, Mother! You won't!' I shouted, and I started hitting and kicking her too.

Jem and Nat had to carry me away while Mother persisted with dressing Saul. I don't know whether he continued to cry. My own shrieks were too loud for me to hear anything else. Nat thumped me hard and shouted at me, Jem held me close and whispered soft words into my ear, but I didn't respond to either brother.

I was lost in the horror of losing Saul. I would never ever have the chance to be a good sister to him. I screamed until my throat was raw. I went on screaming until I slept. When I woke, I had no idea whether it was morning or afternoon. The house was horribly silent, though I could hear a little snuffling noise close by.

I reached out across the bed, but there was no one there. The snuffling continued, from *under* the bed. I leaned out, hung my head down, and saw Gideon curled up beneath me.

'Oh, Gid,' I croaked, barely able to talk. 'Come up into the bed.'

But he wouldn't, so I crawled underneath beside him, lying on the cold dusty floorboards.

'What are you doing, Gideon?' I asked. 'Are you pretending to be a chamber pot?'

I said it to make him laugh but he went on snuffling.

'You cry ever so quietly,' I observed. 'I scream and scream.'

'I know,' said Gideon thickly.

His face was so sodden with tears and snot he could scarcely breathe. I very kindly lifted up my nightgown hem and mopped him dry.

'Is Mother back?' I asked.

'Yes. But Saul isn't,' Gideon whispered.

I swallowed. My throat hurt so much I held it on the outside, clasping my neck with both hands. 'I was a bad sister to him,' I said wretchedly. I wriggled nearer to Gideon. 'I shall be a *lovely* sister to you now, Gid,' I said, putting my arms round him.

I was smaller than him, but he felt very little and spindly in my arms. I could feel him trembling.

'Hetty, will Mother take *us* to this hospital?'

'Hush!' I said sharply. It felt so much worse to have Gideon put it into words. I shook him a little and then felt bad. Hadn't I only just that minute promised to be a good sister?

'Of course Mother won't take us,' I said as firmly as I could. I patted Gideon encouragingly. 'You are her favourite. She wouldn't ever take you. And Jem wouldn't let her take me. Mother won't take us. Never never never. Say it, Gideon. *Never*.'

'Never never never,' we chanted.

I thought I would ask Mother, just to be certain sure, but somehow the words dried in my sore throat when I saw her. She was grey with grief, clutching little Eliza to her bosom, tears rolling down her cheeks.

I asked Jem instead.

'You won't let me go to that hospital, will you, Jem?'

'No, Hetty,' said Jem, hugging me tight.

I looked up at his face. His eyes were very red.

'Have you been crying, Jem?' I asked.

Jem *never* cried. He didn't even cry the day one of the horses bolted and knocked him to the ground. He got kicked in the head, so that one side of his poor face was black with bruises for weeks.

'I'm staying here for ever and ever, aren't I, Jem?' I said again. 'And Gideon is too.'

'Yes, Hetty. Of course you are,' Jem said again and again, but he still didn't seem quite sure enough.

I couldn't get to sleep that night, and when I eventually dozed off I dreamed of Saul. A large cruel nurse was picking him up and plunging him into the water butt, trying to drown him like a newborn kitten. I screamed at her and she seized me too, holding me fast by the scruff of the neck. I struggled in the butt and her hand pushed me down, down, down in the murky water. I woke with a start and found there was murky water in my own bed too.

I thought Mother would be cross with me for being such a baby, but she scarcely said a word. She moved slowly about the house, her head bowed. She fed and changed Eliza, and cooked bacon and cabbage for all of us, but most of the time she sat staring at the floor, wringing her big red hands.

Rosie ushered us out of the cottage to give Mother some peace. We were huddled miserably on the doorstep when Father came striding home.

'Hello, chickens.' He ruffled our heads and sighed. 'Oh dear. No cheeps from any of you,' he said, stepping over us with his great legs.

He said no more until he'd eaten his supper. Then he lit his pipe and called us to come and stand by his chair.

'Nat, go down to the Otter Inn and fetch me a tankard of ale. No spilling a drop, do you hear? Jem, you go with him. Eliza, go and see to your namesake sister. See if you can quieten her grizzling. Rosie, take Mother upstairs – she needs to lie down. Be off, all of you. I want to have a word with Hetty and Gideon.'

When they were all gone, he shook his head at us. 'Such long faces! Are you missing young Saul?'

'Most dreadfully, Father,' I said.

He blinked at me. 'Why, Hetty, you do surprise me,' he said. 'You two were always fighting! No doubt you're full of remorse now?'

I nodded. I wasn't yet sure what remorse meant, but the cold, sour, sick feeling in my stomach seemed to sum it up.

'Poor child,' said Father, patting me.

I climbed up onto his great lap and nuzzled my face against his chest. I could hear his heart going thump against my cheek.

'Mother won't take me away, will she, Father?' I said into the rough cotton of his smock. 'Nor Gideon?'

I waited. I felt Father take several deep breaths.

'Not till next year, my sweetheart, when you are both much bigger.'

'No! No, not then, not ever!' I shrieked, pummelling him with my fists.

'Stop that now, missy!' said Father, catching both my flailing hands in his large one. 'You've shrieked enough today, I'm told. There's no point wailing when it can't be helped. Now hush and listen. Mother and I love you, love Gideon, love little Eliza just like our own children. We still love Saul—'

'And Martha,' I said.

'And Martha,' said Father, seeming surprised I'd remembered her. 'But you're not our children, you're little waifs from the Foundling Hospital. You came to us as tiny babies. Mother has a knack with specially frail babies. She rears you up until you're fat and rosy-cheeked.' He gently poked me in the cheeks with his thumb and finger, but I wriggled free, a new thought having struck me.

I was remembering the pig out in the back yard. Mother had a piglet every year, pale and puny. She fed it and fattened it until it could barely sway on its trotters, and then Father came along, and although we weren't supposed to watch, we heard *squeal-squeal-squeal*, and the next day there was fresh pork on our plates.

'Is she fattening us up to *eat* us?' I said, gazing at Father as if he was an ogre.

He stared back at me, slack-mouthed, and

then he roared with laughter. 'Oh, Hetty, Hetty, you're a funny one,' he chortled. 'Of course no one's going to eat you! Mother will take you back to the Foundling Hospital when you're big enough, and you'll live with lots and lots of other girls. Martha will be there so you'll have one sister. And you'll be with the boys, Gideon, and Saul will be your brother.'

'I want to be with Hetty,' said Gideon, but Father paid him no heed.

'We need to be with *you*, Father. And Mother. And my Jem,' I said. 'Please can't we stay? I promise I'll be very, very, very good. I'll never shout or kick or cry ever again.'

'You're a caution, Hetty,' said Father. 'We would love you to stay here with us. We'd like to keep all our dear foster children, but you do not belong to us. You belong to the hospital. All foundlings must be returned by their sixth birthday. Don't look so worried. I'm sure they will be kind to you as long as you are a sensible girl, Hetty. They will school you properly and teach you to be a good Christian child.'

'Will we live there for ever?'

'No, no, they will train you up to be a servant girl and you will go away into service when you are fourteen,' said Father.

'Like Bess and Nora?' I said.

54

'Just like our Bess and Nora,' said Father. 'And then I dare say you can come home to us once a year just as they do.'

I pondered. Last Mothering Sunday I had admired my big sisters in their fancy print dresses and fine stockings when they'd travelled home on a visit. But they'd told Mother tales of cross cooks who beat them over the head with ladles and sly masters who tried to sneak kisses.

'I do not *want* to be a servant girl,' I said.

'Will I be a servant girl?' asked Gideon.

'Don't be dim-witted, lad!' said Father. 'No, no, I dare say you will be a sailor or a soldier boy like our Marcus.'

'*I* will be a sailor or a soldier and go adventuring,' I said.

'You are a very strange pair,' said Father, sighing. 'Now jump down and give me a little peace.'

'But you must tell us about the hospital, Father!' I demanded.

'Hetty, I don't know anything about the hospital. I've never even set foot inside it. I just know it's a good place for little children and you need never say you're ashamed to come from there,' said Father. 'Now stop plaguing me, girl. My head's aching.'

Father might never have been to this Foundling Hospital – but Mother had.

'Come with me, Gideon,' I whispered as Father sucked on his pipe and closed his eyes.

I tiptoed up the stairs, tugging Gideon behind me.

Rosie was guarding the door to Mother's bedroom, but I was bold.

'Father said we must talk to Mother,' I said.

I heard Gideon gasp at my outright lie. Rosie hesitated, but I pushed right past her determinedly. It was dark in Mother's room, the curtains drawn shut as if it was night-time. I could just make out the shape of Mother lying on her back. I wondered if she'd gone to sleep, but when I clambered carefully up onto the bed, her arm came out and held me tight. I hauled Gideon up too and he nestled on her other side.

'My lambs,' she murmured.

'Mother, Father has told us about the hospital. Is it truly a good place?' I asked.

I felt Mother stiffen. She swallowed hard. 'Of course it is a good place, Hetty,' she said.

I wondered if Mother could be a liar too. I lay thinking about it.

'Did Saul cry a lot when you said goodbye?' I asked.

Mother might be a brave liar, but she wasn't foolish. 'Yes, he cried,' she said.

'And did Martha cry too?'

'Yes, Martha cried too.'

'I shall cry,' Gideon whispered.

'I shall scream and kick and be so bad they won't let me stay, and then Mother can take me home,' I said.

5

I had loved Martha much more dearly than Saul but I had mostly forgotten her. However, I could not get Saul out of my head for months. I thought of him living in this huge hospital with so many other boys. I knew most boys weren't gentle and protective like my dear Jem. The village boys had often jeered and pointed at Saul, imitating the lopsided way he walked. One boy had pushed him hard and then laughed when he toppled over. I thought of all the foundling boys laughing and pointing and pushing Saul, and my eyes brimmed with tears.

Then I thought of all those boys mocking Gideon in turn. My fists clenched. I resolved to fight anyone who dared hurt my special brother. I was certain they would not dare hurt *me*. I was famous for my temper in the village. I might be the smallest but I was always the fiercest in any scrap. Mothers came and told tales to *my* mother about hair-pulling and kicking and sometimes outright punching. Poor

Mother was mortified. She tried reasoning with me but I reasoned back.

'They called me names, Mother. Half-pint and Ginger and Runt. I said my name was Hetty and they just laughed. So I hit them and they stopped.'

'Jesus said to turn the other cheek,' said Mother.

Maybe Jesus wasn't teased the way I was. I thought hard, trying to remember the Bible stories I heard at Sunday school.

'*God* said, an eye for an eye and a tooth for a tooth,' I declared, imitating the solemn holy tone of the Sunday school teacher. I hoped it would make Mother laugh. I knew I was in danger of yet another paddling.

This suddenly started up a new fear.

'Do they punish the children at the hospital, Mother?'

'Not if they're good girls and boys,' Mother said.

This was not reassuring. I thought hard.

'Is that why they're there? Because they're bad?'

'No, no, no. It's because their own mothers can't look after them,' said Mother.

'Why can't they?' I asked.

Mother sighed. 'There never was such a girl for questions. You make my head ache, Hetty.'

'Please tell, Mother!'

'Well, dear, some ladies have babies and they can't look after them,' said Mother.

'Why can't they?' I persisted.

'Perhaps they're very poorly. Or they haven't got a dear husband like Father to give them a proper home. The ladies don't want to go into the workhouse' – Mother whispered the word and shuddered – 'so they take their babes to the Foundling Hospital.'

'Do they cry when they say goodbye?'

'I'm sure they cry a good deal,' said Mother.

'Did my first mother cry?'

'I'm sure it fair broke her heart to part with you, Hetty,' said Mother.

'Why can't I go and live with that mother now, Mother, instead of being sent back to this hospital? I don't need looking after. *I* can earn money. I could sing and dance so that people throw pennies at me.'

'You can't carry a tune to save your life, Hetty, so maybe they'd throw tomatoes,' said Mother. 'No dear, you don't belong to your mother now. You belong to the Foundling Hospital.'

I did not want to belong to an institution. I wanted a mother. I crept off by myself, squeezing into the tiny space at the back of the pigsty and the privy. It was private because everyone else was too big to squeeze through the gooseberry bushes and brambles to sit there. I wasn't comfortable because there were nettles and it smelled bad, but I didn't care. I pulled my skirts down over my bare legs, put my head on my knees and wept.

After a long time I heard them shouting for me. I stayed where I was. Then there were footsteps.

'Hetty? Hetty!' Jem called.

I did not reply to him, but I was sniffing hard.

'Oh, Hetty, I know you're in there,' said Jem. 'Come out. Please!'

I did not budge.

'I'm too big to come in and get you,' said Jem.

I heard the bushes rustling, then Jem swearing.

'That's a bad word!' I said.

'I know it's a bad word. Anyone would say it if they were scratched all over by brambles,' Jem panted. '*Do* come out, Hetty.'

I simply wouldn't.

'Then I will have to try to get in,' said Jem, sighing.

He forced his way forward, thrusting his arm through the bushes until his hand j-u-s-t reached my bare foot. He held it tight. I curled my grubby toes into his palm.

'There now,' Jem whispered.

'Oh, Jem,' I said, sobbing.

'I can't bear you fretting about the hospital,' he said.

'I'm not going,' I said.

There was a silence as we held hand and foot.

'I think you have to go, Hetty,' said Jem. 'But perhaps I could go too. We'll pretend *I* am a foundling boy. Yes, I can take Gideon's place and he can stay with Mother.'

'Dear Jem! I wish you could. But Mother and Father wouldn't let you,' I said.

There was another silence.

'I will be so sad,' I said. 'I will have to stay there soooo long.'

Jem had taught me how to count to ten. I tried to count on my fingers.

'I will be there one two three . . . lots and lots of years,' I said dolefully.

'I think it is nine years, Hetty. And then you will be fourteen and quite grown up. And do you know what will happen then?'

'I will have to be a servant, and cooks will hit me and masters will kiss me,' I said.

'Maybe for a short while. But then I will come to fetch you and look after you, and as soon as you are old enough I will make you my wife. I know I am your brother, but not by blood so we can marry! We will have our own cottage and work on the farm and you will keep house and look after our babies.

It will be just like our games in the squirrel house, but *real*, Hetty,' said Jem.

'*Really* real?'

'I promise,' said Jem.

I didn't always keep my promises, but Jem did. I seized his hand, kissed it passionately, and then crawled out of my hiding place to give him a proper hug.

Thoughts of the Foundling Hospital still loomed, but at least I had a wondrous future ahead of me. I just had to wait one two three four five six seven eight nine years, endure a couple more while I dodged blows and kisses as a servant, and *then* I would be sweet sixteen and Jem's bride.

I dressed up in Mother's best white Sunday petticoat, clutching a posy of buttercups and daisies, and tripped around on Jem's arm, picturing for all I was worth.

'You are my lovely big handsome husband, dear Jem,' I said.

'You are my very fine little wife, dear Hetty,' said Jem.

The others laughed at us, especially Nat, but we didn't care. Gideon didn't laugh but he looked wistful.

'I want to be your husband, Hetty,' he said.

'No, Gideon, Jem has to be my husband, but

you may come and live with us and be our big boy,' I said kindly.

I was out one day in the meadow playing Bride with my husband and big boy when I heard distant cheering and hurrahs, as if half the village were coming to applaud our marriage. I looked over the grass, squinting in the sunlight. I could see no one. They must be processing along the other side of the tall hedgerow.

Then I saw a gigantic grey head poking up above the hedge – a *huge* head with wrinkled skin and a tiny eye and the longest nose in all the world. I knew what it was!

'Oh my stars! E is for *Elephant*!' I gasped. 'There is an elephant walking along the lane.'

Jem was facing the wrong way. He did not take me seriously. 'Has it come to our wedding as a guest?'

'Don't picture T is for Tiger,' said Gideon. 'I don't like his teeth.'

'I'm not picturing! The elephant is *real*,' I said, tugging at them. 'Look!'

They turned and saw the head bobbing along above the hedgerow for themselves. Jem shouted, Gideon shrieked.

'Come on, let's see it properly,' I said, grabbing their hands.

'No, no, it will eat us!' Gideon cried.

'Don't be such a *baby*. Come *on*,' I commanded.

Jem and I hauled him along between us. We ran diagonally across the meadow towards the stile. The clapping and cheering grew louder, the vast head more wondrous the nearer we got.

When we reached the stile, Jem lifted me up, and then Gideon, and then we all jumped out into the lane. There was the elephant plodding along the path, a real true elephant with such wrinkled skin, such huge legs, such an immense belly! A man in a military coat and great black boots strode along beside the beast, leading him like a dog on a chain.

Another man capered about beside them, the oddest creature I had ever seen, with hair sticking up on end and a bright red nose, his feet in great black shoes that flapped comically. He was banging a drum and dancing. Two big boys danced along beside him, dressed in the oddest clothes – sparkly silver shirts and very short breeches and white *tights*. Jem's mouth hung open in shocked horror, but Gideon pointed in awe. These boys paused and suddenly went forward into a tumble, over and over and up in the air and over and over again.

'Oh my stars!' said Jem, overcoming his scorn at their girlish garb. He could go head over heels and stand on his hands, and frequently did so to amuse me, but he couldn't possibly caper like these boys.

Then came great wagons painted scarlet and emerald and canary yellow. There was a message written in curly writing on the sides of each one. I knew my alphabet but I couldn't figure words properly yet.

Jem read it for us:

'The Great Tanglefield Travelling Circus.

Observe Elijah, the largest elephant in the entire world.

See the exotic animals in our vast menagerie.

Gasp at Fair Flora dancing on the tightrope for your delight.

Chortle at the antics of Chino the Comic Clown.

Marvel at Madame Adeline and her star troupe of horses.

Hurrah for Tanglefield's Travelling Circus!'

Almost at the end of this magnificent procession rode a beautiful lady in sparkling pink – wearing no dress at all, just the merest stiff frill. Her long flame-red hair tumbled past her bare shoulders.

'Just look at that lady with scarcely any clothes!' said Jem.

'See her tiny shoes! Oh, I wish *I* had little shoes like that instead of big ugly boots,' said Gideon.

'Look at her hair!' I said in rapture. 'She has red hair just like mine! See, see!' I repeated, jumping up and down.

The wondrous woman raised her hand and waved to us, and we waved back wildly, honoured to be noticed.

Another comical man with a red nose and bizarrely big breeches came capering along at the very end, speaking into a large horn so that his voice boomed out above the hubbub.

'Come to Tanglefield's Travelling Circus tonight at seven, or Saturday at two. The show will be in Pennyman's Field: adults sixpence, children threepence – a total bargain, so come and see and wonder. Come to Tanglefield's Travelling Circus tonight . . .' He recited it again and again until the procession was out of sight and his voice a tinny whisper.

'Oh, Jem, Gideon, we must go to the circus!' I said, jumping up and down.

'We must, we must, we must!' said Gideon, jumping too, pink in the face.

'But we haven't got ninepence,' said sensible Jem. 'I have the two pennies that Mrs Blood gave me at the Otter Inn for collecting up all the tankards, but that is all.'

'We will ask Mother,' I said.

But Mother shook her head. 'Of course I haven't

any spare pennies for such a senseless thing as a circus. And even if I had, I wouldn't let you go. Rosie told me they were near naked in that procession!'

'They were so lovely, Mother, especially the lady all in pink spangles on a white horse. She had red hair, just like mine!'

'Yes, pink spangles!' said Mother, shuddering. 'A grown woman flaunting herself in front of decent folk, and men capering about foolishly, and a dreaded beast all set to run amok and trample everyone. It shouldn't be allowed. Of course I'm not spending precious money on such a wicked show.'

'Don't spend your money, Mother, spend mine!' I said.

'What do you mean, Hetty?' said Mother, frowning. 'You don't have any money, you silly little girl.'

'I do, I do! The Foundling Hospital gives you money for me.'

'Don't talk such nonsense, child. That money is to feed and clothe you, not send you to a heathen show like a circus.'

'Well, don't give me any food any more, and don't make me new frocks or buy me boots. I'd much sooner go to the circus,' I declared.

'I'll certainly send you to bed without any supper,' said Mother. 'Now hold your tongue, miss.'

I *couldn't* hold my tongue. I wanted to go to

the circus and see Elijah the performing elephant and all the other animals I'd heard grunting and growling inside the wagons. Maybe there were lions or tigers, wild wolves, even a white unicorn with a silver horn. I wanted to see Flora dancing on the tightrope, I wanted to see the comical clown, and oh oh oh, I so wanted to see Madame Adeline, the flame-haired lady in pink spangles.

I started to protest bitterly but Jem put his hand over my mouth. 'Be quiet, Hetty,' he said, tugging me away from Mother.

'But I don't want to be quiet! I want to go to the circus!' I persisted.

'Ssh! I might know a way,' said Jem. 'Just keep your mouth shut and wait till I tell you.'

I clamped my lips together and stomped off after him. Gideon stayed with Mother, climbing up onto her lap. He always hated it when I grew stormy. He was so fearful that I'd get paddled – far more fearful than me.

Jem pulled me out of the door and leaned me up against the side of the pigsty. 'I'll take you to the circus tomorrow, Hetty,' he said.

'Oh, Jem! You really will? But how will you get the money?'

'I think I know a way of getting in without needing any money,' he whispered, tickling my ear.

'But the comic man said sixpence for adults, threepence for children,' I said.

'I know, I know. But Nat told me a way to get in for nothing,' he hissed.

'Oh! Truly? Then let's go now!'

'No, no, we can't go now, Mother would know. This is a bad, secret way, Hetty. We will get into terrible trouble if we are caught,' Jem said, looking wretched. 'Perhaps we shouldn't try. I should set you a good example.'

'Oh no, we *must* go! I don't care if we do get into trouble. I want to go to the circus so badly, Jem.'

'I know. And so do I,' said Jem.

'And Gideon does too,' I said.

'Yes, I know, but I don't think we can risk taking Gideon. He will only start wailing or tell Mother,' said Jem. 'This has to be our secret, Hetty.'

'Our secret,' I repeated solemnly.

'What are you two up to?' said Mother, coming to the back door with a bucket of potato peelings for the pig.

'Oh, we – we were just playing circus, Mother,' said Jem. 'Hetty was pretending that our Polly Pig was the elephant.'

'Yes, yes, and I am the lady in pink spangles on her white horse,' I said, hitching up my skirts and galloping round and round.

Mother sniffed. 'No more talk of circuses, you

silly pair. Hetty, you feed that pig, and Jem, you run up to the top field to see if Father needs a hand with the horses.'

'Yes, Mother,' said Jem, rushing off.

'Yes, Mother,' I said too, taking the bucket of peelings. 'Here, Elijah Elephant, eat up – you need to grow a long wavy trunk,' I said, patting our pig on her snub nose.

'Oh, Hetty, you and your picturing,' said Mother. 'Still, at least you've stopped pestering. You can be a good little lass when you really try hard.'

I fidgeted under Mother's warm gaze because I was intent on being as *bad* a little lass as I possibly could. I held my tongue obediently that evening, though Gideon talked non-stop about the circus. He pranced about the table, twirling round and pointing his toes, till Father groaned and gave him a prod.

'Stop that silly flouncing nonsense, lad.'

Gideon's face crumpled and he crouched in a heap on the rag rug.

'He was only dancing, Father, like the circus folk,' I said.

'Boys don't *dance*,' Father said firmly.

I opened my mouth to tell him we'd seen the circus boys dance – *and* tumble head over heels and do handstands – but Jem gave me a nudge. It was never a good idea to contradict Father.

'Boys march like soldiers,' Father said. 'Show him, Jem.'

'Watch me, Gideon. Left, right, left, right,' said Jem, striding about and swinging his arms.

Gideon stumbled along limply, unable to tell his left from his right. 'I don't want to be a soldier,' he said miserably when we climbed into bed that night. 'I want to be a circus boy.'

'I want to be a circus girl, just like the lady in pink spangles,' I said.

'Oh, I wish wish wish we could go to the circus,' said Gideon.

I bit the thumb I was sucking. I badly wanted to take Gideon with me the next day – but I knew Jem was right. He would blurt everything out to Mother, to Father, to Rosie, to the whole family, even to the pig beside the privy. Whereas I knew how to keep my mouth shut when necessary.

6

I behaved in an exemplary fashion all Saturday morning. I even ate all my vegetable soup at dinner time, though I usually fussed and picked out the bobbles of barley and carrot, refusing to eat them because they looked as if they'd been eaten already.

Mother patted me on the shoulder. 'Good girl, Hetty!' she said proudly. 'Now I'm going to feed young Eliza and have forty winks. You children go and play and give me a bit of peace.'

Rosie and big Eliza went off arm in arm, talking big-girl chat of dresses and hairstyles and boys in the village. Nat ran off carelessly, kicking a stone, to meet up with his friends. That left Gideon, Jem and me.

Gideon looked at us happily. 'What shall we play?' he asked.

Jem and I looked at each other.

'Hetty and I were thinking we might play by ourselves right now, Gideon,' said Jem.

Gideon's face fell. 'Are you going to the squirrel house?' he whispered.

'Well, we might be,' I said uneasily.

'But you're not allowed,' said Gideon. 'Mother said.'

'Yes, so you'd better not come, Gideon, or you'll get into serious trouble,' I said.

'But I don't want *you* to get into trouble, Hetty. Or Jem. Please don't go,' Gideon wailed.

'Hush! We *have* to go. Now,' said Jem.

'But I haven't anyone to play with,' said Gideon, and his lip puckered.

'Picture someone, Gideon,' I said. 'Make them up. Here, I can see a little boy standing beside you, a kind, friendly boy. He likes dancing, just like you. You can dance together.'

Gideon looked round wonderingly, as if I'd actually conjured a child out of the ether – and Jem and I seized our moment and ran away.

There were children running from all over the village, courting couples, mothers, fathers, even old grandmothers and grandfathers hobbling along on sticks – all of them bound for Pennyman's Field to see the circus. We could hear the drums and see the top of a great striped tent, with all the red and green and yellow wagons parked in a semicircle behind.

I couldn't see the wondrous flame-haired Madame

Adeline or the tumbling boys in silver. I couldn't even spot enormous Elijah the elephant, but as we entered the field I saw the two clowns with red noses capering at the entrance to the tent. There was a stall selling sweetmeats and another selling little metal clockwork figures, comical cats and mice.

'Oh, Jem,' I said, tugging his hand – and he bought me a penny gingerbread heart hanging on a pink ribbon.

Now we only had one penny left. We needed a whole handful of pennies to get into the tent to see the circus performance. Everyone was standing in a line before the ticket booth, handing over their pennies and getting tickets in return. We watched two boys trying to run right past without paying, but a big man caught them both by the scruff of their necks and sent them flying with a kick to their backsides. I clutched Jem. I was used to being paddled, but I didn't want an ugly big man to kick *my* backside.

Jem squeezed my hand reassuringly. 'We'll go round the back,' he whispered. 'Nat says you can tunnel in under the tent, so long as you're speedy.'

I started trembling with excitement. We ran off, circling right round the tent. My eyes popped. There was Elijah, chained by his huge wrinkled leg to a stake, wearing a red and gold beaded cap with a matching saddle stretched over his vast back. He waved his trunk at us, then lifted his tail – and did an unmentionable thing! Huge dollops of unmentionable things!

I started spluttering with laughter, but Jem put his hand over my mouth.

'Ssh, Hetty,' he hissed.

He'd spotted Elijah's trainer sitting on an upturned tub, smoking a cigarette. Jem pulled me flat against the canvas of the tent so that he couldn't spot us. Three children suddenly came running past, squealing at the sight of Elijah in all his exotic splendour. The trainer man stood up, threw away his cigarette and whistled. Another man dressed in a red tailcoat came running from the nearest scarlet wagon. He held a long whip tight in his hand.

They moved in a flash, seizing the legs of the children as they wriggled underneath the canvas. All three were hauled out, shaken fiercely and shouted at. The redcoat man cracked his big whip and I shut my eyes tight, but I think he simply whipped the ground, not the boys. They were all crying now, even the biggest boy. He wore a blue cap stuck on his head at a jaunty angle. The redcoat man seized his cap and hurled it high across the field, and then all three were shoved and kicked on their way.

My heart hammered hard inside my bodice. What

if the men were to see Jem and me? I shook in my shoes, but Jem held me tight.

'It's all right, Hetty,' he whispered into my ear. 'We won't try while they're lurking here. We'll just have to wait patiently.'

We waited and waited and waited. We heard loud music inside the tent, shouts of excitement, roars of laughter. The circus performance had started. We were stuck outside, still intent on avoiding the eyes of the redcoat man, the trainer and Elijah the elephant. The great beast raised his head every now and then, trunk high in the air, as if he was sniffing us out. He strained against his stake. I held Jem's hand so hard my nails dug into his palm.

Then more men came, pushing a cage of howling hairy beasts. I saw their coarse dark coats, their long snouts, their great teeth – and I thought of grandmothers and little girls in red hooded cloaks. The redcoat man cracked his long whip and strode off after the wolves, all set to subdue them inside the tent.

We heard gasps and cries and sudden bursts of applause. I fidgeted from one foot to the other, desperate, till the caged beasts were eventually wheeled back and off to the side of the field. Elijah and his keeper stayed swaying and sitting, while the two silver-suited tumbling boys came dancing down the steps of another wagon. They paused to rub their hands and coat their sparkly slippers with some dusty stuff in a box.

'It's rosin, to stop them slipping,' Jem whispered.

Then they gave Elijah a fond poke, turned a couple of somersaults for practice, and ran into the ring. We heard more clapping and then a great *'Ooooh!'* as the two boys performed some special trick.

I quivered. I did badly want to see the two boys so I could try to copy their tricks for Gideon. I was tired of standing so still, so scared of these big men with their whips and hard boots, so sad that the circus was happening without me. Perhaps we should simply run away as fast as we could?

Jem felt me fidgeting and put his hands on my shoulders to steady me – just as Elijah's trainer stood up, stretching his arms in the air. I froze – but all his attention was on Elijah. He went up close to the great beast, lolling against the huge front legs. Elijah lowered his head, waved his trunk and opened his mouth. I held my breath, wondering if the beast was about to devour his master before my very eyes. But the elephant looked as if he was *smiling*. He slowly and tenderly wrapped his trunk around the trainer's neck and shoulders so that they stood in weird embrace.

Jem and I stood there, breathless. Then the man muttered something, Elijah unwound his trunk and stood majestically to attention, head up, trunk forward, ears alert. The trainer unhooked his chain from the stake and strode forward in his shiny boots. Elijah followed meekly, like a great grey wrinkly dog on a lead. They disappeared inside a flap in the tent, leaving only a mound of elephant dung on the grass.

'Quick, Hetty! This is our chance,' said Jem, pulling my arm.

We darted forward, praying that no more men would come out of their wagons and catch us. We could see one of the circus men standing by the tent flap – pitchfork in hand! We couldn't simply follow Elijah and his trainer or we'd be skewered. Jem ran round to the side and fell to his knees with a bump, as if in prayer. Then he stuck his head under the tent canvas. He pulled at me to do the same. I copied him obediently, though I was terrified my head would be prodded with a pitchfork on one side of the canvas, my backside kicked by a boot on the other. But I wriggled forward on my tummy into the hot, noisy tent, and at last we were both safe inside!

The ring was brilliantly lit but the spectators all around the tent were in darkness. We could just make out circles of seats, rising in tiers. Jem pulled me up and we edged our way round the back of the tallest tier until we reached an aisle.

Now we had a proper view of the circus ring, scattered with sawdust and edged with a little red wall. Elijah was in the middle of the ring *on his hind legs*, waving his trunk triumphantly while everyone clapped him.

The audience was so absorbed that no one noticed as we crept forward and slipped into two empty seats almost at the front. We watched Elijah perform his tricks, while the silly clowns with red noses darted in and out of the ring, pretending to be scared of him. Then Chino took a clockwork mouse out of his pocket and set it clacking and squeaking, and Elijah lumbered across to a big box and climbed right up on it, as if he was terrified in turn. The trainer pretended to be frightened too, so Elijah bent his head, took him in his trunk, and lifted him high in the air away from the scurrying mouse. Jem and I laughed heartily, loving their antics now that we were safe in our seats.

When Elijah eventually plodded out, the clowns stayed in the ring, capering with some of the children in the audience and playing with buckets of water.

'You can run down and join in, Hetty. I'll save your seat,' said Jem.

I shrank back shyly, not liking the funny clowns with their painted faces and clumsy clothes, scared they might throw their buckets of water over me.

'It's not like you to be bashful, Hetty!' said Jem, putting his arm round me. 'Are you pleased we got into the circus? I told you I'd find a way.'

'I'm very, very, very pleased,' I said.

The band struck up again, and a plump lady in a tight magenta costume came dancing into the ring. She ran over to a vast ladder at the side and started climbing up it, rung after rung, up and up and up, as nimble as a squirrel. She reached a little platform right at the top and clasped a long pole waiting there. We saw a taut rope stretching all the way across the tent, high in the air. She was Flora the tightrope walker!

The lady gave a flourish, seized her pole and stepped out onto the rope! She walked right along it, even pointing her feet and dancing, as if she was a magenta fairy flitting through the air. It hurt my neck to watch her and I could hardly breathe because I was so scared she'd fall. Jem had warned me so many times that I mustn't ever try to edge along the tree branches in our squirrel house. He nudged me purposefully now.

'You mustn't try this lark, Hetty, promise!' he whispered. 'My Lord, isn't she amazing?'

We watched as she skipped along, walked backwards, even *sat* upon the rope, arranging her deep-pink skirts around her and taking a book out of her pocket, pretending to read! These seemed marvels enough, but when she'd advanced all the way over to the other side, she took something from under a cloth on the other lofty platform. It was a little perambulator on two wheels with a baby doll sitting up inside. She took the vehicle, wobbling alarmingly, so that we all went *'Ooooh!'* Then she balanced it on the rope, with dolly still inside. Flora walked steadily back across the rope, as casually as any mother wheeling her baby. When at long last she reached the other platform and took her bow, she seized the doll and made *her* take a bow too.

Then Chino the clown came capering back with his silly friend, Beppo, plus two very little clowns in comical baby gowns with woollen booties on their feet. They had greasepaint on their faces and silly red noses. At first I thought they were simply child clowns, but then I spied a flash of silver beneath the baby gown and realized they were the two tumbling boys dressed up. They kept playing tricks on the clowns, leaping up into the air, landing on their hands and then walking upside down all round the ring. There was a lot of fun and games with bottles and napkins. Jem laughed so much he nearly fell off his seat. Then at last all four clowns took a bow and ran off. That seemed to be the end of the circus, because everyone clapped and then stood up, stretching.

'Oh!' I said. 'Oh dear, Jem.'

'What is it, Hetty? Aren't you enjoying the circus?' Jem asked.

'I think it's wonderful, but now it is ended and I didn't get to see her, the lady in pink spangles with red hair. *My* lady,' I said, nearly in tears.

'It's all right, silly. She'll be in the second half. This is only an interval, Hetty. There's lots more to come, I promise.'

'Really! And so we haven't missed her? We really will see her?'

'Yes, we will.'

'She's the one I like the best,' I said.

'But you haven't even seen her perform yet!'

'I still know.'

'I like the clowns, they are *so* funny,' said Jem, chuckling. 'I should so love to set folk laughing like that.'

'We could have our *own* circus!' I said. 'You could be a clown, Jem, and Gideon can be a boy tumbler, and *I* will wear a short pink skirt and ride on my horse. Let us run away and start our circus, you and me and Gideon, and then I won't have to go to the hospital,' I said earnestly.

'I wish we could, Hetty,' said Jem, looking wretched. 'We could maybe have a circus when we're married. Perhaps we could start a *farm* circus, and you could train the pig to stand on a tub and get the chickens to cluck in time and set all the goats dancing,' he went on, trying to humour me. 'Here now, Hetty. Eat your gingerbread.'

He was trying to distract me. I *did* have a very sweet tooth so I set about eating my biscuit, though it had cracked and crumbled rather when I wriggled under the tent flap. I insisted on sharing it with Jem. We ate every crumb until only the gold star was left. Jem stuck that on my forehead.

Then the band struck up and the clowns capered back into the ring. I fidgeted in my seat, breathless with anticipation. I saw a gentleman throwing daggers at a lady in sparkly drawers, a troupe of seals barking for fish, and a man eating fire as casually as we'd eaten our gingerbread, but I was still restless and unsatisfied. But then, oh, then, right at the end, the ringmaster cracked his whip and announced: 'Now, ladies and gentlemen, girls and boys. Tanglefield's Travelling Circus is proud to present Madame Adeline and her troupe of rosin-backed performing horses!'

I sat up straight as six sleek horses cantered into the ring. I was used to Dobbin and Rowley, the great shire horses in Father's care at the farm. These dancing, prancing horses seemed an elvish breed, so small and dainty. Two were spotted, two piebald and two grey, all with their manes and tails flowing, long and silky. Madame Adeline sat on the first grey, which was almost pure white but with a saucy black patch on one eye, so that he looked as wicked as a pirate. He arched his neck and stepped precisely in time with the music, clearly proud to have Madame Adeline on his back. She looked so beautiful in her pink spangles and short frilly skirt, her flame-coloured hair piled on her head, a black ribbon round her slim white neck.

She stood up on the back of the pirate horse, straight and proud, arms high in the air, never faltering. She smiled at our applause, and called something to the other grey horse. He galloped faster and faster. As he drew alongside Madame Adeline leaped from one horse's back to the other, landing with fairy lightness. She leaped on, from one eager horse to another, she swung herself down till her toes touched the sawdust, then up over the side of the horse, she even stood on her hands while he cantered.

I watched her open-mouthed, marvelling. Madame Adeline jumped through a hoop and landed lightly back on the pirate horse, as easily as if she was skipping down the village lane. I clapped until my hands were sore. She slowed to a trot, still standing, waving at all of us. I waved back wildly, desperate for her to see me.

'Hello, children,' she called.

I piped 'hello' back, standing up in my seat.

'Who would like to come and ride with me?' she said.

I didn't wait for a second. I hurtled out of my seat. Jem tried to catch hold of me by the hem of my dress, but I whisked it away and rushed frantically for the ring. There were already children right at the front, hopping eagerly over the little red wall into the circus ring. Madame Adeline was laughing and pointing, picking her rider.

'No, no, pick *me*!' I screamed, still running. I tried to jump down the steep wooden steps, lost my footing, and hurtled forward, tumbling head over heels.

'Oh my, here's a little acrobat!' said Madame Adeline as I lay with my face in the sawdust, totally dazed.

I felt her strong hands lifting me up. I stood there, trembling. She was even more beautiful close up. Her hair was bright red, her face powdery white though her cheeks were a delicate pink, and her lips thrillingly dark and shiny. I looked up at her and fell totally in love.

'Are you all right, little one?' she asked softly, as if we were alone together, not watched by an audience of hundreds.

'I am, oh yes, I definitely am,' I said, tossing my hair out of my eyes.

'You have lovely red hair, just like mine!' she said, laughing. 'What's your name, child?'

'I'm Hetty Feather, ma'am,' I whispered.

'How old are you, Hetty? You speak up very nicely, yet you can't be more than . . . four?'

'I'm five and three-quarters, ma'am, just small for my age,' I said.

'And you want to ride my horse with me, little Hetty?'

'More than anything!'

She laughed again, her teeth white and perfect, her lips gleaming. 'Then so be it, Little Star,' she said, touching the gingerbread star still stuck to my forehead.

She lifted me up up up and I found myself sitting on the smooth hot back of her horse. She swung herself up behind me, gave a little clucking sound, and the horse started trotting slowly round the ring.

I heard loud clapping all round the circus. Oh my word, they were clapping me! I stopped clutching the horse's beautiful white mane and waved one hand in the air in acknowledgement. Madame Adeline chuckled.

'You're a real showman! All right, Little Star, let's perform a few tricks for your audience.'

She clucked again and our horse started cantering. She held me tightly round the waist but I wasn't a bit scared. I dug in with my knees and arched my back to keep my balance. I heard Madame Adeline laughing approvingly.

'Faster?' she murmured.

'Yes, faster, faster!' I said.

She clucked and our pirate horse gathered speed, galloping now, overtaking all the other horses, round and round and round, so fast that all the seats within the tent seemed to be spinning. My breath bumped from my body. I felt as if I was truly flying, though all the time I was safe in Madame Adeline's grasp. I wasn't sure if the roaring in my ears was my own hot blood or the clapping of many hands.

At long last Madame Adeline shouted a command to the horse and he slowed obediently.

'Now, your star turn!' Madame Adeline murmured into my ear. 'Do you think you could stand up? I will hold you very safely, I promise.'

'Yes! Yes!' I said, scrabbling clumsily onto my knees.

'Steady! Just stretch upwards. I won't let you go,' said Madame Adeline.

I stood right up – but then my foot slipped as the horse cantered forward! I thought for a second I'd go tumbling down onto the sawdust, but Madame Adeline held me firm.

'There now, my Star,' she whispered. 'I told you I would hold you safely.'

I stood still, trying to get my balance, swaying to the left, the right, but after a half-circuit of the ring I started to get the knack of standing with my feet spread, my arms out, my back erect, my whole body moving with the rhythm of the horse. Madame Adeline still held me tight, but I'm absolutely certain I was almost balancing myself. The audience stood up in their seats and clapped, roaring their approval.

Then Madame Adeline clucked to the horse to slow right down. She slid off, taking me with her in her arms. Then she set me down gently.

'Take your bow, Little Star,' she said.

We held hands and bowed low, while the clapping sounded louder than twenty brass bands. Madame Adeline bent and gave me a kiss.

'Well done, my precious child,' she said, and then she patted me on the shoulder to send me back to my seat.

'Oh, Hetty! Oh my Lord, Hetty!' Jem cried when I found my way back to him. He thumped me on the back. 'You were *brilliant*, Hetty.'

'No I wasn't, Jem,' I said modestly, though I wanted to jump up and down and say, *YES, I AM BRILLIANT!*

People right along the rows of seats were turning round, craning forward, calling to me, while my neighbours patted me on the back and added their praises. I scarcely paid attention to them. Madame Adeline was standing on the pirate horse, circling the ring, leaping lightly from one horse to another, flying fairy-like across her steeds, waving and bowing – and then she was *going*, trotting right out of the ring, all five horses in step as they followed her.

'Oh! She's going!' I said, leaping to my feet again. 'It's over!'

'Wait, Hetty. The circus isn't over. Oh, look, it's the clowns again,' said Jem, pulling me back down beside him.

I didn't care for the clowns. I didn't want to watch the tumbling boys. I didn't even wish to see the great golden jungle lion baring its teeth and snapping sullenly at its trainer. I only wanted to see Madame Adeline and I fidgeted and fussed.

'Behave yourself, Hetty,' said Jem sternly, digging me in the ribs. 'Sit quietly. You'll see Madame Adeline again at the end.'

'Will I really?'

'If you are a good girl and sit as still as a mouse,' said Jem.

I tried my best, though I behaved like a very *agitated* mouse, quivering and sniffing. At last the band struck up and all the circus artistes trooped back into the ring. Even great Elijah plodded out, trunk waving in the air. My wondrous Madame Adeline came trotting in on the pirate horse. She waved and smiled at everyone, but her head was turning, glancing this way and that. She was looking for someone. Looking for *me*?

I stood right up on my seat and waved both arms in the air like a windmill, shouting, 'Madame Adeline! Madame Adeline!' Jem had to hang onto me hard by my dress hem.

'Goodbye, Little Star!' Madame Adeline called, kissing her hand and waving just to me.

I waved and waved back. Then everyone paraded out of the ring and the band stopped playing and the audience stopped clapping. Everyone started filing out. Jem pulled at me, but I clung to my seat, not moving until all that was left of the show was an empty tent and dirty sawdust. Then I burst into tears.

'Whatever is the matter *now*, Hetty?' asked Jem.

'I want the circus back!' I wept.

'You're the absolute limit! Aren't you ever satisfied? You've *seen* the circus. In fact you've *been* the circus, doing your double act with Madame Adeline.'

'I want to ride with her again. Oh, Jem, let us go and find her.'

'Don't be so silly, Hetty. She'll be in one of the wagons at the back of the tent, with those big bad men who will catch us and whip us.'

'I don't care. I want to see Madame Adeline. I *have* to see her. She will want to see me. I am her Little Star,' I bellowed, stamping my foot.

'You're a little whatsit,' said poor Jem, giving my arm a shake. 'Why won't you ever see reason, Hetty? I try so hard to please you but it's never *enough*.'

I felt bad then, but not enough to modify my behaviour. I pulled free from Jem when we got outside the circus tent, ready to run right round it to the back. I wasn't looking where I was going and fell headlong over a long rope snaking across the grass. I banged my head hard on a tent peg and it hurt so much I burst into fresh floods of tears.

'It hurts, oh, it hurts!' I wailed.

'It serves you right,' said Jem crossly, but he knelt down beside me and cuddled me close. It only made me cry harder.

'Is that our Hetty screaming?' It was Nat, jostling his way through the crowd. 'Did you get in to see the circus?' he said, sounding awed. 'I tried with some of the village lads, but we were all chased away. You two are so lucky! So why is Hetty bawling? My Lord, she's going to have something to cry for when we get home! Mother is beside herself and Father is furious. You're in for a right royal paddling, you three.'

'What do you mean, you *three*?' said Jem.

I scrambled to my feet, scrubbing at my eyes and

runny nose with the hem of my dress.

'Yes, you're really for it now!' Nat chuckled heartlessly. 'Mother's been searching for you for hours. Seems she wanted Giddy for some trifle, and then she couldn't find any of you. Eliza said you might have gone to the circus but Rosie pointed out you had no pennies. Mother's so demented she feared you'd all been *stolen* by the circus men.'

'I wish they *would* steal me,' I said, sniffing. 'I want to be with Madame Adeline.'

'Madame Addywho?' said Nat. 'Not the woman in the parade showing off all her legs as bold as brass? You should have heard what the lads said about her!'

'Don't you *dare* talk about her in that way!' I declared, flying at Nat, ready to reach up and pull his hair.

Jem hauled me back and shook me hard, shocking me into silence. 'Shut up, Hetty, or I shall slap you,' he said. He turned to Nat. 'You said *three*. Is Gideon missing too?'

'Yes, that's why Mother's in such a particular fret,' said Nat. 'We all told her he'd be fine so long as he was with you – but *isn't* he? Has he run off by himself?'

'He was never with us,' said Jem. 'It was just Hetty and me. Oh, Nat, Gideon is truly lost!'

7

We searched the field for Gideon in case he'd tried to follow us, but there was no sign of him. Jem bravely tried creeping round the back of the tent to see if he had strayed there. One of the circus men shouted at him, raising his fists in threat.

'Please, sir, I mean no harm. I'm looking for my little brother. He's lost!' said Jem.

'There ain't no little brother here. Now make yourself scarce before I give you a boot up the backside!'

'Madame Adeline!' I called, hoping she'd come running to rescue us, but she didn't hear me. Other men did though, and came hurrying out of their wagons.

'Clear off, you little varmints. The show's over!' one growled.

'Come on, you two,' said Nat. 'They're going to cut up rough any minute.'

We all had to run for it. We stopped at the edge of the field to catch our breath. I started crying again.

'We'd best take Hetty home, Jem,' said Nat. 'You never know, Gideon might be back home himself by now. I dare say he just hid himself somewhere in the yard. He's that timid he'd never go dashing off by himself.'

We hurried home, Nat and Jem holding me tight by the hands, but even so I kept tripping. I thought of Gideon, all alone, with no kind big brothers to help him along, and I felt truly dreadful.

I stopped thinking entirely of myself and Madame Adeline. Instead I said over and over again inside my head, *Please let Gideon be safe at home!* But when we ran up the path to our cottage and burst through the front door, Mother was weeping, Father was pacing the floor, Rosie and Eliza were wringing their hands, and even little Eliza was crying piteously in her cradle.

They looked at us, mouths gaping. Then Father and Rosie and Eliza gave great whoops of joy and relief, but Mother stared past Jem and me, her head turning left and right.

'Gideon?' she whispered.

We had to shake our heads.

'Oh, Mother, he's not with us,' I said.

'You have lost your little brother?' Mother gasped.

Gideon wasn't technically my *little* brother – he was born five days before me and was a head taller, though very spindly – but I knew it wasn't the right time to be pedantic.

'Hetty and I went off together,' said Jem, his face as pale as whey. 'Gideon was never with us.'

'You went off to that heathen circus, I'll be bound,' said Mother.

Jem hung his head.

'Shame on you, Jem! How dreadful to lead your sister astray,' said Father. 'You deserve a good thrashing.'

'Oh no!' I said. '*I* must be thrashed, Father, not Jem. *I* wanted to go to the circus to see Madame Adeline. Oh, Father, Mother, I rode with her on her horse and she said I was her Little Star!'

Mother and Father barely reacted. At least Father talked no more of thrashing.

'We must start up a proper search for Gideon. I thought you would all be fine *together* – but that little lad cannot cope on his own. He *must* be found. Do you think he tried to follow you to the circus?'

'He certainly seemed taken with the idea,' Mother wailed. She glared at me, as if it was all my fault . . . which perhaps it was.

Father and Nat went out together to look afresh for Gideon. Mother sent Jem and me upstairs to bed in abject disgrace. I cried and my dear brave brother cried too.

'It will be my fault if anything's happened to

Giddy,' he wept bitterly. 'Oh, Hetty, I should never have taken you to the wretched circus.'

'You only wanted to please me, Jem. Don't cry so. It's *my* fault, not yours,' I said, putting my arms round him, trying to comfort him the way he had comforted me so many times.

It was dark when at last we heard Father and Nat coming back. We jumped out of bed and ran to the top of the stairs – but they didn't have Gideon.

'There's no trace of the lad,' said Father. 'We've had half the village out searching. We've even tried the woods, but it's like looking for a needle in a haystack.'

The woods! I suddenly remembered what Gideon had said: *Are you going to the squirrel house?*

'I know where he might be!' I shouted, running downstairs. 'Oh, Father, Mother, he'll be at the squirrel house. He thought that's where Jem and I were going.'

'*What* squirrel house?' asked Father.

'Oh, Hetty, don't start your silly games. Go back to bed,' said Mother.

'No, Mother, Hetty's right,' said Jem. 'It's an old hollow tree. We used to play there. Gideon asked us if we were going there.'

'Put your jacket on over your nightshirt, boy, and show me,' said Father. 'You come too, Nat.'

I clamoured to come as well, but they wouldn't let me. I stayed shut up in the cottage with Mother and Rosie and Eliza and the baby – and one after another we all wept, longing for Father and the boys to come back, but terrified too, lest they didn't find Gideon.

'I am very wicked,' I wept, sidling up to Mother.

'Yes, you *are* wicked, Hetty,' said Rosie. 'Poor Mother, see what you've done to her.'

Mother had her head in her hands and was crying hard, her whole face wobbling in a distracting fashion.

'What shall I do if my little boy's dead?' she wailed. 'And what will the hospital say? They'll think I'm unfit to care for any more children. They'll take little Eliza away from me—'

'They shan't do that!' said Eliza, cradling her little namesake in her arms. 'Oh, Hetty, this is all your fault.'

I burst out crying afresh, because no one seemed to mind about *me*. I closed my eyes and pictured Madame Adeline.

'Come, my precious Little Star,' she said, holding her arms out. 'Come and live at the circus with me. We will perform every night. I will be the Big Star and you the Little Star. I will give you your own white pony. You will dance on its back and everyone will clap and clap. No one shall ever scold you,

101

dearest Hetty. Jem will come and see us perform in the ring every night, and *he* will clap and clap and you will wave to him. He will tell people proudly that you are his little sister. Rosie and Eliza will beg you to wave at them too, but you won't take any notice of them. You don't want them to be your sisters any more. You don't want Nat to be your brother . . .' But then my vision of Madame Adeline faltered. She could not say the word Gideon. He was my brother for ever and ever, my fellow foundling, almost my twin. If he ceased to be my brother, if he had perished somewhere in the dark woods, then I would go demented with guilt and sorrow.

Madame Adeline faded until she was the merest glimmer of pink. I pictured Gideon instead, howling with terror in the great dark wood, calling for Jem and me until his voice cracked, running and stumbling and falling, lying there in the mud and the leaves, white and limp and broken. Wild creatures scuttled past him but he didn't blink his eyes. They were open for ever in his stark woodland grave . . .

I frightened myself so badly I started screaming. Rosie shook me hard.

'Stop that silly shrieking, Hetty! Shame on you! You just want to be the centre of attention. Stop it this instant.'

I couldn't stop. I managed to quell the noise, but

huge sobs still shook me every second, and tears rolled down my cheeks in a torrent. After a long, long while Mother held out her arms wearily. I crept forward and climbed on her lap. She held me close and whispered soothingly, but she was trembling too, her whole body tensed for the sound of footsteps.

Then at last we heard Father's big boots, the boys' scuffles. Father strode into the cottage and this time *he had Gideon in his arms.* He was holding him like a baby. Gideon's head lolled and his spindly arms and legs dangled lifelessly.

'Oh, he's dead, he's dead!' I cried.

'Hush, Hetty. The little lad's sleeping, but he's fair perished,' said Father.

Mother leaped up, brushing me blindly out of the way, and seized Gideon to her bosom. She wrapped her shawl around him, while Rosie ran for a blanket. Mother had kept the fire burning, so Eliza soon had a stone bottle filled with hot water and bound in a towel, to warm Gideon's icy limbs.

Father knelt beside Mother and spread his own jacket around them both, cradling Gideon's pale face with his big rough hands. Gideon's eyes were half open but he didn't seem to see us. His mouth was open too, but when Rosie tried to feed him a little warm gruel, it dribbled down his chin.

'He *is* dead!' I gasped.

'No, no, he's breathing, dear,' said Mother, bending

her head and putting her ear against Gideon's chest. 'We just need to warm him up a little.'

'He found his way to the squirrel house all by himself,' said Jem. 'But he couldn't hitch himself up into the tree. We found him lying underneath it, shivering and shaking. He cried out when Father picked him up but he's not said anything since. But you mustn't fear, Hetty. I dare say he'll be fine by morning.'

Mother and Father took Gideon to sleep in their own bed, circling him in their arms. I wanted to climb in with them, but they sent me away.

'They don't love me any more because I am so wicked,' I wept.

'Of course they love you, Hetty. You know *I* love you too,' said Jem, letting me scrabble under the covers with him. He wiped my eyes with the sleeve of his nightshirt and stroked my tangled hair. 'I'll always always love you, Hetty, no matter what,' he promised me.

When I went to sleep at last, I dreamed that Gideon never woke up. He lay stiff and white in a glass coffin like Snow White in the storybooks. Mother prayed at his head, Father prayed at his feet, and my brothers and sisters prayed on each side along the length of the coffin. When I tried to join them, they elbowed me out of the way, even Jem.

'Go away, Hetty. I don't love you any more. You are too wicked,' he said harshly.

I crept away by myself. No one noticed when I slunk out of the door. I wandered disconsolately down the lane until I heard the sound of distant drumming. I quickened my pace. By the time I could see the circus I was running fast. There, galloping towards me, was Madame Adeline on her fine white pirate horse. She wore her beautiful pink outfit, with pink roses twined in her flame-red hair. A long gossamer train flew out behind her like a flag.

'My Little Star!' she cried, and she leaned down and scooped me up beside her.

'Oh, Madame Adeline, may I come and live with you?' I said.

'Of course, my precious child!' she said, clasping me close, smelling wonderfully of sweetmeats and roses. She wrapped me tightly in her train. 'Indeed, you *are* my child, my own dear long-lost daughter, and now we will live together for ever. You are not really called Hetty Feather. I named you—'

'Hetty! *Hetty!*'

It was Jem, tugging me.

'Stop it, Jem,' I said furiously, struggling to stay in my wondrous dream.

'But you've wound all the bedclothes right round yourself! You must share them, Hetty.' He tugged hard.

'I'm *not* Hetty,' I said, tugging back because I needed them to be Madame Adeline's train. Then she could bind me close and keep me in the dream.

But it was no use, the dream was fading fast. I vanquished the blanket and lay there, my heart beating hard against my ribs. I relived each dream moment, whispering Madame Adeline's words.

You are my child, my own dear long-lost daughter.

Could it be true? There had been this instant connection between us, almost as if we had recognized each other. We both had flame red hair, pale faces, slender bodies. I had ridden the horse almost as fearlessly as she. Why hadn't I realized sooner? Madame Adeline was my own true mother!

She would not have wanted to be parted from me when I was a babe – but how could she look after me when she rode her horses every day? Folk looked down on beautiful ladies at the circus. I only had to think of Mother's reaction. Perhaps my dear real mother felt she was giving me a better chance in life sending me to the Foundling Hospital? But now I was absolutely certain she was missing me sorely. Perhaps right this moment she was lying awake, wondering if the little child with the red hair and the star on her forehead could possibly be her very own.

I sat upright in bed.

'What is it now, Hetty?' Jem murmured sleepily.

'I have to go to the circus,' I said.

'*What?*' Jem caught hold of me and pulled me back into bed. 'Are you truly demented? It's half past four in the morning. And I *took* you to the circus and look what happened!'

'You don't understand, Jem,' I said.

'I *know* I don't understand! You really are the limit, Hetty.'

'I *have* to go to the circus. Don't you see? Madame Adeline is my *mother*!'

'What did you say? Oh, Hetty, really!' He started laughing.

I pummelled him hard. 'Don't laugh at me! It's true. She told me in my dream.'

'Yes, in your *dream*, Hetty. Not really,' said Jem patiently, trying to catch my wrists. 'Stop hitting me!'

'But you have to believe me. It *is* real. We are so alike, Madame Adeline and me.'

'No you're not! Not the slightest little bit.'

'Look at our hair!'

'Hetty, I don't think Madame Adeline's hair is *really* red, not that bright colour. I think she maybe dyes it.'

'*My* hair is bright, and I do not dye mine. We are so totally alike. Take me to the circus and you will see for yourself.'

'I'm not taking you back to the circus.'

'Then I will go by myself.'

'If you try to do that you will get lost. You are too little to find the way. It will kill Mother if she loses another child. And Father will most likely kill *you* if he finds you – and me, into the bargain. Now lie down properly and go back to sleep like a good little girl.'

He forced me down on my pillow but I couldn't sleep, though I tried hard to seek refuge in my dreams. Eventually I heard Father getting up for work. I slid out of bed quickly and caught him as he went down the stairs.

'Why are you up so early, little minx?' he asked.

'I couldn't sleep, Father,' I said.

'I'm not surprised. I dare say this whole circus escapade was all down to you, Hetty. You have a knack for leading the others astray. Jem's a sensible lad but he's soft as butter where you're concerned.' Father shook his head at me. 'I don't know what to do with you, child. Perhaps it's just as well you won't be with us much longer.'

I felt as if Father's huge fist had punched me straight in the stomach.

'Yes, well might you hang your head,' he said. 'That little lad in my bed was a hair's breadth from death when we found him. He's still icy cold for all he's swaddled in shawls like a newborn babe.'

I dodged round Father and ran into his bedroom.

Mother was lying in bed, propped up on one elbow, crooning a lullaby. Gideon was in a little huddle beside her. I edged towards him, expecting to see a little Jack Frost brother, hair hoary white, icicles hanging from his nose and chin. But Gideon looked almost his usual self, though he was very pale.

I climbed up into bed beside him. Mother put her finger to her lips, frowning at me. She clearly wanted Gideon to sleep – but his dark eyes were wide open.

'Hello, dear Gideon,' I whispered. 'Are you better now?'

Gideon didn't seem able to tell me. His mouth opened and moved but no sound came out.

'I can't hear you,' I said, nuzzling closer, so that my ear was inches from his face.

'Hetty, Hetty, don't squash him! Go back to your own bed,' said Mother.

'But I—'

'I! I! Can't you think of anyone else but yourself, child?' said Mother sharply.

Gideon whimpered at her tone.

Mother glared at me. 'See, you're upsetting your brother. Go *away*!'

All right, I thought. I *will* go away. You don't want me. Father doesn't want me. Even Jem has had enough of me. You're all sending me to the hospital soon anyway. So I'll go away now and save you the trouble.

I stomped out of Mother's bedroom and then crouched at the top of the stairs, tucking my knees up under my nightgown and rubbing my cold feet. I longed for a warm jacket and my boots, but they were in my bedroom and I knew Jem would be suspicious if he saw me putting them on. I took Gideon's boots instead, lying on the landing, still caked with mud and grass from his trek into the forest. They were too big for me but it couldn't be helped. I had difficulty with the laces. I was used to Jem helping me tie neat bows, but I turned and twisted them until they held fast.

I waited, shivering, until I heard Father shut the front door on his way to the farm. I couldn't count beyond ten but I had some idea of time and waited several minutes until I judged it safe. Then I tiptoed downstairs as best I could in my ill-fitting boots. I grabbed a hunk of bread from the larder, and wound an old sack about my shoulders in lieu of a coat. I could not yet write, apart from my name, so I did not leave them a note. I felt a pang for not saying goodbye to Jem, but it couldn't be helped.

I went out the front door, and marched off to join the circus and my true mother.

Oh dear, I am shaking now as I write this. I did not get lost. I was only five then, but I was a very determined child. I hurried through the village, glad that most folk were still in their beds because I looked a queer sight in my sacking and borrowed boots. I could not wait for my own dear mother, Madame Adeline, to clothe me in some beautiful pink outfit so that I looked like a little fairy.

I found exactly the right hole in the hedge to scrabble through to get into the fields. I ran across one, the dewy grass soaking the hem of my night-gown. I stumbled several times, my boots rubbing my bare feet raw, but I was sure I would soon be shod in pink satin slippers. I reached the edge of the field. I fought my way through the second hedge.

There I was, in the circus field – but *where was the circus*? I opened my eyes wide, staring all around. Where was the big tent, the wagons, the horses, Elijah the elephant? Where, oh, where was Madame Adeline?

Had I come to the wrong field after all? Was it on through another hedge? Yes, I had simply miscalculated. But as I wearily started crossing the empty field, I saw the huge circle of crushed grass, scatterings of sawdust, the print of wagon wheels in the earth. Rubbish blew in the wind like gaudy flowers – all that was left of Tanglefield's Travelling Circus.

I had found my true mother – and lost her again.

8

I trudged all the way back home again. What else could I do? I didn't know when the circus had gone. If they'd packed up and travelled all night after the show, they could now be many miles north, south, east or west. And I was too small and scared to run any further. I was freezing cold in spite of my sack, my nightgown was soaked through and stained all over with mud where I'd stumbled, and Gideon's boots seemed intent on paring every inch of flesh from my feet.

I trailed all the way back to the cottage, and as I hobbled homewards I did think with satisfaction that they'd maybe make a fuss of me now. I must have been missing for hours. I thought of the to-do when Father returned with Gideon in his arms. I hoped for just such rejoicing when I limped through the front door. Mother would cast Gideon aside and swoop me up into her arms, Nat would clap his hands, Rosie and Eliza would kiss my pinched cheeks, and Jem . . .

113

I gave a genuine little groan as I thought of dear Jem. How could I have left him without saying a single word of farewell? He would be heartbroken. He might be running crazily round the village this very minute calling for me, striding through the woods, wading through mud and mire, calling my name until his voice cracked. I could picture him so vividly . . .

But I cannot always picture the banal truth. Jem wasn't out searching for me frantically. Jem was fast asleep in his bed, not having missed me for one moment. *None* of the family were aware that I had run away to join the circus. They were all still in their beds, snoring. Even baby Eliza was fast asleep in her cot, though it was past her feeding time.

I thought I'd changed the world but no one had noticed. I got into trouble with Mother later because of the state of my nightgown, but she was too distracted with Gideon to concentrate on giving me a paddling.

Gideon did not get properly better. He warmed up, he ate and drank, he walked around in his uncomfortable boots, he did his few chores – but he seemed like a ghost child now. He was more nervous and timid than ever. If I jumped out at him and went '*Booo!*' he would cower away from me and cry, even though he could see it was only me. He could still laugh, just about, though I laboured long and hard at this. I pulled faces, I tickled him, I said silly rude things, I stood on my hands and waved my legs in the air so he could see my drawers – and yes, Gideon's nose might wrinkle, his mouth twitch into a tiny smile. But he didn't talk any more. He'd always been a quiet child – well, *any* child living with me would seem silent by comparison – but now he didn't talk at *all*.

Mother coaxed him, Father badgered him, the big girls petted him, Nat and Jem tried tricking him and I certainly plagued him, but he stayed resolutely silent.

I could offer him some trinket that I knew he really coveted, perhaps a glass bead as blue as the sky. I'd put it on the table in front of him and say, 'Do you like this bead I found, Gideon?'

He'd nod.

'Would *you* like it?'

He'd nod more eagerly.

'Well, all you have to do is say, "Please may I have the bead, Hetty?" and it is yours.'

Gideon's head drooped.

'Come on, Gid, it's *easy*. You can say it, you know you can. You don't even have to say please. "Can I have the bead?" That's all you have to say.'

Gideon's head drooped further. I took hold of his

jaw and tried to make his lips mouth the words. No sound came out, though tears started to roll down his cheeks.

'Are you *hurting* Gideon, Hetty?' said Mother, bustling into the room.

'No, no, Mother, I'm simply encouraging him to speak,' I said.

Mother paused, diverted by my quaint speech. 'You're a caution, Hetty. I've never known a child like you. I don't know what's to become of you – or Gideon either.' She suddenly sank to her knees and opened her arms wide, hugging both of us to her bosom.

I cuddled up close to Mother. She might not have the starry glamour of Madame Adeline, she might be rough with her tongue, she might paddle me hard for my naughtiness, but she was the only mother I'd known and I still loved her dearly.

'Don't send us to the hospital, Mother!' I begged.

She started, as if I'd read her mind. 'I wish I could keep you, Hetty,' she said, looking straight into my eyes. 'I can't bear to let you go – and it breaks my heart to think of little Gideon there, especially not when . . . when he's not quite himself.'

I wriggled guiltily.

'You will look after your brother when you're at the hospital, Hetty?' Mother said earnestly. 'He can't really look after himself. He'll need you to speak up for him. Will you promise you'll do that, dear?'

'I promise,' I said, though I was shivering so I could hardly speak.

'It's not as if *all* the children will be strangers,' said Mother, perhaps trying to convince herself as well as Gideon and me. 'Saul will be there, and dear little Martha. They will look out for both of you.'

I didn't have Mother's faith in my sister and brother. Besides, the only brother I wanted looking out for me was my own dear Jem.

I started following him like a little shadow, tucking my arm in his, huddling close to him at the table, sitting on his lap. He was so patient with me, playing endless games of picturing: we were pirates, we were polar bears, we were soldiers, we were water babies, we were explorers in Africa – and the simplest and most favourite game of all, we were Hetty and Jem grown up and living together in our own real house, happily ever after.

I was used to dear Jem indulging me, but Gideon was the family favourite. They treated him now like a very special frail baby, dandling him on their knees and ruffling his dark locks. Even Father stopped trying to turn him into a little man. He hoisted him onto his huge shoulders and ran around with him, pretending to be one of his own shire horses.

Gideon squealed in fear and joy, though he still didn't speak.

But suddenly I seemed to be the pet of the family too. Father took me out in the fields with him and held me tight while I rode on the shire's back. The horse was too big to be a comfortable ride and was a simple Goliath plodder compared to Madame Adeline's elegant performing pirate horse – but even so I kicked my heels and held my arms out, pretending I was dressed in pink spangles in the circus ring.

Nat had started whittling simple toys from pieces of wood. He fashioned me a horse and Gideon an elephant. To be truthful, the only way we could distinguish them was by size, but it was kind of my big brother all the same.

Rosie and Eliza were surprisingly sweet to me too, letting me play grown-up ladies in their best dresses, even tying my hair up high and fastening it with pins. We played we were three big girls together and they sprayed me with their precious lavender perfume and told me special big-girl secrets.

Even little Eliza seemed extra fond of me and smiled and waved her tiny fists in glee whenever I picked her up.

'You're like a real little mother, Hetty,' said Mother, sounding truly proud.

I basked in all this praise and attention. For

a child considered ultra-sharp, my wits weren't working at all. It wasn't till the last night that it actually dawned on me. Rosie and Eliza sang baby songs to Gideon and gave us great kisses all over our cheeks until even my pale brother turned rosy as an apple. Nat gave us a bear hug. Father sat us both on his big knees and jiggled us up and down, playing, *This is the way the ladies ride*. Mother made us each a cup of cocoa brimming with cream, a rare treat. Just two cups, one for Gideon and one for me. I looked over at Jem. I knew he loved cream too.

'Can't Jem have cocoa too, Mother?' I asked.

'No, dear, it's just for you two little ones,' said Mother. 'Now drink it all up like a good girl before I get you both ready for bed.'

I went to sit beside Jem, who had been very quiet all evening. 'Take a sip, Jem,' I whispered.

Jem shook his head quietly. He kept his head bent but I saw he had tears in his eyes. My stomach squeezed tight. Why was Jem so sad?

I saw Mother boiling up a great pan of water on the stove: hot washing water, though it wasn't bath night. Then at last it dawned on me. She was going to take Gideon and me to the hospital *tomorrow*!

I'd known for years that I had to go back to the Foundling Hospital. For the past few months folk had referred to it openly and often – I had myself. But it had still seemed distant, long in the future, not anything to worry about right this minute. But now suddenly it had sprung upon me. This was *it* – my last night in the cottage.

The sweet cocoa soured in my mouth. I crept so near Jem I was practically in his lap. He saw I'd realized, and put a finger to his lips, nodding at Gideon. My little brother was smiling as he sipped his cocoa. Mother pulled off his shirt and said, 'Skin a rabbit,' and Gideon made a bunny face, twitching his nose. He was almost his old self again, though he still wasn't talking. I knew if I cried out that we were going to the hospital the very next day, Gideon would be frightened into fits. So I closed my mouth, pressing my hands over my lips to make certain I would not talk.

Jem hugged me tight. 'What a dear brave girl you are, Hetty,' he whispered in my ear.

I didn't want to be brave. I wanted to scream and make a huge despairing fuss, but I could see that would spoil everything for Gideon – and for me too. So I held my tongue and choked down my cocoa, though I couldn't stop my tears brimming as I gazed around the little room that had been my home for the last five years. I could not bear to think I would never see it again. I could not bear to think I would not see Mother, Father and my brothers and sisters, my family. I especially could not bear to think I would never see my dear Jem again.

The tears rolled down my face and I hid my head in my hands.

'Look at Hetty, she's tired herself out!' said Eliza.

'A quick bath in the tub and then you'll be tucked up in bed, Hetty dear,' said Rosie.

I let my sisters undress me and lift me up into the soapy water. Mother washed me all over and rubbed the soapsuds into my hair so hard I thought the red might run away with the water. Then I was towelled vigorously, a nightgown thrust over my head, and I was carried upstairs. I kept my eyes closed all the time, even when everyone gave me a goodnight kiss. I was tucked up beside Gideon, who was already genuinely asleep. I lay there, waiting.

Then Jem crept upstairs. He got into bed beside me and put his arms around me. I buried my head in his chest and wept.

'There, Hetty. There, there, dear Hetty,' he murmured.

'I don't want to go!' I sobbed. 'I shall run away. Yes, I shall run away right now.'

'Where will you run to, Hetty?'

'I shall find the circus. I shall live with Madame Adeline,' I said. 'Perhaps she really is my mother.'

'How will you find the circus? It could be right up in Scotland or way down in Cornwall. The circus is *gone*, Hetty.'

'I'll still run away,' I said.

'But what will you eat? Where will you live? Who will look after you?'

'I will eat berries and nuts, and I will sleep curled up in trees and haystacks and barns.' I paused, trying to work it out in my head. 'And – and if you will run away too, Jem, then *you* can look after me.'

'Oh, Hetty. I wish I could. I've tried to plot it out. I could maybe get farm work far away where they don't know me – though I'm not really big or strong enough yet. And you can't work for years and years, Hetty.'

'You could do the work for me.'

'Yes, but they wouldn't let you tag along too. They would say you needed to be cared for. They would seize you and put you in the workhouse, and that would be much worse than the hospital. So don't you see, Hetty, we *can't* run away, though I wish we could with all my heart.'

'Oh, Jem, please please please don't let them take me away,' I wept, past reasoning.

He held me close and murmured stories in my ear about my time at the hospital. 'Everyone will like you – how could they not? – and you will make good friends there. You will learn lots at school and the years will go by in a blink, and *then*, when you are all grown up, I will come and find you, remember?'

'We will truly have our own house?' I snuffled.

'Yes, our own dear house, and we will live there together. And when I am an old old man with a grey beard and you are an old old lady, hopefully *not* with a beard—'

I giggled in spite of everything.

'Then we will scarcely remember we were ever separated. I promise we will be together and live happily ever after, just like the fairy tales.'

He told me this over and over until I went to sleep in a soggy little heap on his chest – and whenever I woke in the night he whispered it all over again.

Then suddenly Mother was shaking me, easing me out of bed. I clung frantically to Jem.

'There now, Hetty,' he said. 'Let me dress her, Mother. You go and get Gideon ready.'

Jem did his best to dress me in my best clothes, though I did not make it easy for him, keeping my arms pinned to my sides and curling my feet so they couldn't be stuffed into my boots.

'Stop being so difficult, Hetty dear,' he said wearily. 'I will dress too and come with you as far as I can. Try to be a big brave girl.'

I didn't feel big and brave. I felt very very small and very very scared, but I did not make a fuss as Jem fastened my Sunday frock, tied the ribbons of my starched pinafore and buttoned my boots. I washed my face and Jem brushed my hair for me, running his hands through the silky newly-washed strands.

'At least I'll be able to pick you out from a crowd of hundreds, Hetty,' he said. 'No one could ever have as red hair as you. There! You look lovely now.'

I gave him a fierce hug.

'Careful! You'll crease your pinafore,' said Jem.

'I hate silly pinafores,' I said.

Oh, how I longed to be barefoot in my old flower-sprigged cotton dress, ready for a day's larking with my dear brother. I clutched him harder and he held me fast.

'Ready, children?' Mother called.

She had Gideon dressed now, but he was still half asleep, his eyes drooping. We went downstairs and Mother cut us bread and poured us milk. I was too fearful to eat and Gideon too tired. I sat on Jem's lap and Gideon sat on Mother's. It was as if we'd regressed five years and were back to being little babies.

'It's time to go,' said Mother.

Gideon wriggled a little, looking puzzled.

'Come on, my pet. Let Mother carry you,' she said, hoisting him up in her arms.

He held his wooden elephant tight by the trunk. I had my dear old rag baby *and* my new horse, but

I wished Jem had made it for me and not Nat. But Jem had another gift for me, a tiny present in a twist of rag. I opened it up carefully and found a silver sixpence, polished until it shone. I stared at it in awe.

'I earned it running errands. I'll earn you many more sixpences,' Jem whispered earnestly. 'Then, when you're bigger, I can take you to the circus in style.'

'Oh, Jem!' I said. 'Dear, dear Jem.'

'Keep it safe in your pinafore pocket. You can spend it on anything you like.'

I held the sixpence tight in my hand. I knew I would never be tempted to spend a penny of it. I would do my level best to hang onto it for ever.

Father was already out at the farm and Nat and the girls were still asleep. Even baby Eliza was quiet in her cradle. I could not say goodbye to them, so instead I whispered goodbye to my little stool and the scrubbed table and the coloured pictures on the walls. They were mostly scenes from the Bible – baby Jesus in the stable, Joseph in his coloured coat and Daniel in the lions' den. The picture I liked best hung halfway up the stairs: two chubby children in nightgowns with a tall white guardian angel spreading his wings over them protectively.

I ran up to the angel picture and said goodbye.

As I turned back to Jem and Mother and Gideon, I fancied I heard a beat of big wings, a sudden breeze in the thick air of the cottage, as if the angel had stepped right out of the picture and was arching his wings over me.

I tried hard to picture him above us as we trudged down the lane towards the village. We got to the crossroads – and there was Sam waiting with his horse and cart. Gideon clapped his hands, totally misunderstanding. He thought this was a special shopping day. Sam was taking us to town to buy new clothes or new boots, a new kettle or a set of china plates or a washstand, and perhaps a toffee apple or a sugar cane for us children if we were very good.

'Well, the little lad doesn't seem too down-hearted,' Sam said, chucking him under the chin. 'The little missy looks mournful though, bless her.'

'Say goodbye to Jem now, Hetty,' said Mother, lifting Gideon up into the cart.

'No! No!' I said, tears spilling.

'I'll come on the cart with you,' said Jem. 'Hush, Hetty, I'm coming too.'

'You'll miss a morning's school,' said Mother.

'What's school, when I can be with Hetty an hour longer?' said Jem.

'You can't come, Jem. Sam has business in town and won't be able to take you back in the cart.'

'Then I'll walk back,' said Jem. He said it as if

seven miles was a short stroll. He sounded so firm that Mother didn't argue with him further.

Jem lifted me into the cart and jumped up after me. Mother settled herself with Gideon on her lap. He reached out to me and touched my wet cheeks, looking anxious now. Then he looked up at Mother.

'Hush, my pet,' she said, as if he'd spoken.

Then Sam clicked his teeth at his old brown nag and she started trotting along the road and up the hill. Jem held me tight. I craned my neck to see the village for as long as possible. As we got higher up the hill, I could just make out our own cottage on the edge of the village, like a little grey face with thatched hair on top. Then it blurred into a grey dot. I was starting to feel sick from twisting backwards, so I wriggled round and faced forward, my head on Jem's shoulder.

9

Jem and I were both numb with misery and so tired from our broken night that both our heads nodded in spite of ourselves. Every now and then I woke with a start and Jem murmured, 'There now, Hetty, I'm here.' Once I woke first, and when Jem twitched and started awake with a cry, I said quietly, 'There now, Jem, I'm here,' reaching up to put my arms round him.

Then we saw smoke in the distance, and houses started to line the road, and we were almost at the town. On those rare shopping days in the past we'd wriggle around excitedly and start to sing. This time we were silent.

'I meant to tell you a story all the way to comfort you, but the words wouldn't come,' Jem whispered.

'Never mind, never mind,' I whispered back. 'I do love you so, Jem.'

'I love you too, my Hetty. You have your sixpence safe?'

'In my pocket, look. Oh, Jem, I've nothing to give you!'

'Give me a kiss, Hetty, that's all I want.'

I leaned even closer and carefully blew a big kiss into his ear.

'There, my kiss is inside you now,' I said, imagining it flying around like a little caged bird.

Sam drove his cart through the crowded streets of the town towards the big station. It loomed above us, its great steel archway a gaping maw. I'd always loved peeping inside at the huge trains blowing out steam with a roar like gleaming dragons – but now I shrank back. We clung to the sides of the cart, shivering. Then Mother saw the great clock and gasped.

'Look at the time! Oh Lordy, we'll miss the train if we're not hasty. Set us down, Sam.'

She jumped from the cart, taking Gideon in her arms. He moaned at the noise and hid his head under her shawl.

'Come, Hetty. Jem, you have to go home.'

'Let me go on the train too, Mother, I beg you.'

'No, son. I haven't got the fare for you. The hospital sent the exact amount, one third-class seat and two children.'

'I can hide from the ticket man, Mother,' said Jem. 'I can run right through the barrier and—'

'Nonsense! Do you want to get us all into

130

trouble? Now we're late, the train is due to leave any minute. Get *down*, Hetty!' She pulled me from the cart, twisting my arm in her haste, so that I started bawling.

'Stop that noise!' said Mother. 'We must go to find our carriage.' She looked anxiously at Jem. 'Take care going home, for goodness' sake. If you lose your way, find a kindly-looking lady to set you on the right path. Promise me you'll be a sensible lad and go straight back. I can't take any more worries.'

'But, Mother, I *have* to come too,' said Jem, jumping down from the cart and putting his arms round me. 'Hetty needs me so. I have to look after her.'

'You *can't* look after her. You're only a silly little boy,' Mother snapped in her distress and frustration.

It was as if her words were some dreadful antidote to our magic spell. Jem had always towered like a giant, but now he shrivelled into a small boy scarcely bigger than me – a boy who started sobbing.

'Say goodbye *now*, Jem,' Mother commanded.

Jem reached up to Gideon in her arms and kissed his white cheek. Then he bent and kissed me too, on both my cheeks and then my lips.

'Goodbye, Hetty. I love you so,' he mumbled.

'I love you too, Jem. I love you, I love you, I love you.'

'You won't forget me, will you, Hetty?'

'Never ever ever ever ever ever . . .' I still chanted it as Mother tore our hands apart and bustled Gideon and me past the barrier and the ticket man, urging us towards the train. I craned my neck and saw Jem waving and waving. I sawed my own free arm wildly in the air until Mother found the third-class carriages at last and tugged us up into the train as the whistle went.

I sat on the seat by the door, my legs sticking out. I fingered the leather strap to open the window. As we started chugging slowly out of the station, I wondered if I dared leap right out. I could jump onto the platform, rejoin Jem, and then we could run away together . . .

Mother slapped my hands away from the strap. 'Stop that, Hetty! Do you want to fall out to your death?'

'Yes!' I declared, deciding I did indeed want to die if I couldn't be with Jem.

As the train gathered speed and hastened through the town and out into the countryside, I pictured myself leaping out of the window. My guardian angel would scurry down and snatch me up in his strong arms. We would fly up and up to Heaven. I would wear a snowy nightgown and build castles in the clouds and jump from star to star . . .

'I definitely want to die,' I declared.

'That's a dreadful thing to say, child,' said Mother, shocked. 'You can't mean it.'

'Yes, I do. I'd like to go to Heaven right this minute.'

'If you choose to kill yourself, you'll go straight to the Other Place, Hetty,' Mother reminded me.

I thought about H-e-l-l. I remembered the time a hot coal fell out of the fire and glanced against my leg. It had hurt so badly I screamed and screamed – and then I'd had to stump around with a rag bandage for a week or more. I pictured burning my whole body, cooking for all eternity.

I decided I didn't want to die just yet. I stopped fiddling with the carriage door and slumped in my seat, my chin on my chest. Gideon reached out and clutched my hand. His eyes were wide with fear now. He burrowed hard against Mother.

'There now, my lambkin, Mother's here,' she said automatically.

Gideon kept quiet, but he started crying, tears seeping down his cheeks. I cried too, clutching my rag baby, using her soft legs as a handkerchief when I got too damp and soggy. Mother pulled me closer, her arms round both of us now.

The train started slowing down. I peered out of the window in agitation. Were we there already?

Mother saw my expression. 'It's a long

133

journey, Hetty. A couple of hours until we get to London town.'

Gideon wailed fearfully, understanding properly now. The train stopped at a little country station and a large woman in a purple gown squeezed herself into our carriage. She smelled very sweet and her cheeks were very red. I thought she must have been running hard to catch the train, but Mother sniffed slightly and edged away from her.

The purple lady beamed at all three of us. 'Hello, my dearies. Why the tears and long faces?' She peered at Gideon's pale face and dark-circled eyes. 'Oh dear, is he not well, the little lad?'

'He's been poorly,' Mother said shortly. She stuck out her shoulder, trying to protect Gideon from the purple woman's glance.

She looked at me instead. 'And what about this little mite?' she asked. 'Why are you crying so, my dearie?'

I sniffed, not knowing what to say. 'I don't want to go to Hell,' I mumbled – though I wanted to go to the hospital even less.

'Hetty!' Mother hissed.

The purple women shook with laughter. We could hear her stays creaking. She threw back her head, her chins wobbling. Then she reached into her reticule for a lace handkerchief and dabbed at her streaming eyes. 'Children!' she said to Mother. 'Oh my Lord, the things they say!' She looked at me, pinching my cheek with her fat fingers. 'Cheer up, little girlie. Have you been a bad girl plaguing your mother, is that it? Here, I know what will cheer you up.' She ferreted around at the bottom of her bag and came up with a fruit drop as red as a ruby. 'Aha, what have we here? Pop it in your mouth quick!'

'Thank you kindly, but Hetty's not allowed—' Mother started, but the drop was in my mouth before she could finish her sentence.

'There, that worked a treat, didn't it?' said the purple woman triumphantly. 'Shall we find one for your brother now?' She discovered an emerald-green fruit drop and offered it to Gideon.

Mother sighed. 'Oh, very well.'

She stoppered Gideon's mouth with the sweet.

'Say thank you, children,' said Mother.

I thanked the purple woman and Gideon nodded his head.

'Think nothing of it, my dears,' she said. 'How old are you, missy?' she asked me.

'I'm five going on six, ma'am,' I said.

'And what about you, little boy?'

Gideon said nothing. Mother didn't seem inclined to answer for him.

'He's five too,' I piped up.

The purple woman seemed surprised. She peered at Gideon, she peered at me. Then she looked at

Mother. 'They're never twins! They don't look a jot alike.'

'They're not twins,' Mother said uncomfortably.

'Oh my. But they *are* brother and sister?' She pulled one of my red plaits. Then she lowered her voice. 'Do they perhaps have different *fathers*? Neither child favours you, my dear.'

Mother snorted down her nose. 'I don't care to discuss it. Particularly not in front of the children.' She couldn't have been plainer if she'd said *Mind your own business* – but the purple woman would not be put off.

'No need to be so humpty-tumpty, missus,' she said, chuckling. '*My* two kiddies have two fathers, and neither father was my husband, but we've managed just fine and dandy – and I've a real husband now to support us all.'

She showed off the gold ring on her fat finger. She was talking in riddles as far as I was concerned, but Mother was outraged.

'I'm a respectable married woman,' she said. 'These two dear lambs happen to be my *foster* children.'

'Really, my dear? Well, there's a thing! Foster children, eh? That's a fine idea. So are their real mothers dead then?'

'*No!*' I said.

Mother usually told me off when I used that tone,

but she patted my shoulder now. 'They've never known their mothers. These are children from the Foundling Hospital.' She said it with her head held high, as if it was something to be proud of.

The purple woman certainly seemed impressed. 'The Foundling Hospital, hmm? I dare say they pay you royally then. How much do you get for their keep, if you don't mind me asking?'

Mother clearly *did* mind, but she murmured, 'Eighteen pence a week.'

'For the two of them?'

'Per child.'

'My Lordy, that's a fortune, especially as these two are the size of sparrows, hardly likely to eat you out of house and home.'

'I look after my children for love, not money,' said Mother. Then her voice broke. 'And now I have to take them back to the Foundling Hospital and my heart is breaking.' She started sobbing. Her arms were still stretched round us so she couldn't hide her face. She wept openly, tears dripping down her dear big face.

The purple women seemed taken aback. 'Don't upset yourself so, dearie. I'm sure they'll be well cared for. It's not as if you're putting them in the workhouse, now, is it? They'll do very well back at the hospital, and you can always get yourself another baby or two to keep your income steady.'

137

'You don't understand,' Mother sobbed. '*I* didn't understand. These children seem like *mine*.'

We understood, Gideon and I. She was our mother. She'd been Martha's mother too, and Saul's.

I threw myself against her chest, winding my arms round her neck. Gideon was fairly suffocating but did not protest. We three hugged each other hard. All thoughts of Madame Adeline rode right out of my head on that white pony. At that moment I was hugging the only mother I wanted.

The purple woman was at last subdued. She stopped talking until a new woman joined our carriage at the next station. Then they set up a conversation together, their voices low so we could scarcely hear them. It seemed they were talking about us.

We clung tightly to Mother the entire journey. At long last the train hissed and puffed into a vast echoing station with steel buttresses arching overhead, like a smoky cathedral. Doors opened and slammed, and there was a scurrying and clamour that unnerved all three of us. We stood still while people pushed us and jostled us and complained in harsh, high voices.

'Let's go back home, Mother!' I begged.

Mother looked at us. Her hands tightened on our shoulders. She bit her lip. For a moment I thought she was actually going to bundle us back on the train. But then she took a deep breath.

'We *can't* go back home, Hetty,' she said very sadly. 'You are my dear children, but you are not allowed to stay with me. You have to go to the Foundling Hospital now.'

She led us across the station forecourt to a public lavatory. This was such a novelty to us that in spite of our misery we marvelled at the white porcelain and brass chain and the proper paper for wiping ourselves. When we had relieved ourselves, Mother washed the train soot from our hands and faces and then fumbled in her purse. She brought out two bone lockets, each hanging on a silk ribbon.

'These are for you,' she said, tying one round my neck.

'Is Gideon having a necklace too, Mother?' I said, surprised.

I picked up my locket and peered at it. There was a long number engraved on one side. I read it out with difficulty: I didn't know my numbers yet the way I knew the alphabet.

'This is your number at the hospital, Hetty. You are foundling number 25629 and Gideon is number 25621.'

'So are there thousands and thousands of children at the hospital, Mother?'

'No, no, the hospital has been open a very long time. All the first foundlings have grown up and maybe had children and grandchildren of their own, and now they are in their graves. So many children,' said Mother. She bent closer to us. 'And you two – and Saul and Martha – are the best foundling children ever. Take no notice if folk spurn you or cast aspersions because your real mothers could not care for you. You hold your heads up high and let me be proud of you.'

We stared back at her earnestly, tipping our chins up and stretching our necks. She gave us each a warm kiss on the lips and then took us by the hand.

'Come then, my children.'

We emerged into the loud, hissing bustle of the station. Mother led us outside, where the hansom cabs were waiting.

'Please take us to Guilford Street,' said Mother, fingering her fat purse to show she could pay the fare.

'The Foundling Hospital?' said the cab driver. He sucked his teeth and shook his head at us. 'Poor little mites.'

We clambered inside his cab and peered out in awe and terror at the crowded London streets. Mother might have been a country woman, but she proudly showed us St Paul's Cathedral as we passed slowly over Waterloo Bridge. We could not believe the traffic everywhere. We were used to seeing one cart at a time in the village lanes. There seemed to be *hundreds* of cabs and carriages and carts and huge omnibuses crowded with city folk. Men in smart dark suits marched on foot over the bridge. I wondered if they could be some strangely garbed army, but Mother said they were simply businessmen on their way to and from work. There were ladies too, their skirts drawn up in comical bustles at the back, trit-trotting in their tiny shoes. They had to hold up their skirts and tread warily when they crossed the streets, which were covered in horse dung.

We were country children and used to horse dung – *and* clearing out the pigsty – but we'd never smelled it so strongly before. The river smelled sour and strange too, with a greasy slick shining in the water. What sort of city was this where you couldn't stroll along the streets or swim in the river?

Once we were over the bridge, the cab travelled through such a muddle of streets, some very broad and big, some narrow twisting alleyways, so that I was hopelessly muddled and confused. My heart thudded whenever I spotted any great grey building in case it was the hospital. At last the cab slowed and came to a stop outside great iron gates enclosing a plain wide building with many arched windows.

Mother drew in her breath and clutched our hands tight. She didn't need to tell us. We were at the Foundling Hospital.

10

Gideon and I huddled in the cab. Mother had to pull us out.

'Please be so good as to wait,' she said to the cabman, and approached the porter. 'If you please, sir, I'm bringing my two foster children back to the hospital,' she said.

He nodded and let us through the forbidding gates.

Mother walked us along the long gravel path towards the doorway. We stared up at all the windows but we couldn't see inside. There were no children peeping out at us, no children playing on the grass, no children anywhere. I strained my ears but could hear no chatter, no singing, no laughter.

Mother rang the doorbell, and a tall woman in a dark dress and white apron opened the door. She had a white cap tied on her head and a long grim face. She did not smile.

'Foundlings 25621 and 25629?' she said.

'Yes, ma'am,' said Mother huskily. 'This is Gideon Smeed and Hetty Feather. They are such dear

143

children. Hetty is very bright indeed, and Gideon is very good and loving, though he doesn't speak just at present. He needs a little extra cosseting—'

'We treat all our foundlings in exactly the same manner. We have no favourites here,' said the nurse. 'Come along, children.'

She held out her hands. We shrank backwards, clutching Mother.

'Say goodbye,' the nurse said firmly.

I was struck as dumb as Gideon. I couldn't believe it was actually happening. Not now, not so coldly and quickly.

Mother gathered us together and kissed us, first me, then Gideon. 'Goodbye, my dear lambs. Try to be good and make me proud of you,' she whispered. 'Hetty, look after your brother.'

She straightened up and took a step backwards. Then she turned and ran down the path, her hand over her eyes.

'Mother!' I called.

Before she could look back the nurse shut the door, trapping us inside the hospital. She clasped our hands determinedly. Her own hands were icy cold and startlingly smooth – we were used to Mother's big work-roughened hands.

'I am Nurse Beaufort. Come with me,' she said, setting off at a quick march.

We had to scurry fast to keep up with her. Gideon

tripped once and she jerked his arm impatiently, hurting him. He started crying then, big tears splashing down his cheeks.

'Don't cry so, Gideon. I am here. I will look after you,' I said desperately.

'Ssh, child. You are not allowed to talk until outdoor playtime,' said the nurse, yanking my arm too.

She pulled us up a long flight of stairs. There was another nurse standing there, waiting. She was dressed in an identical dark frock and white starched apron, but she was smaller and very squat. Her dress strained at the seams and her white cap seemed too small for her dark-pink face. She had little eyes, prominent nostrils and several chins, looking for all the world like a pig in a bonnet. I gave a little snort, half laughing, half crying.

'Be quiet, child,' she snapped. She seized me by the shoulders and propelled me to the right. My head jerked round. Tall, grim Nurse Beaufort was propelling Gideon *the other way*.

'Oh no, if you please, Nurse, Gideon and me, we have to stay together!' I said, struggling.

'I am not a nurse! I am Matron Peters. Now come *along*, child. You cannot go with your brother. The small girls' wing is *this* way,' said Pigface Peters.

'But you don't understand! He's only little. He can't manage without me.'

'Nonsense.'

145

'It is *not* nonsense!' I shouted, stopping in my tracks. 'I have to look after Gideon. I promised Mother.'

'You must forget all about your foster mother now. You are a foundling child and you will obey *our* rules. Our boys and girls live separately – and so will you.'

'Then let me say goodbye to Gideon! Let me explain to him. Oh *please*!'

'Stop this ridiculous fuss this instant, Hetty Feather!'

'I *won't* stop! You are very cruel and wicked and I hate you!' I cried.

I twisted my wrist out of her grasp and ran the other way, after Gideon.

'Gideon! Oh, Gideon!' I shouted.

He was dragging his feet and drooping, his boots barely supporting him. He looked round, his eyes wide, his mouth a great O of terror.

Then fat pig-trotter fingers seized me by the shoulders. She hauled me along, kicking and screaming, marching me to the right, away from my poor brother.

'How *dare* you behave so atrociously! You will be sorry, my girl, very sorry.'

She pushed me into a strange cold room with small bathtubs in orderly rows.

'Right, missy, take your clothes off instantly. You need a bath.'

I stared at her. 'But I've *had* a bath. I'm clean as clean, look!'

'*Country* clean,' she said scornfully. 'You need a good scrubbing to get rid of all those nasty bugs and beasties. Get those clothes off while I fill the tub.'

I took off my coat and then sat down to start unlacing my boots. The matron crumpled my good coat up into a little ball and dropped it into a basket. I gave her one boot and she threw it on top of my coat, careless of the muddy soles. She saw my shocked expression.

'You won't need these any more,' she said, giving the basket a contemptuous shake.

I blinked at her. Were the foundling children required to run around *naked*?

'You will wear our uniform now,' she said.

'Can I wear my best clothes on Sundays, miss?'

'You must call me *Matron*. No, you wear your white tippets and aprons on the Sabbath, with bands around your cuffs, specially snowy white. And woe betide you if you get them dirty. Now hurry *up*, child. Get the rest of your clothes off and step into the bath this instant.'

While she was topping up the bath, her back turned, I took Jem's precious sixpence out of my pinafore pocket. I stuck it inside my mouth for want of a better place to hide it. The coin tasted unpleasantly metallic and felt as big as a dinner plate against my cheek, but it couldn't be helped.

I was right to be so cautious. Once I had my pinafore and dress and drawers off, standing shivering in my shift and stockings, the matron darted at me, snatched my rag baby and threw her in the basket too.

'She's not clothes! She's my baby!' I protested, though it was hard to talk distinctly with the sixpence wedged in my cheek.

'It's nasty and dirty. And you're not allowed dollies here.'

'But I can't sleep without her!'

'Then you will have to stay awake,' said the matron.

She pulled the shift over my head, plucked my stockings from my feet, lifted me up and plunged me into the bath. Then she took a cake of red carbolic soap and started scrubbing me viciously. I wriggled and squirmed at the indignity, especially when she started washing my long hair, digging her fat fingers into my scalp and kneading it as if my head was a ball of dough. I put my hands up, trying to protect my poor head. My fingers scratched her wrists and she dug harder, furious.

'Keep still, you fiery little imp,' she said, lathering me into a foam. She fetched another jug to rinse the suds away. 'This will quench that fire!' she said, pouring icy cold water over me.

I gasped in shock and would have screamed at her, but I had to keep my mouth stoppered because of the sixpence. Then she hauled me out onto the cold floor and wrapped a thin towel round me.

'Well, dry yourself, child, hurry up, hurry up!'

When I was halfway dry she sat me on a stool and picked up a pair of scissors. I started trembling. What did she intend to do now? Cut off my fingernails? Cut off my *fingers*?

She attacked my head with a hairbrush, smoothing out all the tangles so that my hair fell in a silky curtain past my shoulders – and then she started snip-snip-snipping, cutting my hair off right up to my ears.

'Oh, *please* don't cut my hair!' I begged, but she paid no heed. She snipped until my hair was shorter than a boy's and I was covered in damp red tendrils. She brushed them off me with the towel and then fetched another basket, the clothes inside this one neatly folded.

'This will be your clothes basket, Hetty Feather. You are to keep your clothes in it at night, and woe betide you if you rumple them.'

She pulled out boots and stockings and bade me put them on. The stockings were stiff and bunched at the toes with repeated darning, and the boots were much too big for my small feet. I told Matron, but she didn't appear to care.

'Put your dress on now – the *right* way round, you silly child. I will tie your apron for you.'

I hesitated. Where were my new undergarments? I saw something white in my basket, but it was simply a strange old-fashioned cap. There was no shift, no drawers, nothing!

I sidled over to my old clothes.

'Leave them alone! They're going to be disposed of straight away.'

'But, miss – Matron – I have no drawers!' I said, agonized.

The matron's pig face went even pinker. 'You do not wear such garments here,' she said. 'Now put that dress on at once.'

I stuck my poor shorn head through the stiff brown serge. It felt hard and scratchy against my scrubbed skin. She did up my buttons at the back for me, tied on the apron, and then stuck the cap upon me.

'There!' Matron marched me over to a speckled mirror above the stone slab sinks. 'Respectable at last!'

I stared at the forlorn figure in the mirror. Was that weird little creature in the cap really *me*? I shook my head violently, but the girl in the mirror shook her head back at me.

'Now you will join the other infant girls. Come with me.'

I hung back, fidgeting. 'Please, miss – Matron – I need the privy,' I blurted.

She consulted the watch pinned to her chest. 'The infant relief break is not for another hour. You will have to wait.'

'But I need to go *now*! Please, I'm nearly wetting myself!'

She sighed impatiently. 'The privies are outside in the yard. I'm not trailing you all the way there. You will have to use a chamber pot. Go in that little room and be quick about it. You must learn to control your bladder as well as your temper, Hetty Feather.'

I ran into the room, selected an ugly pot and sat on it, trembling. What sort of a madhouse was this? I put my fingers up under my cap and felt the shorn ends of my hair. I gave a little sob. Even if I managed to run away back to Jem, maybe he wouldn't love me any more because I looked such a fright.

'Hurry up, child!' Pigface grunted outside.

Safe behind the door, I took the sixpence out of my mouth, stuck out my tongue and waggled it at her. Then I hid the sixpence in my new tight cuff and jumped up from the pot.

'Now wash your hands!' she said as I came out of the little room. 'Dear goodness, do you know nothing of hygiene?'

I didn't think it at all hygienic to run around without underwear. I wondered if the matron wore drawers herself. I imagined her big piggy-pink bare bottom.

'What are you smirking at?' she said suspiciously.

I lowered my eyes and shook my head. 'Nothing, Matron.'

'Then come along with me. You will join your class at their afternoon tasks.'

She took hold of me by the wrist. I looked back at the little basket of my Sunday clothes, so lovingly washed and pressed by Mother. They were all in a muddy jumble now, my poor rag baby sprawling on top, arms and legs akimbo.

'Come on! You've no need of those nasty old clothes any more, I've told you that already,' said Matron Pigface.

'Mayn't I just kiss my baby goodbye?' I begged.

'I've never heard such nonsense. It's only a bundle of rags!' she said, and she would not let me.

I pictured my poor baby so forlorn without her mother. I heard her wailing, abandoned in the basket. I wished she was little enough to hide about my person, like the sixpence. But there was nothing I could do. I had to leave her there, tumbled about in my clothes. I never saw her again.

As Matron Pigface marched me along to my class, I thought at least I would meet up with Gideon again – but there was no sign of him. I was thrust into a room of some forty or fifty girls of five or six or seven, but there was not a single little boy. The girls were sitting at small wooden desks, all startlingly similar in their white caps and mud-hued dresses. They all stared hard at me and then whispered. I shifted from one sorely-shod foot to the other, feeling so shy and strange.

'This is Hetty Feather,' said Pigface.

Several of the little girls giggled. My hands clenched into fists.

'Thank you, Matron Peters,' said a starch-aproned nurse at the front of the class. She wasn't pink and pig-faced, she wasn't grim and pale. *This* nurse had rosy cheeks and dimples and wisps of curly hair escaping from her cap. She was as sweet and fresh-faced as Rosie or Eliza or any of the village girls. She smiled at me.

'I would watch this one. She's got a *very* contrary way with her. Redheads are always little vixens,' said Matron Pigface Peters. 'She needs that temper quelled. Spare the rod and spoil the child, remember!' She shorted, and then waddled out of the room, her stays creaking loudly.

'Hello, Hetty dear,' said this new nurse, beckoning to me.

I crept up to her desk. I saw a leather strap lying across it. Oh Lordy, was she about to punish me already?

No, she leaned towards me and said gently, 'Do not look so fearful, child. It must seem very strange your first day here, but I promise you will soon get used to life at the hospital. You seem very small. Are you turned five yet?'

'I am almost six,' I said.

'Excellent! Then I think you are old enough to learn how to darn, Hetty.' She brought out a stocking and a needle and wool from her desk. 'Did your foster mother teach you how to sew, Hetty?' she asked.

The word Mother made my eyes well up. I shook my head wordlessly.

'Then I will show you.'

She threaded the big needle, squeezing the end of the wool over with practised skill, and then put her hand inside the stocking. She started looping the wool across the hole in neat lines.

'There, do you see?'

Then she started weaving the wool the other way, making the neatest, smoothest patch. I watched, fascinated in spite of my misery. My head was itching horribly after my haircut and I put up my hand to scratch, knocking my cap sideways.

'Try not to scratch, dear, it's not very ladylike,' said the nurse. She put down the beautifully darned stocking and took my cap off. She smoothed my poor shorn hair, drying now, and sticking straight up in the air.

'My goodness, I think I remember you!' she said. 'You were the smallest baby I'd ever seen – and you had the reddest hair!'

She was the nurse who had cradled me when I was newborn and wouldn't suck properly! She was dear kind Winnie, though now she told me to call her Nurse Winterson. She bade me sit on a stool beside her while I struggled to darn a stocking myself. I badly wanted to impress this gentle nurse and show her I could act like a big girl, even though I was so small – but I couldn't get the hang of darning at all.

I pulled the needle too hard so that it came right off the wool, and then I had no end of bother re-threading it. Nurse Winterson kept threading it for me, and patiently guided my hands, but I could barely do a single stitch. I was in such a state I came near to flinging the stocking upon the floor.

I heard whispers and giggles from the other girls. Every now and then I looked up from my wretched task and glared at them. They all seemed identical at first, but when I peered harder I saw some had rosy cheeks and some had pale; some had snub noses and some had freckles; some had blue eyes and some had brown. There was one girl with a pair of spectacles on her nose who had her head bent right over her stocking, examining her stitches. There was something familiar about the bend of her head, the little frown lines above her nose . . .

'Martha!' I cried out. I jumped to my feet in my excitement, my stocking rolling to the floor. 'Oh, Martha, it's truly you!'

I ran down the line of desks and threw my arms around her neck. The other little girls squealed and squawked at my behaviour. Martha herself edged away from me, looking alarmed.

'Hetty, Hetty!' Nurse Winterson came speeding after me. 'You must not be so passionate, child! And you have to learn to stay still in your seat like a good little girl.'

'But it's *Martha*, my sister Martha!' I cried. Martha still looked dazed. 'Tell them, Martha! I am your sister Hetty.'

Martha blinked her poor squinting eyes. 'Hetty?' she said. 'Did I have a sister Hetty?'

'Oh, Martha, you can't have *forgotten* me!' This was such a terrifying thought that I burst into floods of tears.

'Oh yes,' said Martha, nodding now. 'You were the little one who cried a lot.'

She really seemed to have no other clear recollection of me. The girls on either side of her giggled, and Martha blushed and wriggled further away from me, clearly embarrassed.

I let Nurse Winterson lead me back to my chair. I picked up my stocking and applied myself to darning, but tears kept brimming and the stocking blurred in my hand. I was so shocked that Martha had barely remembered me, her own sister. Did she not remember any of us – Rosie, Eliza, Nat, Jem?

Surely she must remember Saul. I wondered when we were to meet up with all the boy foundlings.

A bell rang at four and all the other girls stuffed their stockings into workbaskets in their desks. Nurse Winterson took my poor cobbled stocking and held it up, examining my enormous stitches.

'Oh, Hetty, you've sewn the sides together! How could anyone get their foot into this stocking?' she said, wafting it gently in front of me.

The other girls giggled and grinned. I felt my cheeks turn fiery red.

'We will try again tomorrow,' said Nurse Winterson. 'Cheer up, Hetty. We will make an expert seamstress of you yet. Now, run and play outside with the other girls.'

I followed them forlornly. I did not want to play with any of them and I was sure they did not want to play with me. They scurried along the corridor and down the stairs, calling to each other, though they subsided abruptly when another nurse appeared on the stairs. She clapped her hands crossly.

'*Quietly*, girls! No talking at all until you get outside,' she said. She noticed me skulking at the top of the stairs. 'Come along, child, don't loiter. The girls' playground is down the stairs and through the big door.'

'Please, miss – Nurse – mayn't I go to play with the boys?' I asked.

She drew herself up, hands on her hips. 'Of course not, you bold little girl!'

'But I need to see my brother Gideon. He will be so wretched without me. Please, Nurse, I need to see my brother so badly,' I begged.

Nurse Winterson came and stood beside me, her hand on my shoulder. 'Perhaps it will help Hetty settle down if we let her see her foster brother for a few minutes,' she suggested.

But the other nurse shook her head firmly. 'Really, Winnie! Will you never learn? You can't afford to be so soft-hearted with the children. If we change a rule for just one child, they will all be clamouring for special privileges.' The fierce nurse turned to me. 'Now run away and play or you shall be whipped!'

I ran because I certainly did not want to be whipped. The other girls were playing games of tag, or strolling around together arm in arm, or sitting in little circles telling secrets. I did not have anyone to play with.

I peered around desperately for Martha. She was walking with a girl on either side, all of them singing a song. I sidled nearer until I was walking two steps behind. One of the girls craned round.

'Stop following us!' she said.

'I'm not following *you*, I'm following my sister,' I said fiercely. I ran round them and stood right in front of Martha. Her eyes blinked anxiously behind her spectacles.

'I am so happy to find you, Martha. I have so much news to tell about Mother and Father and dear Jem, and did you know that Gideon is here too, we travelled together in a big steam train, and there is a new little baby Eliza, and do you ever see Saul, and that horrid matron took all my best clothes and my rag baby, and I've been to a real circus and ridden on a white horse . . .' I was babbling now, trying to get some kind of reaction from poor Martha. She looked bewildered.

'I don't really remember,' she said. 'That was long ago. I only remember *now*.'

'But now is so horrid!' I said, starting to cry again.

'Don't cry!' said Martha. 'Please don't. It hurts my head. All right, Hetty, you can walk with us. This is Elizabeth and this is Marjorie.'

They both sighed, but let me trail after them. When they resumed their silly song, all tra-la-la's and tootle-tootles, I did my best to imitate them.

Nurse Winterson rang the bell at the end of playtime. She smiled at me. 'There, Hetty, you've made friends already,' she murmured to me.

She didn't understand that Martha was simply trying to be kind because of our dimly remembered kinship – and Elizabeth and Marjorie certainly did not wish to be friends.

We were all marched to the privies, where we took

it in turns to relieve ourselves, ten girls at a time. We then washed our hands with the horrible carbolic soap. I could barely reach up to the basin and got water right up my arms, wetting the uncomfortable cuffs on my sleeves. My hidden sixpence was rubbing a bruise on my skin, but I bore the pain proudly.

Then we were marched again – one two, one two, one two – into a large echoing dining room set with very long tables. The little girls scrambled onto benches. I stood bewildered in the crush and lost my chance of sitting next to Martha. I had to squash right on the end of a bench next to a fierce-looking fair girl with a high forehead, who dug me hard with her elbow when I took a bite of the bread on my plate.

'You're not *allowed*, not yet!' she hissed.

We had to wait as endless lines of big girls filed in too, until the whole hall was filled with girls girls girls, all scarily alike in their brown dresses and white caps.

My stomach was rumbling because I'd missed having any dinner on this most terrible day, but I still had to wait until Matron Pigface said, 'Let us say grace, girls.'

I did not understand and mumbled, 'Grace.' The fierce girl snorted derisively.

'For what we are about to receive may we be truly grateful, amen,' she chanted with all the others.

We'd never said grace at home, we'd just grabbed our bowls from Mother and started spooning, but I *was* truly grateful for my slice of bread and my wedge of cheese. I wolfed them down in four bites and waited. And waited. There didn't seem to be anything *else*, apart from a mug of watered-down milk.

I was a country child. We might have been poor but Mother believed in giving us big platefuls and our milk was always creamy rich. I wondered if my helping was minute because I was the smallest girl here, but when I peered around, I saw that even the very big girls with chests filling out their tippets had the same size slices.

I wondered how I was going to bear the enormous emptiness inside my stomach. I didn't realize that it wasn't simply hunger, though that was a small part of it. An entire loaf of bread and a round of cheese could not have eased the ache of my loneliness.

I wondered how Gideon was faring in the boys' wing, unable even to ask for what he wanted, and my tears brimmed again. The fierce girl beside me took no notice, but a big girl with long plaits came over to our table.

'You can go and play for a little, you babies,' she said. She stopped in front of me. 'Oh dear! Are you feeling monk?'

'She's new today,' said the fierce girl. 'They're *always* monk when they're new.'

I didn't know what monk meant exactly, but I certainly felt it.

'Don't cry, baby,' said the big girl, and she lifted her own apron and dabbed at my eyes. 'You're so *weeny*. Don't worry, I'll look out for you. My name's Harriet.'

'My name's Hetty.'

'My, they're very similar. Some of the girls call me Hatty.'

'I had long hair like yours,' I said, taking hold of her long silky plaits. 'But that nasty horrid matron with a pig face cut it all off.'

Harriet giggled but put her hand over her mouth. 'You mustn't talk like that about the matron! She wasn't being deliberately nasty or horrid, all the new girls have their hair cut off, it's the rule, in case of lice. But don't fret, yours will be as long as mine in two or three years.'

Two or three *years*! I'd been in the Foundling Hospital for less than a day and yet it already felt like a lifetime.

'Do you know your way around all this great big building, Harriet?' I asked.

'Of course I do. Don't worry, you'll learn your way around soon too.'

'Do you know where all the boys are?'

'Yes, they are in the west wing.'

'Do you know how to get there?'

'Yes, but I have never been. It's not allowed.'

'Have you never seen the boys?'

'Oh, yes, yes, sometimes we see them across the yard at play, and we watch their sports day once a year. We see them in chapel too, though we're not supposed to peer round.'

'Couldn't we go together now, just to have a peep at them?'

'Of course not, Hetty. We would be seen and then we would get into fearsome trouble.'

'I don't care. I need to see my brother,' I said.

'Ah.' Harriet was silent for a moment. 'I had a brother. Two brothers. They are here too. Michael and John.'

She said their names uncertainly, as if she wasn't sure. I felt my throat tighten. She didn't seem to remember them properly, and yet she was a big girl, not a small girl who was easily muddled, like Martha. I resolved even more strongly that I would never never never forget my dear brothers (especially Jem) or my sisters, and that *somehow* I would find the boys' wing and seek out Gideon.

Harriet wouldn't take me to the boys' wing but she *did* take me to the big girls' room. There was no nurse keeping order so the girls chatted as they mended clothes, sewing up split seams in the ugly brown dresses and hemming torn aprons.

'Come here, Hetty, let me show you something,' said Harriet.

I feared I was in for another sewing lesson and I'd already proved myself spectacularly untalented at darning – but Harriet pulled off a long length of cotton thread, tied it together, and then placed it round her outstretched hands.

'Watch carefully! I will teach you how to play cat's cradle.'

I watched, though I didn't see a cat or a cradle, just strange patterns forming as Harriet fiddled the cotton with her fingers. She tried her best to show me what to do, and praised me extravagantly when I managed to flip the thread into the right zigzag pattern.

'*Clever* baby!' she said.

I felt a little indignant – she seemed all too ready to treat me like a two-year-old – but I didn't protest. It was wonderful to have found a friend in this huge and horrifying hospital, *two* friends, if I counted kind Nurse Winterson.

But at night-time I was utterly friendless. All the little girls were lined up and washed by a big girl. She had long plaits like my Harriet, but she was nowhere near as kind. She scrubbed at our hands and faces with the horrid carbolic soap, not caring in the slightest if it went in our eyes.

Then we were led to the infant dormitory, a vast room of fifty iron bedsteads. I was taken to a bed right beside the door and my clothes pulled off me by another big girl. She stuck a nightgown over my head. It was so long it trailed on the floor. My shorn hair stuck out wildly in all directions. Some of the other girls laughed and pointed. I licked my fingers and tried to make the tufts stick to my scalp.

'Stop doing that, you look so silly!' said the big girl. 'Fold your clothes up neatly – *neatly*, I said – and put them in your basket at the end of the bed.'

I did as I was told. I hid my lucky sixpence in my basket too, resolving to find a safer hiding place when no one was watching.

'Now say your prayers. Don't take too long about it, mind. Then get into bed.'

I knelt down, put my hands together and shut my eyes. 'Dear God, please get me *out* of this horrid, hateful place,' I prayed. 'Please don't let the matron and the nurses and the other boys be plaguing Gideon. I know it is all my fault he cannot speak any more and I am such a sorry girl. Please bless my dear family at home and don't let me ever forget them. Please especially bless Jem. Please—'

But the big girl was tugging me impatiently. 'That's enough. Into bed. Now!'

I opened my eyes and saw that all the other girls were already under their covers. I hurried into bed myself. The big girl dimmed the light and said, 'Goodnight! No talking now.'

She went out of the door and closed it tight. Immediately a whispering started. The girls called each other, chatting about their day. They started talking about me as if I wasn't there!

'What about the new girl, Hetty Feather?'

'She looks a sight. That hair!'

'She's so small and scrawny.'

'I saw her sucking up to Harriet.'

'She's so stupid at darning.'

'She went down on her knees to pray, pretending she's so holy.'

'She's just acting monk to make people sorry for her.'

'I don't like her at all.'

I jumped out of bed and ran to the nearest girl. 'Well, I don't like *you*!' I cried, and I pulled her ear hard. She screamed and I ran to the next bed. 'And I don't like you!' I pulled another ear, then ran on. 'Or *you* – or *you*!'

They all set about shrieking, and then the door burst open and someone stood there, an oil lamp held high, illuminating her ugly features. It was Matron Pigface!

'What is this terrible noise? How *dare* you behave so badly! And who is this child *out of bed*?'

She seized me, shining the lamp in my face. 'Hetty Feather! Behaving like a child of Satan on your very first night here! Get back into bed this instant, and if you put so much as a foot on the floor all night you will be whipped severely.'

She smacked at me as I dodged past her and dived into my bed.

'Now you are all to go to sleep *this instant*!' Pigface commanded.

After she'd waddled out of the room there were several muttered remonstrances, but soon every girl was breathing heavily. Some murmured as they dreamed, some snored. I was the only one awake.

I lay on my back, feeling so wretchedly lonely in my narrow bed. I longed to snuggle up beside Jem or Gideon. My arms ached for my dear rag baby. I lay trembling hour after hour. I felt so small in this huge room of spiteful girls. I seemed to grow smaller and smaller as I lay there. I clutched myself in fear that I was actually shrinking. I did not seem myself any more. I gripped my elbows tightly and gritted my teeth. I had to hang onto myself. I was not going to become just another foundling girl in hideous apparel. I might have to wear the dress, cap, apron and tippet, I might have to obey all their dreadful rules, but inside my head I still had to stay Hetty Feather.

11

I woke to the clamour of a bell. A new big girl strode up and down the dormitory, shouting at us to get up. It was cold and my bladder was bursting, but I had to strip my bed, roll up my mattress and put on my hateful uniform before I could shuffle to the privy. A big girl – yet another, so *many*, how would I ever learn who was who? – washed our hands, inspected our necks and brushed our hair. Then we had to line up and walk two by two to the dining room. I did not have anyone to walk with. I decided I did not care. I pictured to myself another Hetty, and we held hands and walked downstairs together, whispering to each other. Several times the other girls tried to elbow me out of the way, but Hetty and I elbowed back. We had small arms but *very* sharp elbows.

'Stop pushing and poking each other!' a nurse called. 'Who is that girl there, the little one?'

'Hetty Feather,' the other girls chorused, triumphant that I was in trouble again.

'You must learn patience and decorum, Hetty

169

Feather. We expect little girls to queue up quietly for their food at the hospital, not trample and grunt like little pigs in a sty.'

She said it humorously but she nearly set me off crying again, because I thought of our pig in the sty, and Jem and Mother, and a wave of homesickness washed over me.

'So you're a new little girl,' said the kitchen maid at the end of the table, serving out bowls of porridge. She was small and slight – if it wasn't for her careworn face I might have mistaken her for one of the big girl foundlings. Her maid's uniform hung about her, her skirts trailing past her boots. 'I'm new here too. It feels very strange, don't it?'

I nodded forlornly.

'I'm sure we'll both settle down soon,' she said. 'Here, specially for you!' She took a twist of paper out of her apron pocket and sprinkled the contents on the top of my porridge. 'Sugar!' she whispered.

All the other girls had entirely plain portions.

'Get on with it, Ida! There isn't time to *talk* to the children,' the fat cook called from the serving hatch.

Ida winked at me. I did my best to wink back, though I hadn't quite mastered the art and I fear I squinted dreadfully. Ida's unexpected kindness cheered me even more than the sprinkle of sugar.

I still had to face the ordeal of morning school. We had a proper mistress, not a nurse, an elderly lady called Miss Newman. She did indeed resemble a new kind of man: she was tall and square-shouldered, with a severe bun scraped back from her wrinkled forehead. She could control her hair, but her eyebrows wriggled in unruly fashion above her small spectacles. She was plainly dressed in a grey blouse with a white collar and a dark grey skirt, with just a silver clasp on her belt to break the monotony – but she looked exotically glamorous in comparison with the dull uniform of all the nurses.

She stood at the front of our classroom and peered hard at all us girls. She saw me and raised her formidable eyebrows. 'What is your name, little girl?'

'Hetty Feather, Nurse – miss.'

'You will address me as Miss Newman, if you please.'

'Yes, Miss Newman.'

'Did you attend school in your foster home?'

'No, Miss Newman.'

She sighed. 'Well, you are going to have to concentrate very hard, Hetty Feather.'

She held up a large placard with four pictures. There was a round rosy fruit, a big brown furry creature, a yellow piece of furniture, and a black and white animal waving its tail. Each picture had writing underneath it.

'A is for Apple, B is for Bear, C is for Chair and D is for Dog!' I declared.

Miss Newman stared at me. 'I thought you said you had never attended school, Hetty Feather.'

'I haven't, Miss Newman.'

'So how have you learned to read?'

'My big brother Jem read to me,' I said proudly. 'So I learned all my letters.'

Miss Newman nodded approvingly. 'Then he was a kind brother to you, child.'

'Oh, he *is*, the kindest brother in the whole world,' I said fervently.

Miss Newman led all of us through the alphabet with her coloured placards – and then we progressed to the much duller but still interesting spelling out of little words. It was not long before I could stutter 'The c-a-t is on the m-a-t', and in the second half of the long morning's lesson I grasped a scratchy pen and wrote line after line of shaky *a*s and *b*s and *c*s. Then I wrote my first sprawling word – *c a b* – and drew a picture of the London cab that had taken me away to this grim new life.

Miss Newman liked my picture, she liked my word, and when she had showed me how to sign my artwork *H e t t y*, she embellished it with a gold star.

I was pleased and proud, but the star made me think of the wondrous night of the circus and Madame Adeline and then the awfulness of Gideon going missing, and I had to fight to stop my tears brimming all over again.

'She thinks she's so clever just because she can read and write, but look, she's nothing but a crybaby,' Sheila hissed to her friend, Monica. Sheila was the fierce fair girl with the high forehead and I already detested her.

However, Martha came and peered very closely at my picture, running her finger along the lines as if it helped her to see. 'Very good, Hetty. And you have a gold star! I've never had a gold star yet. I won't either. I am a total dunce.' She sighed, though she said it cheerily enough.

'Well, *I* think you're very clever,' I said loyally. Even if Martha did not remember me properly, I remembered *her*. We were still sisters, no matter what.

Martha was truly very good at our singing lesson. We had to stand in lines and sing long dreary hymns. I did not know the words yet so I could only hum uncertainly to the piano music, but Martha's voice soared high above the others, making me shiver with its sweetness.

Wait till I tell Mother! She will be so proud that Martha can sing like an angel, I thought. Then I realized I would never be able to tell Mother. I had to fight the tears this time, knowing that if I cried again the other girls would torment me. I screwed up my face desperately.

'Look at Hetty Feather!' sang Sheila, keeping in time to the hymn. *'She looks like she's about to w-e-t herself!'*

I *did* actually need to go to the privy. I couldn't get used to the idea of only being able to go when the nurses commanded. My bladder and bowels had a will of their own and I prayed I would not have an accident. One girl was wriggling and jiggling towards the end of the line and Miss Newman spoke to her sharply.

'Stop fidgeting, Sarah Barnes!'

Sarah jumped – and then water started trickling down her legs, spreading in a pool about her boots. The girls on either side of her sprang away, and everyone stared and pointed. Miss Newman sent Sarah out of the room in disgrace. She shuffled soggily away, her head bowed, her face scarlet with shame.

I had a desperate private conversation with my own bladder. I had seen a pig's bladder at home so I had some idea of what mine looked like. I pictured tying the end up tightly with string, making many knots. It worked so well that when we were eventually allowed a trip to the privy, I sat there for several minutes before I could squeeze out a single drop.

'Come *along*, Hetty Feather. For goodness' sake, child, you must be finished now! You're just being contrary.'

A nurse came and dragged me off while I was still weeing. A little splashed down my legs, but not enough to make a puddle. I thanked the Lord for my long skirts, though it wasn't comfortable.

We had our dinner in the great dining hall. I saw Harriet and tried to go and sit with her, but I was hauled back to sit on a bench with the other girls my age.

We had a different kitchen maid to dole out a few morsels of boiled mutton and carrots and potatoes. I received a standard portion, but when the other kind kitchen maid passed behind my bench, taking her great dish back to the kitchen, she slipped one more potato onto my plate. It had a little dab of butter on top and tasted especially delicious. She watched me eat it up, smiling at me.

'Did that new kitchen maid give you an extra potato, Hetty Feather?' Sheila demanded crossly.

'She had one left so she gave it to me. Because I'm little and I look sweet,' I said. 'Not like *you*.'

Sheila had a very high frowny forehead and a fierce expression, her mouth drooping like a dog. I pulled my own features into a Sheila-face, and the two girls opposite laughed. Even Monica sniggered, though she was Sheila's best friend.

It was a stupid mistake to ridicule Sheila, especially as she was much bigger than me. She cornered me out in the playground when there wasn't a nurse in sight.

'I'll teach you, Hetty Feather,' she said, and she punched me in the stomach, so that I doubled over.

Then she ran behind me and pushed hard. I toppled down onto my chin. I grazed my hands painfully, tore the knees out of both my stockings, and sliced my poor chin right open.

Monica squatted down beside me, looking aghast. 'Oh, Sheila, you've hurt her! She's bleeding frightfully, look!'

'Only a little bit,' said Sheila, but she looked worried too.

'What if she tells Matron?' said Monica. 'You will be whipped, Sheila!'

'Good!' I said, struggling to my feet. I wiped my stinging chin with my hand. I was startled when I saw the bright red on my fingers but I decided to be brave. I'd played soldiers often enough with Jem at home. I knew you had to show courage when you were wounded. I marched off, swinging my arms, my dripping chin held high.

Matron Pigface came into the playground just then, bell in hand, ready to ring for us to go indoors for our needlework session. She took one look at me and gasped. 'Hetty Feather! Whatever have you done to yourself, you wretched child?'

Every girl in the playground stood still, staring at me. Out of the corner of my eye I saw Sheila and Monica clasping hands.

'*Answer* me, Hetty Feather!' Pigface bellowed.

I did not want to answer her. I did not want to admit to all the infant foundlings that Sheila had knocked me down and I had failed to punch her back. It was too shaming.

Matron Pigface was peering closely at my chin, inspecting my hands, lifting my skirt to see my torn stockings and oozing knees. 'Have you been in a *fight*?'

I shook my head, because I hadn't had the wit or strength to fight Sheila back.

'So did some girl here *attack* you?' Pigface demanded.

I opened my mouth at last. I looked at Sheila. I didn't want to give her the satisfaction of everyone knowing she had triumphed over me. 'No, miss . . . Matron. No one attacked me. I fell over because these blooming boots are too big.'

Pigface shook me by the shoulders for impertinence until my head waggled. Then she seized me by the wrist and hurried me off to the washroom. She scrubbed at my chin and hands and knees with carbolic soap. It stung horribly but I stood still and stiff, because I was a wounded soldier and would not show weakness to any enemy. Then she painted my chin with strange purple liquid from a medicine bottle. This stung even worse than the soap and I wriggled just a little.

'Keep *still*, Hetty Feather,' Pigface said, but when she'd finished applying the violet medicine and replaced my blood-splattered tippet with a fresh one, she gave me a nod that was almost approving. 'Run along to join the other girls at needlework, Hetty – and watch where you're going this time!'

She did not accompany me. I was supposed to know my own way around the building after twenty-four hours' residence. I darted off, but I was concentrating on the pain of my chin. I darted in the wrong direction, to the left instead of the right. I blundered down a long echoing corridor, turned a corner – and seemed to find the washroom all over again.

I stared at the big white room, my hands over my sore chin, wondering how I could possibly have come full circle – when a small snivelling *boy* came rushing in, with ink all over his hands.

We stood staring at each other, equally taken back.

'What are you doing in the boys' wing, little girl?'

'I – I got lost,' I said honestly, then sighed in irritation. Why, oh, why could he not be Gideon?

'You will get whipped if they find you,' he said.

'I know. I don't care. I'll go in a minute, but please could you tell me first, do you know my brother Gideon? Is he all right?'

'Gideon?' said the little boy, sneering. 'You mean the idiot boy?'

'He is not an idiot!' I shouted fiercely. 'I shall hit you if you say he is!'

His hands went to his mouth, smearing ink all over his face.

'Now you're all black and it serves you right,' I said.

I ran out of the washroom, right along the corridor until I saw a whole troop of boys bustling out of a big room. I peered hard at this army of brown, but I couldn't spot Gideon at all. However, all the boys could see me. They let up a whoop and a shout.

'Girl! Girl! Girl!'

A nurse came running, shouting at me furiously. I knew I had to make a quick escape. I flew back back back along the corridors, back to the safety of the girls' wing, where I slowed down and walked sedately, trying to look innocent. I joined my class at their darning.

'Where have you been, Hetty Feather?' asked Nurse Winterson. 'Oh dear, your poor chin! What happened to you?'

All the girls looked up expectantly, Sheila clearly anxious. I wanted to get her into trouble with Nurse Winterson. But I still did not want it made plain to all that she had got the better of me. I held my tongue a second time.

'I tripped and Matron took me off to put this purple stinging stuff on my chin,' I said.

'It is gentian violet, Hetty. I dare say it hurt a great deal. You have been very brave, dear.'

I thought the girls might groan to see me singled out so favourably, but they nodded at me, almost in a friendly fashion. I did not know then that I had avoided the worst sin of all at the Foundling Hospital.

No matter how a child is teased or tortured, they must never ever ever tell a nurse or matron. If they do, the others will torment them until their last day at the hospital.

I had unwittingly kept to this rule and won everyone's respect. I sat and stitched demurely, while Nurse Winterson read us a story. I loved stories, and this was a splendid fairy tale – but for once I could not concentrate.

My mind was whirling. I knew how to reach the boys' wing, but I would be spotted immediately if I went back there, unless . . . Unless I could find some way of disguising myself.

I did not see how this was possible, until later in the day, when Harriet sought me out.

'Poor Hetty! Look at your sore chin. Oh dear, oh dear,' she said, making a great fuss of me.

I rather enjoyed this, and even managed to squeeze out a few tears so she could pet me. She took me to the big girls' room and sat me close by her side while she started sewing. She took a pair of boys' trousers from the big basket and started patching a knee. I stared at the trousers on her lap – and smiled. I knew how to obtain the perfect disguise!

I waited until Harriet had to go to a cupboard for more thread, peered round quickly, then seized another pair of trousers from the brimming basket. I could not be seen carrying them so I thrust them up my skirts, wedging them in a bunch as best I could.

I positively waddled on my way back to my dormitory, but I managed to deposit the trousers safely in my mattress.

The next day I purloined a jacket – and I was ready! I decided my best chance of reaching the boys' wing undetected was during the playtime after dinner. There were fewer nurses on duty, many of them dining themselves. I stood in the playground awaiting my opportunity. The other girls took no notice of me. Sheila seemed disconcerted that I had not told tales on her, and left me alone.

I hesitated, standing near the girls' entrance, suddenly in a funk, frightened of being caught and whipped. I made myself think hard of Gideon. I pictured him so clearly that he seemed to be standing before me, white and trembling, tears running down his face, his mouth opening and shutting soundlessly. It was such a sad image, it galvanized me into action.

I gave one last glance to check I was unobserved, and then I ran into the entrance and up the stairs, all the way to the dormitory. I tore off my cap and tippet and apron. I struggled out of my scratchy brown dress. Then I pulled my stolen jacket and trousers out of my mattress and put them on. The trousers were too large and much too long, but I rolled each leg up at the hem until they rested on my boots. The jacket was too big too, but it was easy enough to shrug it up on my shoulders. My shorn hair suited my purpose well. I had no mirror, but looking down I could see I appeared a convincing boy, though I was on the short side. I clenched my fists and tapped myself on the chest.

'Courage, Hetty,' I whispered.

I hastened out of the dormitory, hating the heaviness of the jacket on my shoulders, the chafing of the trousers on my skinny legs. I sped along the corridor, but then heard the squeak of a nurse's boots marching along the polished floor.

If she caught me in boys' apparel, all would be lost. I darted into the girls' washrooms and hid behind the door, trembling. *Squeak squeak squeak* came the boots, louder now. They paused at the door of the washrooms. A head poked in and peered, but I was crammed right back into the corner and she didn't see me. She went marching on her way, while I breathed out at last. Once she was out of earshot I peeped anxiously out of the doorway, and then resumed my journey.

I turned to the right until I found the boys' washrooms, and then I carried on down the corridor until I reached the stairs. I ran down them, but there at the bottom, right by the door, stood a nurse watching the boys playing outside. I stopped still, pressing back into the shadows. I could not bear to be thwarted now, when I was so nearly there. I waited, willing her to move, and eventually she yawned and stretched and sauntered off.

I hurtled out into the playground, blinking at the sight of so many small boys in brown. They were so lively too. We girls wandered aimlessly up and down, or talked in tiny groups, or played decorous clapping games. These boys were all running and capering and kicking stones and shouting – all but one. A spindly boy with a stark haircut stood all by himself, his head bowed, his hands weirdly splayed as if he were searching for something that wasn't there.

'*Gideon!*' I called.

He looked up and I ran over to him. He cowered away as if I was going to hit him.

'It's me, Gideon! It's Hetty, your own sister!' I cried.

He peered at my shorn hair and breeches, looking doubtful.

'It's really me. Oh, Gideon, I've missed you so!'

I embraced him, my arms tight around his neck. I felt him crumple, his head on my shoulders, and then he started sobbing.

'Oh, Gid, it's so hateful hateful hateful, isn't it? If only we could be together it wouldn't be too bad.'

He straightened up and looked at me imploringly.

'I can't stay, Gideon. The nurses would see I'm

not a real boy – especially when I went to the privy!' I giggled – and Gideon smiled through his tears. 'How has it been for you, Gid? Have they been horrid to you, the other boys?'

Gideon hung his head.

'What about Saul? He's here, isn't he? Does he look out for you, stand up for you?'

Gideon hunched up further. Saul was clearly not a protector.

'Well, you must fight back. If you cry, it will only make them worse. The other girls are hateful to me, but I punch them and pull their hair and stamp on their feet until they scream,' I said, exaggerating fiercely. 'You must do the same.'

Gideon stared at me. We both knew this was a ridiculous suggestion.

'*Try*, Gideon. And you must *say* things. They will think you are stupid if you won't talk. They will call you bad names like Idiot Boy.'

Gideon flinched.

'But you're not an idiot, you're clever, just like me. You can talk perfectly, you just *won't*. Please say something to me now, Gid.'

Gideon shook his head helplessly.

'For my sake – because you stopped talking when you got lost in the woods that night I went to the circus, remember?'

It was clear from Gideon's eyes that he did.

'I've felt so bad since, knowing it was all my fault. It would make me feel *so* much better if you said something. Anything. You can call me names if you like. You can say, "Hetty Feather is a mean, nasty, pigface, smellybottom sister!" Go on, say it!'

Gideon resisted, but he smiled again.

'Well, say it in your head if you won't say it out loud. Talk to yourself every day. Talk about *home*. We mustn't forget, Gideon. It's the most important thing of all. Martha can barely remember anything, not even me! But if we talk to ourselves and picture home again and again and again, it will stay true in our heads. We must picture Mother—'

Gideon moaned softly.

'Yes, remember Mother, her dear red face, her lovely warm smell, her big chest, our mother. And great Father, remember him galloping around with you on his shoulders. And Nat with his jokes and his whittling. Did they take your wooden elephant, Gid? They took my dear rag baby. But I've still got Jem's sixpence safe. Oh, Gideon, picture Jem, remember our dearest brother, and listen to me, listen hard: Jem is going to come for me when I'm older, and he'll come for you too, and we'll all live together and be happy again – and you will be free to dance, Gid. You can even wear a silver suit if you like. Remember the tumbling boys and their dance?'

Gideon's face suddenly lit up. He pointed his foot in its clumsy boot and then twirled round, while I clapped. But the other boys were watching. They started pointing and jeering.

'See the idiot boy dancing!'

'He is *not* an idiot,' I said, clenching my fists. 'I will punch any boy who calls him that.'

They laughed harder, because they all towered over me.

'Who *is* this little red-haired runty lad?'

'Is he new? I've never seen him before.'

They were gathering round us, which made me nervous.

'He's a rum little fellow! Where's his waistcoat and cap? He's only half dressed!'

'What's your name, boy?'

'I'll tell you his name – it's Hetty Feather!' someone said.

I spun round – and there was Saul, grown thinner and taller, his face pinched. His bad leg bent sideways and he clutched a cane for support.

The other boys roared at my name. 'The cripple's talking such rot! Hetty Feather! That's a girl's name.'

'She *is* a girl. She is my foster sister,' said Saul. He looked at me, his cheeks flushed. 'Remember, remember, remember, Hetty Feather. You tell Gideon to remember – but you forgot *me*!'

'He's a *girl*?' said the biggest boy. He seized

hold of me and thrust his hand down my breeches, though I struggled and shrieked. 'He *is* a girl!' he yelled triumphantly.

'There's a girl over here!'

'A girl, a girl, a girl in breeches!'

'Come and see the girl, the red-haired girl!'

They were all running towards me. I saw a nurse in the distance raise her head and stare over at the hubbub.

'I have to go, Gid, or I shall be in terrible trouble. But you remember, promise? Remember everyone at home. Remember *me*, your Hetty.'

I gave him a quick kiss on his cheek. I might have tried to kiss Saul too, but he spat at me. So I spat back, then dodged round him and ran.

The boys shouted after me, some of them running in pursuit. I heard a wail. I turned. Gideon was waving wildly at me. His mouth was open.

'My Hetty!' he called, his voice cracking.

There was uproar as they all heard him speak, but I could not stay to congratulate or comfort him. I shot inside the entrance and ran like a rat, desperate for cover. I heard bells clanging and knew it was the end of playtime. I made it undetected all the way back to the girls' dormitory. I tore off the jacket and breeches, tugged on my dress and apron and tippet and thrust my cap upon my head. I was a girl again. I had got away with it!

12

Each day was so alike: up in the morning as the bell rang; dressing, washing, eating, even going to the lavatory at the allotted hour. We learned the same lessons every day, reading and writing and singing and scripture, then the wretched darning every afternoon. We ate the same meals – porridge for breakfast, boiled beef or mutton for dinner, bread and cheese for supper every Monday, Tuesday, Wednesday, Thursday, Friday and Saturday, all identical – so *Sundays* came as a total surprise.

We were handed special snowy-white Sunday tippets and aprons, and given a severe warning by Matron Pigface Peters to keep them spotless. Woe betide any girl who dribbled her porridge down her front at breakfast! Then we all trooped off to chapel, marching in a crocodile. I still did not have a friend in my own class so I had to trudge along beside Matron Pigface herself, while Sheila and Monica walked directly behind and kept kicking the backs of my legs and treading on my boot-heels.

I turned to try to kick them back, but Matron Pigface tugged my arm and glared at me.

'Behave yourself, Hetty Feather! Pray to the Lord above to make you a good meek little maid, not the total varmint that you are.'

I wasn't sure what a varmint was, but I decided I wanted to stay one if I possibly could. I didn't want to be good or meek. I certainly didn't want to stay little so that all the others could squash me flat. I didn't much care to be a maid either. If I had to be a foundling, then the boys seemed to have far more fun.

The Sunday service in the chapel wasn't fun for any of us, girls or boys. We had to sit as still as statues on the hard pews. If we so much as swung our legs, Matron frowned and tapped us. If any small foundling fidgeted or fell asleep during the long, long sermon, a big girl would poke her hard in the back – and doubtless the little boys over on the other side of the chapel were being subjected to similar nips and knocks.

The foundlings who formed the choir were the only children who could mingle, girls and boys together. I was surprised to see my own sister, Martha, up there at the front, the smallest child in the whole choir, looking especially earnest with her spectacles on the end of her snub nose. She had a very short solo and sang like an angel, hands folded, head high, mouth wide open. I felt true sisterly pride, goose pimples on my arms at the sweetness of her voice. If only Mother could have been present to hear her!

I blotted out my pew of foundling girls sitting hip to hip in their ugly brown frocks. I pictured my entire family, Jem beside me, whispering loyally that he was sure I could sing every bit as sweetly as Martha, Nat surreptitiously whittling a piece of wood, Rosie and Eliza in their Sunday print frocks with their hair specially curled, Father large and lumbering, holding his neck awkwardly because the collar of his starched Sunday shirt was rubbing, and Mother rocking the sleeping baby, her eyes shining to see us all together. Gideon would be with us of course, sitting bolt upright, dancing his toes in time to the music. I suppose Saul would have to be here too – but right at the other end of the pew, away from me.

I peered round to see if I could possibly spot the real Gideon and Saul in the distant sea of brown boys – and got poked hard in the back for my trouble. I had to sit still, and pray and sing and listen while the vicar preached endlessly about miserable sinners. I was *very* miserable and I knew I was a sinner, so I decided I had better pray hard inside my head so that I wouldn't tumble straight down to the fiery flames of Hell.

'Dear Lord, please make me a better girl,' I prayed earnestly, over and over – but as the sermon droned on and on, I switched the prayer to 'Please God, let this service finish *soon.*'

When it was finally over, I had pins and needles from the tips of my toes right up to my bottom and I stumbled when I stood up. We filed out of the chapel, row after row, while the rest of the congregation gawped at us. I wondered who all these strange ladies and gentlemen were. They certainly weren't hospital staff. I had a sudden wild fancy that they were parents come to seek out their lost children. Perhaps my real mother was there, looking for her lost babe. Perhaps she really *was* Madame Adeline. I peered at all the ladies, trying to spot a flame of red hair under all the Sunday bonnets, a flare of pink lace at the throat of a stark Sunday dress.

'Stop staring, Hetty Feather!' Matron Pigface snapped.

'But they're staring at me!' I muttered, but not quite loudly enough for her to hear.

Harriet was one of the big girls supervising our privy visit when we got back.

'Who *are* all the ladies and gentlemen?' I asked her.

'They are the Sunday visitors,' said Harriet.

'Why are they here?'

'They like to look at us,' said Harriet. 'They will watch us at our Sunday dinner too. So mind your manners, little Hetty!'

I was not sure whether she was serious or not, but when we marched into the dining room, one two, one two, there they were, the ladies and gentlemen all lined up expectantly. We stood behind our benches while a big girl said grace in a very loud sing-song, making her voice extra holy because it was Sunday, and everyone was staring at her. Then we clambered onto our benches and the kitchen maids started serving.

It was roast beef, one slice each, with roast potatoes and carrots and cabbage from the garden. My special kind maid pushed her way quickly down to my table and gave me the biggest slice of beef and the largest, crispiest potato. She winked at me as she did so.

The ladies and gentlemen surrounding us were making such a noise I dared to speak myself.

'Thank you!' I whispered, smiling at her. 'You're very kind to me. What is your name?'

'I'm Ida Battersea.'

'Do I call you Matron or Miss?'

'You can call me Ida. What is your name, dear?'

'I'm Hetty Feather.' I wrinkled my nose. 'It's a silly name.'

'I think it is a very distinctive name,' she said.

'Oh, I do *like* you, Ida!' I said. I forgot to whisper, and a nurse came bustling up, glaring at me.

'Were you *talking*, child?' she demanded.

'Oh no, ma'am, it was me. I'm very sorry, ma'am,' said Ida.

'You must learn to hold your tongue,' said the nurse, as if Ida was one of us girls.

She flushed and bowed her head, but when the nurse moved away, Ida pulled a comical face at her back. I laughed and choked on my hot potato.

Ida had to serve the next table, and as soon as she was gone, three fine ladies stepped right up to our table and watched us eat.

'My, they're so neat and dainty! See how they spoon their gravy so carefully!' said one.

Of course we were neat and dainty. We knew that if we spilled anything down our Sunday tippets we'd get our knuckles rapped.

'Aren't the little ones sweet! Do you see that one with the high forehead? That's a clear sign of intelligence,' said another, singling out Sheila, who smirked at her in sickening fashion.

'I'm rather taken with the very little one. She's not much more than a baby,' said the third. 'Poor little scrap, I doubt she'll survive the winter.'

I scowled at her, which was a mistake.

'Oh dear, look at that expression! She's a surly little thing. No, no, *my* one's smiling prettily,' said the second lady, fumbling in her purse. 'Here, my dear, a little treat for you.'

She put a wrapped sweet beside Sheila's plate. Sheila popped the sweet down the front of her tippet before anyone else could see. Aha! So *that* was why she'd smiled so.

I knew how to play this game now. The three

ladies trotted further down the dining hall, and their place was taken by a gentleman and a lady, arm in arm.

'Oh, I do like the little ones,' said the lady.

I sat up, opened my eyes wide, and smiled.

'That's a dear little love, the one at the end. Look, she's smiling!'

'Bless the child, she's taken a shine to us!'

I grinned and gurned deliberately while they oohed and cooed – but they sauntered off without giving me anything. Sheila saw my face and laughed at me. She patted the tiny bulge in her tippet where her sweet was and licked her lips.

But then another lady and gentleman came nearer, both so fat that his waistcoat buttons were a-popping and her corsets were strained to bursting point. They were exclaiming over the meagreness of our portions, though this Sunday fare was practically a feast to us.

'I'm sure the children are half starving!'

I sucked in my cheeks and looked mournful.

'See the little one at the end! What a shame, she needs feeding up. Here, my dear, this is for you.' The gentleman pressed a slab of toffee in my hand. I gave him the greatest grin of my life and tucked it into my tippet immediately, with a triumphant little nod at Sheila.

Dear Ida came back with a second course for us, a

milk pudding with a splash of red jam. Ida served out the pudding *and* the preserve, so I got a whole spoonful of raspberry jam. My spirits lifted considerably. I hoped Gideon was faring equally well in the boys' dining room. Ladies often made a pet of him so I thought he might get singled out and given sweetmeats.

I collected four more boiled sweets myself, so that I was growing quite a chest under my tippet. I planned to eat my feast in bed, but as soon as we got outside after our Sunday meal, the big girls pounced on us little ones.

'Come on, give us your sweets, fair dos!' they said, feeling up our cuffs and down our tippets, practically turning us upside down and shaking us in their search for our sweets.

One girl snatched my precious slab of toffee, another gathered up my boiled sweets. I cried and tried to fight them off but there were too many of them.

'Poor little Hetty! Leave her alone, she's my baby!' Harriet shrieked, rushing to my rescue.

She managed to save one last sweet, a barley sugar. 'There you are, my pet. Eat it up quickly before someone grabs it. Shame on you, girls, descending on the babes like a swarm of locusts!'

She swept me off with her. I cuddled up close and sucked my barley sugar while she petted me.

I learned to be more wily the next Sunday, stowing my sweets under my cap. They made my shorn hair a little sticky but I didn't care. It had a good scrubbing on bath night. Meanwhile sucking my sweets helped the long nights seem less lonely.

I dreamed of home when I eventually fell asleep. It was so sad to wake and find myself imprisoned in the bleak hospital dormitory. I wondered how they were managing at home without me – especially Jem. I knew he would be fretting, frantic to know if I was all right. It gave me an added incentive in my writing class with Miss Newman. As soon as we could master our pens sufficiently, we were allowed to write home.

It was a long letter and it made my hand ache terribly. Miss Newman wrote it on a board and we copied it out laboriously:

Dear Mother

I now have the greatest pleasure in writing these few lines to you, hoping to find you quite well and happy, as it leaves me at present. Please give my love to all the family.

I remain
Your affectionate girl
Hetty

We were told to copy it exactly, neither adding nor deleting anything. Older girls who were fluent enough occasionally tried to add a few more personal lines, but Miss Newman had to approve them before they could be sent.

I was exhausted by the time I reached 'affectionate' and didn't concentrate hard enough. If I didn't insert enough *f*s and *t*s, or got my *i* and *o* the wrong way round, Miss Newman put a line through it and I had to start all over again. I longed to add my own personal message:

I detest it here and I miss you so and Sheila is mean and I hate Matron Peters and she stole my rag baby and I don't wear drawers nowadays.

However, I'd seen other girls have their letters confiscated if they so much as commented on the monotonous food or complained about being stared at on Sundays. I simply inserted two words after *Please give my love to all the family – *<u>*especially Jem*</u>.

After I'd signed my name, I filled the rest of the page with kisses.

Now that I could write, more or less, I tried hard to copy some of my picturings down on paper so that my stories were preserved. It was very hard to *find* any paper. I dared to steal a sheet from Miss Newman's special supply in the stationery cupboard, but it was mostly kept under lock and key. Harriet once obligingly tore a couple of pages from her exercise book, but my steadiest supplier was dear Ida. She slipped me paper bags and greaseproof paper from the kitchen. I stuffed them down my tippet and went around crackling all day until I could hide them in my mattress.

It was hard to find a place to write privately. Sometimes I sat up in the middle of the night and scribbled in the dark with a stolen stick of charcoal, though in the morning I saw my lines of writing wobbled up and down and sometimes crossed right over each other.

It wasn't enough to write *my* stories. I wanted to read new stories too. I had the Bible, and some of the stories were exciting, but the words were very hard to decipher. Miss Winterson lent me her book of fairy tales, and I read them over and over again. I went to the ball with Cinderella in my glass slippers, I let down my long hair like Rapunzel, I swam in and out of underwater coral palaces with the little mermaid.

Ida spotted me reading on my lap during dinner time. 'Watch out or one of them nurses will be after you, Hetty,' she hissed.

'I just love reading, Ida. I don't know what I shall do when I have to give the fairy-tale book back to Miss Winterson.'

She chewed her lip. 'I'll see if I can find you some

stories, Hetty. It's a wonder a tiny girl like you can read so well. You need encouragement.'

'What's that you're saying?' Matron Pigface came waddling up, snout quivering.

I quickly sat on my book, not wanting to get Nurse Winterson into trouble for lending it to me. I thought Ida would mumble something and move on, but she stood her ground.

'I said she needs encouraging, Matron,' she said.

'And why's that, pray? Matron Pigface enquired.

'Because she's clever,' said Ida.

'Clever as a cartload of monkeys, I'll grant you that,' said Matron. 'She needs watching all the time, that one. She doesn't need encouraging, she needs *suppressing*.'

Ida still didn't give up. 'She learns so fast. I think she could become a real scholar.'

Matron Pigface snorted with laughter. 'A foundling? Don't be ridiculous, girl. She'll be a servant, like all the others. That's all she's fit for and don't ever think otherwise. Now get back to the kitchen and stop wasting time! You're here to serve the food, not give your impertinent opinions. And don't let me see you favouring Hetty Feather or I shall make sure you lose your position.'

Ida swallowed. 'Beg pardon, Matron,' she said, and scurried off.

I sat uncomfortably atop the book of fairy

tales, fearing that I'd got Ida into serious trouble.

Ida didn't serve my table at supper. She stayed up at the end where the big girls sat. Matron Pigface bustled past me. She said nothing, but the look on her face said it all. *There! You've lost your friend now. You've been put in your place, Hetty Feather. I'm mistress here.*

But the next morning at breakfast Ida hovered at my table. I looked round anxiously for Matron Pigface but couldn't see her.

'It's her day off,' Ida whispered. 'I wish she'd stay off for ever. I can't abide her.'

'I call her Pigface,' I said.

'Well, you're very bad,' said Ida, but she grinned. 'Here, Hetty, shove this down your tippet.' She pulled a paper out from under her apron. 'It's Cook's, her special *Police Gazette*. She's read it now. She says there's lots and lots of stories in it.'

'Oh, Ida, thank you!'

I don't think Ida was a keen reader herself. She can't have read the *Gazette* stories or she wouldn't have passed them on to me. They weren't remotely suitable for small girls: tales of grisly murders and violent passion. I read them in a rush of excitement, my eyes popping.

I became a remarkably fast reader because it was so hard to find a private place where I could read in secret. I had to hide in cupboards and crannies and lurk at the back of buildings, with maybe five minutes to read in peace before the wretched bell started ringing. My eyes flew down each page. It was as if I had a minute to eat a whole meal. I bolted down each story in a great undigested lump – and it frequently kept me awake half the night.

When the matron put the light out and the whispering started, I stoppered my ears with my fingers and told myself the stories inside my head, but the other girls would not leave me alone. Sheila was especially tormenting, continually making reference to my red hair and temper.

'Oh, sew your lips up with a darning needle!' I responded. 'You'd better mind I *don't* lose my temper like mad Flora Jackson. She was a maid in a big house in the country and her mistress scolded her all the time, so one dark night Flora took leave of her senses and seized a ball of string and the sharpest carving knife in the kitchen. She trussed up her nagging mistress in her nightclothes and cut off her tongue, so she could not scold her any more. So be warned, Sheila Mayhew. I know where the knives are kept in the kitchen!'

There were stifled shrieks up and down the dormitory.

'How silly you are, Hetty. You certainly don't frighten me,' and Sheila – but her voice was high and squeaky and she certainly *sounded* frightened.

'What happened to Flora's mistress, Hetty? Did she *die*?'

'Oh no, she was left with her poor tongue cut in half so she couldn't speak any more – she just *gurgled*, oogle-oogle-oogle!'

'Ooooh!' the girls shrieked, so loudly that Matron Pigface came stomping back to give us all a severe scolding.

'Matron Peters had better watch out too,' I murmured darkly when she'd gone at last.

The next night the girls all begged for more stories of mad Flora and her mistress, and I recited the whole story again: there had been three whole pages devoted to this grisly tale in the *Police Gazette*. The next night I told them a new story, the night after that another, and when I had used up all the *Police Gazette* horror tales, I found it easy enough to make up my own.

Everyone begged for more, even Sheila and Monica, though half the girls woke up shrieking with terrible nightmares. Several took to wetting their beds and suffered horrible public humiliation, trailing their smelly wet sheets behind them – but these were the very girls who cried, 'Tell us a story, Hetty, a really bloody one,' the moment the lights went out.

I carried on like Scheherazade (Nurse Winnie was reading us *Tales of the Arabian Nights* during our darning sessions now), but one night I woke up to hear desperate sobbing coming from the bed opposite.

I was used to hearing the other girls cry – I sometimes cried myself – but this was different. I climbed out of bed and pattered over. It was the new girl, Polly. I seemed to have frightened her into fits.

I wasn't the new girl any more. There had been three new girls since me – Jane, Matilda and Maria – and each time my heart beat faster in the hope I might make a new friend. I tried to be kind and reassuring, I guided them to the privies, the dining hall, the classroom and the playground. I protected them when Sheila and Monica and the others starting their teasing, I helped them learn their letters, I even showed them how to darn, though I still found it a struggle myself.

But somehow my attempts didn't work. Jane was a dull, dull, dull girl who stared blankly with her mouth open when I tried to get her to picture things. She was shocked by my night-time stories.

'You're a very bad girl, Hetty Feather, telling about them things,' she declared, and would have nothing to do with me.

Matilda was more fun and I liked her big brown eyes and ready smile. She was a little slow at picturing herself, but marvelled when I turned the grey wastes of the playground into the hot sandy desert or the salty ocean as we played explorers or pirates. She begged for more when I told her my gory *Gazette* stories. Oh, Matilda seemed a perfect friend, and for a week or two I was actually happy at the hospital – but then Maria came.

Her bed was beside Matilda's and she sat next to her in class, so Matilda looked after her a little, which I thought only kind and fair, but soon Matilda and Maria were going round arm in arm, whispering secrets. *They* were friends now and I was the girl who was allowed to trail round after them on sufferance.

I resolved to give up my search for a friend. It was too painful. I made up my own companions in my head and we got along well enough. My imaginary friends all adored me, and begged to link their shadowy arms through mine, and listened spellbound while I told them stories.

Polly had appeared at midday, a plump girl with watery blue eyes. She had arrived with long white-blonde hair to her waist, but after a session with Matron Pigface and her dreaded scissors, she now looked like a dandelion puffball under her cap. She cried on and off in a dreary way throughout the day, but none of us took much notice. It was standard new-girl behaviour. She made not a peep of protest when I told my stories in the darkness of the dormitory. When we were settling down to sleep, I did call out, 'Goodnight, Polly,' but she did not reply, so I thought she must be sleeping already.

She was clearly not asleep now, though she still didn't answer when I whispered her name. She tried to lie still, her face in her pillow, but she could not stop sobbing.

'Don't cry so,' I said softly, patting her heaving shoulder. 'I know it's horrid here, but you will get used to it.'

Polly went on sobbing.

'I'm so sorry I told the story. I did not mean to frighten you so. I won't ever tell about the Meat-axe Murderer again, I promise. And he's all locked up in prison, so he can't hurt you.'

'It's not the Meat-axe Murderer man,' Polly sobbed. 'I want to go *home*.'

I sighed. 'So do I,' I said. The longing for Jem and Mother and everyone overwhelmed me again. I bit my lip hard to stop myself crying too. 'Oh, Polly, so do I.'

I reached out to pat her shoulder. She jumped at my touch.

'What is it? I didn't hurt you!'

'You're so cold.'

'It *is* cold. Here. Move up.' I burrowed under her covers, getting right into bed with her. 'Oh, your pillow's soaking wet! You must have been crying for hours.'

I moved her head and turned the pillow over. 'There, that's better, isn't it?'

She put her hands up over her head. 'I look so ugly now,' she wept.

'It does look a little strange, but it will grow soon. I quite like mine now. I look like a boy.'

'I don't *want* to look like a boy!' Polly sobbed.

'Oh, I do. They have much more fun. I have a wonderful big brother, Jem. He is going to come and fetch me home when I am old enough, and I have another even bigger brother, Nat. I have two more brothers here, in the boys' wing, and a sister, Martha, who sings in the choir very beautifully. I was very worried about my brother Gideon, so I dressed up in boys' clothes and went and found him, and I shall go again soon to check on him. I have another brother, Saul, but I don't think much of him at all. Don't you have brothers? I have yet another brother who's a soldier – his name is—'

And then I was stuck. I held myself rigid, hands over my mouth. I couldn't remember! I was forgetting my family already. I had never known this big brother, but we had talked of him often. Mother had always sighed when she said his name and kept his letters tied up with blue ribbon.

I started trying to say each member of the family, mumbling their names under my breath.

'Are you praying, Hetty?' Polly asked.

'Marcus! Oh, I have remembered!' I said, hugging Polly hard in my relief. 'I must never ever forget them. I shall say them over and over again each night. You must remember all your brothers and sisters, Polly.'

'I have none,' she said. 'My foster mother is Miss Morrison, who used to keep the school, Miss Morrison's Seminary for Young Ladies. She took a fancy to bringing up a foundling babe when she retired. She is my foster mother and I miss her sooooo.' Polly started wailing again. 'Every night I sat on my bed with its lovely rose quilt and she brushed my hair one hundred times.' She clasped her shorn head despairingly. 'There's nothing left to brush now!'

'We will picture it together,' I said. I started running my fingers through her sad, feathery tufts. 'There, this is the brush, and your hair is growing again, feel, growing and growing, it's past your ears now. I'll keep brushing, my goodness, how it's growing! There, feel it resting on your shoulders now?'

I felt Polly put her hands up in the dark and I braced myself, thinking she was going to be another Jane. But no, she felt the thin air and then whispered, 'Oh, it's back, and so long, and *this* time it's curly.'

'Oh, Polly, you can picture! Will you be my special friend?'

'I should like to be your friend more than anything, Hetty,' said Polly.

I stayed cuddled up with her until dawn, then I hurtled back to my own bed only a few moments before the big girl monitor burst into the room.

I helped Polly smooth her apron and tippet into place when we got dressed. When I placed her cap upon her head, I whispered, 'There, all your new curls are tumbling down past your shoulders.'

When Ida smiled at me at breakfast, I said, 'This is my new friend, Polly.'

Ida nodded at Polly in a kindly way.

'Ida is quite the nicest maid in the whole hospital,' I told Polly.

Ida blushed deeply, the pink in her cheeks making her look almost pretty. 'Hetty is quite the most *artful* girl in the whole hospital,' she said sprinkling sugar on my porridge. She sprinkled a little on Polly's plate too.

I made sure Polly sat next to me in lesson time, and I resolved to help her with her ABC very patiently. But I didn't need to! Polly's schoolmistress foster mother had taught her charge well. Polly could read as fluently as me, though I was now top reader of the entire infants class. She could write neatly too, in a curly copperplate that sent Miss Newman into raptures.

'Look, girls, mark this penmanship! See with

what style Polly writes her lesson, and not a single mistake!' she said, showing us all Polly's page.

If Polly had not been my true friend, I would have been a little irritated. Half the girls groaned jealously. Sheila and Monica started making up a vulgar verse together about Polly Penmanship. I quelled them with a terrifying look. No one should be allowed to tease my friend!

Polly proved gifted at darning too, sewing neatly and smoothly, an accomplishment that proved more popular. Our clothes were not marked in any way. We were handed out our clean clothes randomly on Sunday. If you were given badly darned stockings, the toes all cobbled together, you knew you'd be driven mad by the irritation, forever forced to take your boot off to ease the stocking this way and that.

Polly and I pictured together every playtime. We'd spread our arms and pretend we could fly. We might look as if we were simply running up and down the playground with our arms outstretched, but we knew we were swooping high above the sooty rooftops of London town. One day we'd fly to visit Polly's foster mother and sit at Miss Morrison's skirts and eat seedcake for our tea; the next day we'd fly to my village and sit with Jem in my squirrel house and eat gingerbread.

I told Polly about Madame Adeline and Tanglefield's Travelling Circus. I invited her to take part, though privately I was a little unsure about her as a circus performer. Although she got no more food than the rest of us, she remained a very sturdy child, flat-footed in her institution boots. But I need not have worried. Polly had as much imagination as me.

'There was a parrot at Miss Morrison's. He was called Polly too, though I think he was a boy. He used to squawk dreadfully and nip everyone, but he was very good with me. It was my special job to feed him, and he'd say, "Good girlie, good girlie." So I'll be a bird trainer at the circus and teach parrots to sing songs, and great hawks and eagles and albatrosses will fly about my head and do such tricks,' she said. She waved her hand and I *saw* her performing birds and marvelled.

I shared my purloined *Police Gazettes* with Polly, and we gasped and giggled together at their grisly stories. I wondered if Polly would wish to terrify the dormitory with her own version at night, but she was a tactful girl and left the public tale-telling to me.

She did still cry at times, long after the other girls slept, but I always slipped into her bed and cuddled her close and comforted her.

13

Polly and I even got ill together that winter. I'm not sure which of us started sniffing and sneezing first, but within a day we both had red and running noses and hacking coughs. Matron Pigface Peters gave us a rag each to wipe our noses, but they were made of harsh, hard cloth and rubbed us raw. Our heads were aching and our arms and legs hurt. All we wanted to do was lie down, but we were forced up into our everyday routine. It was especially cold and we stood shivering at playtime, barely able to stand.

'Run around, children! You need plenty of fresh air to blow those horrid colds away. Don't pull those long faces at me!' said Matron Pigface.

'But we're so cold, Matron. Mayn't we stay indoors just this once?' I snuffled.

'Cold? Of course you're cold if you loll around like that! Do some skipping! Take some exercise, you lazy little girls. And stop that shivering! You've got your good thick coats.'

We had our coats, but we had no woollen scarves or mittens. We had no underwear, so the icy wind blew straight up our skirts. We staggered miserably up and down, our faces grey, snot running freely. By bedtime we were both wheezing and dizzy with fever. I could not croak out a story for everyone. I could barely breathe. I lay there, head throbbing, while my bed seemed to rise up and down, voyaging to the ceiling and back. I lifted my head and was violently sick all over my pillow and coverlet. I crouched, shivering and sniffing, desperate to know what to do. I was sure I'd be punished for making such a terrible stinking mess. I had to try to clear it up, but I didn't know *how*.

'Oh, Hetty Feather, have you been *sick*?' Sheila called. 'I can smell it from here. How disgusting you are!'

'She couldn't help it,' said Polly. 'I feel sick too. Oh no—!' She vomited as well.

'Stop it! You're *both* disgusting,' said Sheila.

Some of the other girls woke too and groaned and complained.

'Ssh! I hear footsteps. It's Matron!' Monica hissed.

I started crying then, unable to lie down in my bed, terrified I might be whipped for being out of it. But it wasn't the dreaded Matron Pigface Peters. Lovely Nurse Winnie was on night duty. She came in with her lamp.

'Oh dear, oh dear, who's been sick?' she said. 'Is it you, Hetty? And poor Polly too!' She came up to me and felt my forehead. 'You have a fever, dear. You need proper nursing – and you too, Polly. Come along with me, girls.'

She ushered us out of the dormitory and down the corridor, into a room we'd never been in before, like a small dormitory with twelve beds.

'This is the infirmary, girls. Let's strip off those soiled nightgowns and get you washed and clean again, poor lambs.' She was so gentle with us that we both started crying, unused to such tenderness. When we were in our clean nightgowns, we were tucked into bed in the infirmary with new softer rags to blow our noses and bowls beside us in case we were sick again.

'There now. Try to get some sleep. I'll go and check the other girls and strip your soiled beds. Don't cry so. You'll feel better soon.'

'We're not going to be punished?' I said.

'Goodness, Hetty, you're both ill with the influenza. Of course you're not going to be punished.' Nurse Winnie sounded shocked. 'Dear goodness, what must you think of us!'

'I think *you're* lovely, Nurse Winterson,' I said.

She was truly angelic to both of us: she held the bowls when we were sick again; she lifted us onto the chamber pot; she wound wet towels round us to bring down our fever; she gave us sips of sugared water; she read aloud to us when we were restless; she clasped our hands when the doctor came to examine us. By this time the infirmary was full of sneezing sick girls, with further beds lining the corridor.

'Half the hospital has gone down with this wretched virulent influenza,' he said as he listened to Polly's chest. 'However, you're a sturdy child with excellent lungs. You'll be running around in a day or so, as right as ninepence.'

He looked graver when he undid my nightgown to listen to my chest. He bent closer, till his pomaded hair was right under my nostrils. He kept prodding me with the cold end of his stethoscope, shaking his head. 'This child is nowhere near as robust,' he declared. 'Severely undernourished. She has a sparrow's bones, no meat on them at all. She needs feeding up!'

'I eat the same as Polly, sir,' I said, but he took no notice.

'Give her black beer in the mornings, and full cream milk and plenty of porridge – or you'll lose her,' he said bluntly.

I shivered, with excitement as much as fear, because I could not help delighting in the fact that *I* was the child so sorely ill. I hated it when Polly was sent back to the dormitory the next day, almost fully recovered. I was so worried she might form a friendship with another girl in my absence – but I could not help basking in the attention of dear Nurse Winnie at nights. Mercifully Matron Pigface Peters went down with the influenza herself and kept to her room. Several of the nurses were also ill, so during the day we were looked after by anyone available. Sometimes it was a big girl. One glorious day Ida came with a specially ordered bowl of creamy porridge for me. She sat beside my bed and insisted on feeding me, spooning porridge into my mouth as if I was a little baby. I was still feeling sick and kept shaking my head, but Ida tapped my mouth gently with the spoon, coaxing me.

'There's a good girl, Hetty. Another few spoonfuls just for me, eh? And look what I have for you here – a little slab of my own home-made toffee. You may suck on a square when you've finished your porridge.'

I cried a little then.

'Don't cry, dearie. Does your chest hurt bad? Perhaps you need a piece of flannel at your throat?'

'No, no, it's just you're being so kind to me. It's almost as if I was at home,' I wept. 'I miss Jem so much – and Mother.'

'What was your foster mother like, Hetty?' Ida asked.

'She was just . . . Mother.'

'She was kind to you?'

'She was very kind. Though she paddled me when I was a bad girl.'

'I'm sure you could never be truly bad,' said Ida. She lifted me up off the pillow to drink my milk. She had her arm round my shoulders, and I leaned against her gratefully.

I decided I was in no hurry to get better when Ida and Nurse Winnie were making such a fuss of me, especially when Nurse Winnie smuggled me a reassuring note from Polly.

Dear Hetty,

I do hope you are not too ill. I miss you so dreadfully, it is HORRID without you.

From your very loving friend, Polly.

Dear Polly I replied,

It is ENORMOUSLY horrid not being with you, but I am trying hard to bear it. I will get better soon, I promise. Nurse Winnie is my friend and Ida is my friend too, but you are my most very SPECIAL friend in all the world and I am very affectionately
    Your Hetty

I was still not very strong and I had to labour long and hard over my letter. I asked Ida how to spell the great big words like *enormously* and *affectionately*, but she blushed and looked wretched.

'I'm not very good at writing, Hetty. I can't rightly say,' she said.

'Well, never mind, I'll ask Nurse Winterson,' I said, sad that I'd embarrassed her.

'I never had much schooling, see,' Ida said. She looked at me earnestly. 'That's the good thing about the hospital. You girls get a proper education. You're brought up almost like young ladies.'

'Yes, but we're *not* young ladies. We have to be servants,' I said, wrinkling my nose. 'I don't want to be a servant.'

Then it was my turn to blush because I realized I'd been tactless. 'I am sorry, Ida,' I said, taking her hand.

'There are worse positions in life,' she said flatly. 'And you're very bright, Hetty. Perhaps – perhaps you'll get a position as a lady's maid and wear a fine uniform and never have to do any hard work. Should you like that?'

I considered. 'Perhaps I should like it if she was a very *kind* lady, and let me dress up in her silks and velvets and gave me cake at tea time,' I said.

Ida laughed. 'You have wheedling ways, but I doubt any lady will let you do that.'

'Then I won't be a servant at all. I shall run away to the circus.'

'Oh yes?' said Ida. 'And what will you be there? A performing monkey?'

'I shall be a fine lady on a white horse,' I declared.

'With rings on your fingers and bells on your toes?' said Ida, not taking me seriously.

'No, I shall join my real mother, Madame Adeline, and she will give me a costume of pink spangles and we will ride our horses together in the circus ring,' I said.

'Whatever makes you fancy your mother is a circus lady?' said Ida.

'Oh, I am absolutely certain of it,' I said. 'Madame Adeline told me herself. More or less. And when I am big enough I shall go and find her, just you wait and see.'

'Well, you're not big enough yet, Hetty. You're still the smallest girl in the whole hospital. You must eat up all the milk puddings I bring you, every last morsel, and then you will get better.'

I *did* get better, though I think it was due to the love and attention of Ida and Nurse Winnie, not their milk puddings and medicine. But one of our sick girls, Sarah Barnes, grew worse. The nurses wrapped her in soaking sheets, but she was still burning hot when I touched her and she could barely sip her sugared water. She was so weak they had to lift her onto a chamber pot like a baby. And all the time, morning, evening, all through the night, she coughed and coughed.

I slipped out of bed and went to stand beside her, shivering. 'Poor Sarah,' I whispered. 'Is your throat very sore?'

'Yes!' she mumbled. 'Yes, it hurts.'

'Shall I get Nurse?'

'No. No, I want—'

'Who?'

'I want my *mother*,' Sarah sobbed.

I told Nurse Winnie and she looked stricken.

'Poor lamb! I wish she *could* see her foster mother, but it's strictly against the rules.'

'But she's so ill.'

'I know, Hetty, I know,' she said wearily, and she covered her face with her hands.

'Nurse Winterson . . . is Sarah *dying*?' I whispered.

'I hope not. But she is very, very poorly,' said Nurse Winnie.

Sarah started crying again that night, calling for her mother. She wouldn't quieten, no matter how Nurse Winnie tried to soothe her.

I got out of bed and crept nearer. I had the fanciful idea that I could picture Sarah's mother for her, tell her that she was coming very soon, that she loved her little daughter – but Nurse Winnie took hold of me and forced me back to bed.

'I know you mean well, Hetty, but you must not get too near poor Sarah, especially while she is coughing so. You must not risk re-infecting yourself. You're still quite a sick girl. Now go back to sleep, there's a good child.'

I tried to do as I was told, pulling my blanket high over my head to cut out the sound of Sarah. When I woke up in the morning the room was strangely quiet. I sat up. Sarah's bed was empty, her sheets pulled off, her mattress bare.

'Where's Sarah? Is she in the washroom?' I called anxiously.

'No, Hetty.' Nurse Winnie came over to me, her face very white, purple shadows under her eyes. 'No, Hetty, Sarah's gone to Heaven. She's with the angels now.'

I sat still, stunned. I'd asked if Sarah was dying, but I hadn't really meant it. Sarah was such a *real* girl, with her cough and her running nose and a tendency not to reach the privy in time. Yet now she was an angel in a long white dress, with wings sprouting out of her small shoulder blades? I was accomplished at picturing, but it was very hard imagining Sarah lolling on heavenly clouds, a halo over her lank brown hair.

'Don't be sad, Hetty. Sarah is happy now, and her poor cough is better,' said Nurse Winterson – but she didn't sound at all sure.

I lay down again, my heart beating fast. They said I was getting better, but might *I* die too? A new nurse came to take over from Nurse Winnie, a little sharp-faced woman I'd not seen before. It seemed she usually worked in the boys' wing, but was now working a shift with us because three of our nurses were ill themselves.

Nurse Winterson told her the news about Sarah. She was whispering but I could still hear her.

'Let's hope she is the only one we lose,' said Nurse Winnie.

'One of our boys is failing fast,' said the new nurse. 'A sad little lad, much troubled. Calling for his mother, and his father, and all his brothers and his sisters—'

'That's maybe my brother! I must go to him!' I said, getting out of bed.

'No, Hetty, don't fret, it won't be *your* brother,' said Nurse Winnie – but the sharp-faced nurse seemed taken aback.

'He *has* a sister Hetty!' she said.

'I have to see him. He's calling for me! I have to see him before he goes to the angels like Sarah,' I said frantically.

'Hush, child, it's not allowed,' said the sharp-faced nurse.

'*I* will allow it,' said Nurse Winnie.

She wrapped my blanket around me and lifted

me in her arms. She must have been exhausted after a long traumatic night, but luckily I was very light.

'You can't take her!' said the other nurse.

'Yes, I can,' said Nurse Winnie.

She carried me out of the infirmary, along the corridor, all the way to the boys' wing.

'Oh, Nurse Winterson, I love you dearly! Thank you so much. I need to see my brother Gideon so badly,' I said.

'I know you do, Hetty. I will make sure you see him.'

She pushed open a door with her hip and we entered a room with the familiar smell of carbolic and sickness. There were boys in the beds, sniffing and coughing, and a nurse bending over a boy at the end, looking grave. She was startled at the sight of us.

'Don't be alarmed. I have brought Hetty to see her brother,' said Nurse Winnie.

'Gideon! Oh, Gideon, I'm here!' I cried.

But it wasn't Gideon lying in the bed.

'Oh goodness! It's *Saul*! But . . . is Gideon all right?' I begged the nurse. 'My brother Gideon? He's very frail, with a weak chest. Where is he? Oh please, he hasn't died and gone to join the angels?'

'Hush, child, keep your voice down. Saul is very

sick. But Gideon is perfectly healthy. He has not caught the influenza,' said the nurse.

'You promise that's true?' I said, not certain I could trust her.

'Hetty!' said Nurse Winnie. 'Now, dear, do you have some words of comfort for your brother Saul?'

He was the *wrong* brother. I really wanted to rush out of the infirmary and find Gideon so I could see for myself that he was truly well – but I knew that in the circumstances this would not be looked on favourably. So I took a deep breath and stared down at Saul.

He was lying wretchedly in bed, his curls damp with sweat, his cheeks flushed with fever.

'Hello, Saul,' I said softly. 'It's me, Hetty.'

'I'm not sure he'll know you, child. He's very fevered,' said the nurse.

But Saul's brown eyes were open, staring straight at me. He knew me all right. He'd heard me burble about Gideon. He knew I'd never have begged to come and visit him. I suddenly felt terrible.

'Oh, Saul,' I said, wishing I could cry to look truly sorry. 'Oh, poor Saul, you look so ill. I've been ill too, but not as much as you. It must hurt so much. Here, let me hold your hand.'

I tried to take it, but he pulled away from me.

'I know you don't like me, but never mind, because I like *you*,' I said. I was lying now, but it seemed only right and fair. 'You are my dear brother and I wish I could comfort you. I wish Mother could come.'

Saul's eyes filled with tears. I tried desperately hard to think what it must be like to be him.

'I think Mother loved you best,' I whispered, bending down beside him. I started stroking his damp hair. This time he didn't try to push me away. 'Yes, you were her special baby, her little lamb, but then Gideon and I came along and she had to attend to us. You got pushed out of the way. No wonder you did not like us. But Mother still loved you best. When she took you to the hospital she was so sad. She could barely speak for days after, she just moped in a corner, missing her special boy.'

'Hetty, Hetty, try to *cheer* your little brother,' said Nurse Winterson.

But Saul was smiling a little and I knew my words were cheering him immensely. I stayed crouched by his side, whispering to him about Mother, and he stopped tossing restlessly and curled closer. His hand was near mine, and this time when I took it he clasped me back.

His eyelids starting drooping. When they closed, I started uneasily, fearful that he might be dead – but I could hear his laboured breaths and the wheezing of his chest.

'Come, Hetty. He is sleeping peacefully now. I must take you back,' said Nurse Winnie.

I staggered to my feet, stumbling over something on the floor. It was Saul's crutch.

'He'll not be needing that any more,' said the sharp-faced nurse ominously, tidying it into a cupboard.

I burst out crying then. It was almost as if she'd taken Saul himself and stowed him in the cupboard. I cried all the way back to the girls' wing, though Nurse Winnie did her best to console me. She was sorry for me, and doubtless frightened lest any other nurse asked why I was crying so. I tried to stop, because I didn't want to get her into trouble, but I felt too sad. For all I prided myself on my picturing skills, I'd never before imagined what it was like to be Saul. I had pitied myself often enough, and fretted about dear Gideon, but I'd never cared a jot for Saul.

I resolved to be a true sister to him if by some miracle he made a full recovery. I'd disguise myself in breeches again and slip along to the boys' wing on a regular basis. I'd make a great fuss of *both* my brothers. I'd wheedle sweets out of the Sunday visitors and hide them away from the thieving big girls. I'd keep every one for Saul and Gideon, and take pleasure in seeing them suck them. They'd give me sticky embraces, telling me I was their dear sister Hetty.

But the next morning I heard the boys' nurse whispering to Nurse Winnie. I heard Saul's name – and I knew he was dead. I started crying anew.

'Oh, Hetty, you have such sharp ears! You poor lamb, I am so sorry. Still, at least you were able to say goodbye to him,' said Nurse Winnie.

'I can't bear it if he's really dead,' I sobbed. 'I haven't had time to make him like me!'

'Of course he liked you, Hetty. You were a lovely sister to him. You must try not to grieve so. He will be happy now in Heaven. He will be there with our dear Sarah.'

I tried to imagine Saul and Sarah playing together in white angel nightgowns. I did not think Saul would care for Sarah. Her nose would run and she would start wailing. He would provoke her and prod her with his crutch.

'Nurse Winterson, will Saul be lame in Heaven?'

'No, that is the joyous thing. God will cure him. Saul will be able to run around on two strong legs. Isn't that wonderful?'

'Why couldn't God cure him *here*?' I said.

'Oh, Hetty, you're such a child for questions, even when you're ill,' said Nurse Winterson, sighing hard.

They let me out of the infirmary the next day. Polly greeted me with a great hug.

'I thought you might die and then I couldn't bear it,' she said fervently.

'I think I *nearly* died. Sarah did – and my brother Saul.'

'Will you go to their funerals?' Polly asked in awe.

I rather hoped I *would* go. I had never been to a funeral, but it seemed to be a very grand and sombre occasion – and anything was better than the monotony of the hospital routine. I think they must have *had* funerals, but I wasn't invited. We sang a special hymn in chapel on Sunday – and that was the last time their names were ever mentioned.

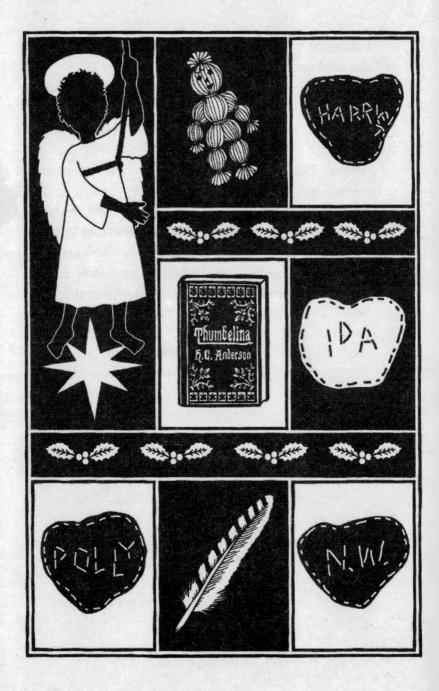

14

Christmas was coming but I didn't know whether to get excited. I asked Harriet how it was celebrated at the hospital.

'Christmas is rather like a special Sunday,' she said, which depressed me utterly.

I hated the long cold hours in chapel. I'd started to hate Sunday dinner too. I still simpered so that the ladies and gentlemen would give me sweets, but the big girls were wise to me now, and stole them all from me the moment I stepped outside the dining room.

I tried looking to Harriet for protection, but she had developed a ridiculous passion for one of the younger gentlemen visitors and hung back, blushing and smiling, frequently the very last foundling out of the dining room.

He wore a gold tie-pin in the shape of a P, so Harriet spent entire *hours* wondering if he was a Philip, a Peter or a Paul.

'I think I heard his wife calling him *Peregrine*,'

I fibbed, making up the silliest name I could think of.

'Nonsense, Hetty! And that lady isn't his *wife*, she's far too old, years and years older than him. She might even be his mother, though I rather think she is his older spinster sister.'

She was a very plain, pale, serious-seeming lady who always wore plain charcoal-grey dresses with no adornments – so perhaps Harriet was right.

She certainly seemed convinced he was fancy-free and conducting a full-scale flirtation with her, though as far as I could see he didn't so much as glance in her direction. But she was happy to dream.

'Will all the ladies and gentlemen gawp at us when we eat our Christmas dinner too?' I said.

'Oh yes!' said Harriet happily. 'And they will be in the chapel for the Christmas service with the choir and the *tableau vivant*.'

'What's a *tableau vivant*?' I asked.

'Oh, it's very pretty, a representation of the Nativity. I hope each year that I might get picked as Mary. I would so love to play the virgin mother in all her holiness with everyone gazing – especially *him*.'

I knew all about the Nativity. Every Christmas time Mother hung up a big picture of baby Jesus in the manger, with all his visitors adoring him.

'So is this *tableau vivant* like a play?'

'There are no words, Hetty, and you have to keep very still. It's like a living picture.'

This wasn't such good news. It didn't sound as if anything *happened*. I longed for drama, angels proclaiming at the tops of their voices, innkeepers turning away the holy couple, wise men processing with their exotic gifts.

'How do we know who is who if no one moves or says anything?' I said.

'Don't be so silly! They wear special costumes. Mary has a beautiful dress of brilliant blue and a long white veil,' said Harriet, sighing wistfully. 'Imagine!'

Oh, I could imagine. I suddenly understood. Harriet had been wearing an ugly brown dress and a ridiculous cap since she was five years old.

'I do hope you get to be Mary,' I said. 'Or if not, perhaps *I* could be Mary?'

My heart beat fast at the thought. I pictured myself in that blue dress, felt the soft bright silk on my arms, the long veil brushing past my shoulders.

'Oh, Hetty!' said Harriet, and I saw she was trying not to laugh. 'You are much too little. And you have red hair.'

I was rather put out by this. Harriet was meant to be my friend.

'I could stand on a box. And my hair wouldn't show much underneath my veil,' I said, a little sulkily. However, I had another idea. 'Or as I am really little, perhaps I could be baby Jesus? I could crouch inside a box, and be like baby Jesus in the manger.'

This time Harriet couldn't help laughing heartily. 'You are so comical, Hetty! You couldn't possibly pass as Jesus! No, they have a *real* baby, one of the new foundling babes from the nurseries. Last year it cried so loudly that it almost drowned out the singing of the choir.'

'I could do that. I am very good at crying,' I said. 'Who chooses the children for the *tableau vivant*?'

'I'm not sure,' said Harriet. 'Perhaps the matrons and the nurses?'

I had no chance at all if Matron Pigface Peters had any say. But dear Nurse Winnie would surely put in a good word for me.

'Or maybe it's the teachers,' said Harriet.

Aha! Miss Newman was too strict a teacher to have obvious favourites, but we all knew she favoured Polly and me because we were the cleverest. Perhaps she would pick both of us? I thought hard about costumes. I did not wish to be a shepherd or a guest at the inn. Their costumes would be very commonplace. But the wise men would surely wear fine gowns of velvet and brocade – and if they were kings, they should have golden crowns on their heads!

'Oh, Harriet, we could be the three wise men!' I said. 'You could be the big one and you could be first to bow down to baby Jesus and give him a big present. And then Polly could be the middle-sized wise man and give a middle-sized present. Then I could come last and be a teeny tiny wise man with a very teeny tiny present.'

Harriet laughed so hard that tears rolled down her cheeks. 'It's not *Goldilocks and the Three Bears*, Hetty! You are so funny! And besides, we are girls, so we only play the lady parts. The boys always play the wise men.'

'But that isn't fair!' I reckoned it up, counting on my fingers. 'There are heaps and heaps of men parts. There are only two lady parts, Mary and the innkeeper's wife. Unless – is an angel a man or a lady?'

Harriet did not look sure. 'I think an angel can be either,' she said.

'Then I could be an angel and wear a long white nightgown. Oh, and I could have *wings*, great feathery wings. Do you think I could have wings that really fly?'

'*Pigs* might fly before they let you be an angel, Hetty,' said Harriet. 'Everyone says how fierce and bad you are. And you fidget so. You could never be part of a *tableau vivant* where you have to stand still as still throughout the entire service. Now stop plaguing me about the *tableau vivant*. Tell me, did you happen to notice the exquisite cravat my gentleman was wearing this morning?'

But I was in a sulk and did not want to discuss Philip-Peter-Paul-Peregrine. I didn't care if he was choked by his own exquisite cravat. I just wanted to be in the *tableau vivant*.

I told Polly all about it that night.

'We could both be angels, Polly. Well, perhaps not the big special angel who tells the wise men about Jesus.'

'Gabriel,' said Polly.

'Yes, that one. But there are lots of *other* angels – the hymn says, *A host of heavenly angels*, and I'm sure a host means a great deal. So we could be small angels, baby ones—'

'Cherubs,' said Polly.

'Yes, cherubs!' I thought back to the Nativity picture at home. 'There were definitely cherubs at the Nativity. They were up at the corners, flying above the stable, but they didn't have any clothes on, just little wisps.'

'We would have to wear clothes, Hetty,' Polly said firmly.

But we weren't chosen to be angels, wisps or no wisps. *Monica* was picked to be a small angel. We were astonished. She was such a thin, colourless girl with very little personality. She just echoed everything Sheila said. Sheila seemed equally taken aback, convinced that she would make a far superior angel. She started to tease and torment Monica – but Monica didn't retaliate. She had become irritatingly holy since being chosen.

'You're making Jesus very unhappy calling me silly names and pinching me, Sheila,' she declared. 'I shan't play with you any more until you say sorry.'

'I'm not a bit sorry,' said Sheila, marching off. 'I'd far sooner play by myself.'

She stood stamping her feet and glowering in a corner of the playground while Monica smiled in a maddening saintly way and struck angelic poses. I walked arm in arm with Polly past Sheila and felt almost sorry for her. A truly kind child would have invited Sheila to walk with us – but I am afraid I am only kind when I want to be.

I definitely tried to be kind to my real friends. I decided I wanted to give a Christmas present to Polly, to Harriet, to Nurse Winterson, and to Ida. I did not have any money apart from Jem's precious sixpence, safely hidden inside the knob of my bedhead. I did not have an opportunity to go shopping in any case. I had not been outside the grounds of the hospital since arriving.

This meant I had to make my presents. I certainly wasn't a competent needlewoman. Besides, I had no materials. But I was an opportunistic thief. I was sent in disgrace to Matron Peters's room for cheeking one of the nurses. While standing there being seriously scolded, I saw she had a Chinese bowl of dried lavender and rose petals on her little table. This gave me a wonderful idea. I edged nearer and nearer the bowl, my hands behind my back.

When Matron Pigface consulted her punishment book to check just how many times I had been in trouble, I grabbed a big handful of dried flowers and stuffed them up my sleeve.

I worried a little when I said my prayers at night, in case thieves went straight to Hell, so I told God I was very sorry. But it didn't stop me snatching a torn apron from the mending basket the next day, and hanging onto my needle and thread instead of handing them in to Nurse Winterson after our darning session.

I made four little lavender sachets with my stolen snippets. I tried to fashion them into hearts, but they were woefully lumpy and lopsided. I wanted to sew long loving messages on each, but I didn't have the skill or the time, so I simply stitched each name. Ida was mercifully short, and Polly was simple enough. I had to write Harriet in very tiny stitches, but even so her name had to wind round the edge of her heart. I could not possibly attempt Nurse Winterson in its entirety, and I was fast running out of time, so she had to make do with a hastily stitched NW. She seemed delighted all the same, and kissed me on the cheek. Harriet kissed me too, and gave me her own presents. She had fashioned me a very little dolly out of scraps of wool. She was too small to cuddle close so was no real substitute for my rag baby, but I was still very grateful and gave Harriet many kisses back.

Polly had a present for me too – a pen! She had found a jay's feather in the playground and fashioned the end into a proper quill.

'I can't quite figure how to get any ink,' she said, a little anxiously. 'It would spill if I tried to smuggle some from the classroom inkwells.'

'Never mind, Polly. I can write secret stories in *invisible* ink, or perhaps I could prick my finger and write in blood, though it would have to be a very *short* story. But I *love* my quill pen.'

'And I love my scented heart,' said Polly, and we gave each other a fierce hug.

Ida gave me a present too. I was rather hoping for one, but I thought it would be some delicious titbit, maybe another slab of toffee or a little iced cake.

'Here, Hetty,' she whispered at Christmas Eve supper. 'Don't open it until tomorrow morning, now!' She dropped a little square parcel in my lap.

Definitely a cake, I thought, my mouth watering. I hoped it would have extra-thick icing, and maybe yellow marzipan too, and a surplus of cherries. I was in such a greedy daze of anticipation I almost forgot I had a present to give to Ida too. I fumbled up my sleeve where I had hidden it.

'Are you looking for a handkerchief, Hetty?'

'No, no. Where's it *gone*?' I said, wriggling and scrabbling.

Ida's present had gone right up my sleeve and down inside my dress. I tapped my front. There it was, a little lump above my own real heart. I edged it up towards the neck of my dress.

'Is it moving? Oh dear Lord, have you got a mouse down your dress?' Ida squealed, backing away from me.

'No, silly Ida! It's *your* present.'

'You have a Christmas present for me?' said Ida.

'Yes. Ssh!' I said, peering round to make sure we weren't being observed. I scrabbled down my dress. 'I haven't got any fancy paper to wrap it with, so

240

you will see what it is right this instant. Perhaps you can wrap it up yourself and try to forget what it is, and then when you open it on Christmas day it will come as a splendid surprise. Ah!'

I fished the lavender heart right out into the open. It had got squashed out of shape during its journey up and down my frock and my stitches seemed very big and uneven. I offered it shyly, hoping Ida wouldn't laugh at my efforts.

Ida didn't laugh; she *cried*. She stared at the crumpled heart in her hand and tears welled in her eyes, spilling down her cheeks.

'Oh, Ida, don't cry. I'm sorry it's such a small and shabby present. I will try harder next year,' I said earnestly.

'It's a *wonderful* present – so kind of you, Hetty – oh, bless you, child,' Ida mumbled, and then hurried away to the kitchen, forgetting her serving tray in her haste.

Sheila glared at me. 'What have you done to make Ida cry, Hetty Feather?'

'I have made her *happy*,' I said stoutly, though I wasn't quite sure if this was true.

I couldn't wait till Christmas morning to open my present from Ida. I got up in the middle of the night, clutching my precious small parcel. I tiptoed the length of the dormitory to the washroom. I knew where the nurses kept a candle and matches, in case a child was taken poorly in the night. I took the candle into a corner and lit it with a match. Then I sat down cross-legged and opened my parcel.

It wasn't cake. It wasn't anything to eat at all. It was a tiny book, bound in red, with gilt lettering: *The Story of Thumbelina*. I opened it up with trembling fingers. The story was about a very, very small girl called Thumbelina, and there were *coloured illustrations*! I saw Thumbelina with pink cheeks and very yellow hair, tucked up neatly in a brown walnut-shell bed. I stroked her hair and patted her tiny quilt and then read the first few pages, though I had to squint in the candlelight and it was fearfully cold in the dank washroom.

Dear Ida! She had chosen the smallest book she could find so I could hide it easily about my person. Thumbelina was even smaller than me, yet she was the heroine of her fairy tale, and when I peeked at the ending I saw she lived happily ever after.

I was frozen solid when I eventually stole back to bed, but glowing inside, warmed by Ida's loving generosity. At breakfast I waited until she came to serve us our porridge and then I grabbed hold of her hand tightly.

'Thank you, Ida!' I said passionately. 'I do love you so.'

The other girls giggled, thinking I was simply thanking Ida for my porridge. But Ida understood.

She gave my bowlful an extra sprinkling of brown sugar and patted my shoulder, smiling all the while.

I marched off to chapel feeling very happy. For once I sat through the long, long service without fidgeting, because I had the wondrous Nativity *tableau vivant* to gaze at. The participating children kept still as statues. Even the newborn babe in the cardboard manger slept peacefully throughout. Mary was one of the big girls in Harriet's class, thin and dark and a little gawky, but strangely graceful now. She knelt before the baby, hands clasped in awe, her beautiful bright-blue dress draped decorously about her.

Joseph was one of the big lads, tall as a man, splendid in his orange striped robe. The shepherds were arranged artistically on the left, some standing, some kneeling. There was even a stuffed sheep, and the smallest shepherd clutched a toy lamb. The three wise men paraded on the right, wearing large gold crowns studded with glass jewels. Each boy sported a long false beard to show they were very old and very wise. Oh, how I longed to have a beard too!

Best of all, there were the angels, an entire flock of them, standing aloft upon the stable roof, in gauzy white with great feathery wings, Monica amongst them, pink and pious, her eyes raised upwards.

There was one angel who seemed to be truly flying, dangling on a rope from the chapel rafters, his bare feet on the points of a silver star; the most wondrous angel, with a halo illuminating his dark curls. You will never guess who it was! My own little brother, suspended in mid-air, his arms gesturing gracefully, his toes pointed, dancing down from Heaven.

'It's Gideon!' I whispered proudly to Polly. 'My brother Gideon.'

I felt I could sit there in the chapel for ever. I was so happy for Gideon, and so relieved that he was well and making such a grand job of this angel acting. I glowed with pride when I heard the ladies and gentlemen talking as we ate our Christmas dinner afterwards.

'Bless the children, they looked so splendid in the *tableau vivant*.'

'They kept so still, even the tiny ones.'

'The little boy angel was by far the best.'

'Oh, I agree! A true little angel up there in mid-air!'

I nudged Polly, and happily munched my way through my roast goose and my plum pudding. We each had an orange too. Some of us little ones were inexperienced orange eaters and tried to bite into the bright dimpled skin. I might have done the same because we never had oranges at the cottage, but I watched Polly and copied her as she peeled the skin away and divided her orange into segments.

We had no official presents as such, but when we lifted our mugs to take a drink, we discovered a brand-new polished penny. I hid mine later on top of Jem's silver sixpence. I went to sleep that night with Polly's pen under my pillow, Harriet's doll tucked in beside me, and my tiny book clutched to my chest.

15

We were given an orange and a new penny the next Christmas – and the next and the next and the next. That was the worst thing of all about the hospital: the sheer sameness of every single day.

If things *did* change, it always seemed to be for the worse. Harriet left the hospital to go into service as a nursery maid. She cried when she said goodbye, telling me she'd never care for any of her new nursery charges the way she cared for me. I missed her dreadfully. She had been so kind to me, and I'd loved sitting on her lap and being babied. Thank goodness I still had Polly!

We moved into the upper school, into a different dormitory. Of course I remembered to transfer Jem's sixpence to my new bedpost. I had to say farewell to dear Nurse Winnie and Miss Newman. Thank goodness Ida could still serve me every day in the dining room, giving me illicit gifts of raisins and jam and knobs of butter when no one was watching.

'How are you doing, Hetty?' she'd always ask.

'I'm doing very well, Ida,' I mostly said.

I wasn't doing well, I was doing very badly. I didn't care for my new teacher, Miss Morley, and she certainly didn't care for me – or Polly either. Miss Newman had been strict but she liked both of us. When we answered correctly or asked an interesting question, her eyes lit up behind her spectacles and she seemed delighted to teach us.

Miss Morley stopped asking us to answer questions, because she knew we'd get them right, and this seemed to irritate her.

'Don't sit there with that smug expression on your face, Hetty Feather. We all know *you* know the answer,' she'd say, and she'd give a false yawn and encourage all the others to laugh at me.

I couldn't *help* knowing the answers because our lessons didn't progress. We could mostly all read and write by now, and do the simplest sums – and there we stuck, not working our way forward at all, going over the same dull facts again and again.

There were maps all round our classroom wall and I'd stare at all the different countries and picture a flea-sized Hetty sailing across the blue sea and landing on each pink and yellow and green land.

'Stop daydreaming, Hetty Feather, and attend to your dictation,' Miss Morley snapped.

'Can't you tell us a little about the countries on the map, Miss Morley? I wonder what it is like in great big Africa or India or Japan? Do the children do dictation there? Do they wear long dresses and caps, or do they wear short clothes – or maybe if it's very very hot, no clothes at all?'

The others sniggered and Miss Morley flushed, though I hadn't meant to be impertinent.

'Stop these ridiculous questions, Hetty Feather. You don't need to know the answers. It's not as if *you're* ever going to voyage to foreign parts. You're going to be a servant like all the other girls. You only need to write a decent hand, read a recipe and add up your groceries correctly.'

I felt I needed to do so much more! I still hated the idea of being a servant. I feared I would be a very bad one. We were taught how to wash clothes and scrub floors now, helping out with all the household chores in the hospital. I hated getting hot and wet. I was so bored I distracted myself by telling stories in my head, not concentrating on the tedious housework.

'Use some more elbow-grease, Hetty Feather!' they'd scream at me. 'Watch what you're doing!' they'd yell when I started and knocked over my pail of water.

Polly was as bored as I was, particularly in lessons. She could not bear our arithmetic sessions because Miss Morley frequently made mistakes. Polly pointed out a simple subtraction error on the blackboard early on, waving her arm earnestly.

'What *is* it, Polly Renfrew? I haven't finished the sum yet.'

'I know, Miss Morley, and I'm sorry to interrupt, but I don't think you've noticed that you've subtracted an eight from a three and put the answer as five, and yet you haven't borrowed ten from the next line so that nine is incorrect,' she said helpfully.

She wasn't being impertinent. At this stage she didn't realize that Miss Morley's grasp of arithmetic was extremely shaky. She thought she'd simply made a silly slip and would be grateful for her intervention.

Grateful! Miss Morley flushed an ugly scarlet and rubbed the entire sum from the blackboard. 'How *dare* you admonish me, Polly Renfrew! Come out here.'

Polly stepped forward uncertainly.

'Hold out your hand.'

Polly held it out politely, as if Miss Morley was going to shake it. But she seized her long ruler instead and went *whack whack whack* across Polly's soft white hands.

We all jumped. Our eyes stung. We'd been threatened with whippings and beatings many times in the infant school, but the only actual physical punishment any of us had received was an impatient tug on the ear or a light tap on the backs of our legs. This was a cruel assault. We could see the painful red weals on Polly's palms. Polly's face crumpled and she started crying.

I was beside myself. 'How dare you hit her when she's done nothing wrong at all, you cruel, wicked woman!' I cried, and I seized her ruler and hurled it into a corner of the classroom. The whole class gasped. I was a little shocked myself. I hadn't quite meant to say those words, they just spurted out of my mouth in a torrent.

'Come here, Hetty Feather!' Miss Morley said. 'I will not stand for this behaviour!'

I thought she would retrieve her ruler and beat me to within an inch of my life. I decided I would not cry like poor Polly. I would hold my head up high and be a brave, unflinching martyr. She could beat me three times, six times, even a dozen; she could beat my hands into a bloody pulp but I would not murmur or shed a tear. I would stare back at her like a basilisk, wishing her dead.

But she didn't beat me even once. She seized hold of me by the wrist, digging her nails in hard, and tugged me right out of the classroom. I thought she was simply standing me in the corridor and decided I didn't mind in the least. I could just stand and picture the past in my own private daydream. But Miss Morley marched me right along the corridor. I realized she was taking me to Matron.

My heart started thudding then. The senior school matron made Pigface Peters seem sweet as sugar. Matron Bottomly was thin and pinched, with a permanent pucker in her forehead. She had a big hooked nose like a beak and always looked as if she'd like to peck you very hard. Matron Bottomly had already told me off several times for talking in corridors, she had chastised me for tearing my dress when I fell over playing tag, she had made me scrub a whole floor twice over because I'd left one or two slimy soap smears. (Oh, how I wished Matron Bottomly had slipped on them and landed on her bony stinking bottom!) What might she do when she knew I'd shouted at a teacher, taken her ruler and thrown it away?

I felt I *might* cry now, but I stared hard, scarcely daring to blink in case the tears started spilling. I was pushed unceremoniously into Matron Bottomly's room and forced to stand there in front of her while Miss Morley gave a highly exaggerated account of my rebellion.

'It was total insubordination, actual physical violence!' Miss Morley declared dramatically, drops of spittle on her chapped lips.

Matron Bottomly rose from her desk and looked me up and down. I started trembling but I looked her up and down back, my fists clenched.

I will not cry, I said inside my head. *I will not cry,*

no matter what they do to me. I can bear it, whatever it is. They cannot kill me. I will be brave.

'You are a child of Satan, Hetty Feather,' said Matron Bottomly. 'You have his Hell-red hair and his flaming temper. We must quench this devilish fire. You must be taught a severe lesson.'

I was so crazed with fear I thought she meant a literal lesson. I dared to breathe out, because I knew I was always quick to learn. But this punishment had nothing to do with books.

'Take hold of her, Miss Morley,' said Matron Bottomly.

They each seized a wrist and pulled me to the door. They dragged me down the corridor. I thought they were taking me to the boys' wing. We'd heard fearful rumours that the baddest big boys were beaten with a cat-o'-nine-tails. Perhaps they were now going to whip me with this dreadful instrument! I gritted my teeth, though they were chattering now.

But when we reached the grand staircase, they dragged me up one flight of stairs and then another, right to the very top of the building, to a little attic room in the tower.

They opened a door at the end. It was empty apart from an old blanket and a chamber pot.

'No!' I cried. 'No, please – you can't put me in there!'

'Oh yes we can, Hetty Feather. You stay here and

pray to be a better girl,' said Matron, and she thrust me inside. The door slammed shut and I heard the sound of a key turning. I was locked in! I heard their footsteps retreating. Perhaps they were simply trying to frighten me. They would come back any minute. They couldn't leave me locked in here!

There was only one very small window, set high up in the wall. It had bars across, as if this was truly a prison. I tried jumping up but could only catch a glimpse of sky. I was very small, but there was no way I could ever wriggle through those bars – and it was a sheer drop anyway.

I tried hurling myself against the door, knocking all the breath out of my body. It held fast. I was truly a prisoner.

'Well, what do I care?' I said aloud. 'I will show them. It is not so very dreadful to be locked in for an hour or two. They will have to come back soon because it is nearly dinner time. Meanwhile I shall amuse myself. I shall pretend I am a princess locked up by two evil wicked witches in a tall tower.'

I pictured this determinedly, inventing a magnificent Prince Jem who climbed the tower and rescued me. We lived happily ever after in his wondrous kingdom – while the two witches were locked up in their own tower for ever.

I amused myself with this story for quite a while, but my stomach started rumbling. I could not hear the clock chiming from my isolated prison but I was certain it was long past dinner time now. So they intended to starve me, did they? Were they going to keep me locked up right until supper time?

I kept staring at the chamber pot. It was clearly there to be used, so perhaps I truly was to be left for hours yet. I decided I would not sit on the pot, no matter what. It would be too humiliating for the contents to be inspected by Matron and Miss Morley.

The hours went by, and I fidgeted on my blanket, trying to divert myself. In the end I simply had to squat on the pot in an undignified fashion or have an accident. I waited further hours, and after a long, long while all my picturing skills faded. I could think of nothing to divert myself. Surely it would be supper time soon?

They *had* to let me out for supper. They couldn't leave me locked up in this tiny room until I starved to death. I listened desperately for the sound of approaching footsteps, but there was just endless silence. I tried singing to make a sound in the room, but my voice sounded too high, too weird, as if I was a crazy girl.

I tried to lie down on the blanket, but the floorboards were hard and the blanket smelled stale and musty when I nuzzled into it for comfort. I remembered my long-ago rag baby, and started weeping. Once I'd started I couldn't stop. I sobbed frantically, but still no one came.

'I'm sorry!' I shouted. 'Please come back, Matron! I've learned my lesson now!'

But she didn't come. It seemed to be getting darker in the small room. Oh my Lord, was it evening now? Were they going to keep me locked up all night long?

I shouted until my voice cracked, but still nobody came. I threw myself about the attic, kicking and screaming. I tore off my stupid cap and pulled my own hair. It was long again now, in two tight plaits, but I undid them and shook my head in despair, my hair wild about my shoulders.

I was so thirsty from crying I could barely swallow. How could they leave me without even a few sips of water? They *had* to come back soon or I would surely die. Was that what they really *wanted*? Oh dear Lord, what if they never came back? What if I mouldered up here in my dark prison for ever? What if they waited until I was a grisly skeleton in scraps of brown, crumbling to dust?

Then, at long, long last, when it was getting really dark, I heard footsteps coming along the corridor, and the sound of a key in the lock.

'Oh, at last!' I said. 'I'm so sorry. You will let me out now, won't you?'

It was Nurse Macclesfield, one of the senior school staff. She was carrying a bucket and a plate and a mug. 'Of course you are sorry, Hetty Feather – and you'll be sorrier still by morning!'

'What! You're not going to keep me locked up here all night!' I said in horror.

'You must learn the error of your ways, you wicked girl.' She seized my pot, pulling a face of disgust, and emptied it into her bucket. Then she put the plate and mug down on the floor and went to close the door on me again.

'No! Oh, Nurse Macclesfield, have pity on me! Let me out!'

I tried to cling to her, but she pushed me away.

'Don't you dare try to attack me the way you attacked poor Miss Morley. She said you were like a wild beast. It's time you were tamed!'

She slammed the door shut on me, rattled the key in the lock and marched off.

'Please come back, please, please!' I screamed, though I knew she would not relent.

At last I drank the water down in three great gulps, and ate the single slice of dry bread. It was almost pitch dark now, and I hunched up on my blanket. I could not think up a single new story, but old tales from the *Police Gazette* started swirling in my mind. Mad Flora crouched beside me, knife clutched at the ready. The Meat-axe Murderer slavered at the door, dripping with blood.

I pulled the blanket right over my head, but

they crept underneath too. I put my hands over my ears because they were whispering menacingly, threatening me.

'Oh, Hetty, are you in there?'

Wait! Was this a real voice, outside my attic prison? I heard knocking at my door.

'Hetty? Have they locked you in there?'

I knew that husky voice.

'Is it really you, Ida?'

'Oh dear God, they've really locked you up inside.'

'Ida, please, turn the key and let me out!'

'I can't, my love, those witches have taken away the key,' she said. She sounded as if she was crying herself.

'How long are they going to keep me here?' I asked desperately.

'I don't know. I think maybe all night long. I'm so very sorry, Hetty. I only just found out. I didn't see you at dinner but I thought I'd simply missed you. When I did not see you at supper either, I asked Polly and she said they'd taken you away to punish you. She was in tears too, poor girl, saying it was all her fault, that you were trying to protect her from Miss Morley. What did you *do* to her, Hetty?'

'I snatched her ruler away when she'd struck Polly. Oh, how I wish I'd struck her with it. I hate her. I hate them all.'

'I hate them too. You must try to be brave, dear Hetty. They will have to let you out tomorrow. If they don't, I will go to a governor's house and report them for wicked cruelty,' Ida said wildly.

'I'm not sure I can manage a whole night,' I wept. 'It's so dreadfully dark and I'm so scared all by myself.'

I thought of little Gideon then, all by himself in the squirrel house the night we went to the circus. No wonder he'd been so traumatized. Was I going to be shocked senseless too?

'You're not alone, Hetty,' said Ida. 'I will stay. I cannot get in, but I am only the other side of your door. I will wait until you go to sleep.'

'But you will get into trouble if they catch you.'

'They won't catch me. If I hear anyone coming, I'll run along the corridor and hide, and then creep back afterwards. I'm not leaving you here so frightened.'

'You're so good to me, Ida.'

'I'd give anything to look after you properly, Hetty. For two pins I'd slap those evil witches until they gave me the key, and then I'd let you out and have you sleep in my own bed – but I have to keep my position. I'd never get any other work without a good reference, and I'm not going to end up in the workhouse. I'll tell you a secret, Hetty. I spent three years there, and it was a dreadful, dreadful place.

No, I'm doing well for myself now and saving up my wages. I've the future to think of.' She paused for a long moment. 'Shall I tell you . . .?'

'Tell me what, Ida?'

'No, no, maybe not now, not yet.' She was silent.

'Are you still there, Ida?' I asked anxiously.

'Yes, of course I am. You curl up, my dear, and try to go to sleep. Did they give you a mattress?'

'I've got a blanket, but it smells so horrid.'

'Put your cap over your nose – that will smell of fresh laundering and hair oil, good smells. Now, you're the girl for picturing. Picture you're lying on a soft scented pillow, so fresh and dainty, and you have a feather mattress and a beautiful warm quilt. Oh, you are getting so cosy now, aren't you, dear?'

'I didn't think *you* could picture, Ida!'

'I can do lots of things, Hetty. Now nestle under your splendid quilt. Shut your eyes, dear. You're getting very sleepy. You're going to go fast asleep and have happy dreams, *such* happy dreams. One day all your dreams will come true, Hetty. All my dreams too . . .' Ida's voice murmured on and on, and somehow the stout door splintered away and we were together, both of us in our soft feather bed, lying on fresh pillows . . .

Then I woke up with a start, my neck twisted, my whole body aching, locked in the dark all alone. But somehow it wasn't quite as bad as before because Ida's voice echoed in my head, helping me picture the bed, and after a long time I fell asleep again.

Then I heard the key in the lock. The door opened and I was blinking in daylight.

'Well, well, well, Hetty Feather!' Matron Bottomly peered in at me, a look of triumph on her ugly face. 'You look suitably chastened, child. Are you truly sorry, or do you need another twenty-four hours to teach you your lesson?'

'I am very sorry, Matron,' I said meekly, my head bowed, because I could not stand the thought of further imprisonment.

'I am glad to see you truly penitent at last,' said Matron Bottomly, smiling grimly. 'I'm pleased that vicious spirit of yours is broken at last. Now perhaps you will show suitable respect to your elders and betters.'

Oh, how I hated her, talking about me as if I was a tamed wild beast. Of course I wasn't the slightest bit sorry I'd stuck up for poor Polly. I had no respect whatsoever for Matron Bottomly or Miss Morley. They were undisputedly my elders but they certainly *weren't* my betters. They were cruel, wicked women, not fit to look after children. How dare they beat us and lock us up like criminals and act as if it was for our benefit!

16

I resolved to run away.

'Oh, Hetty, I will run away too,' Polly said, hugging me.

Her hands were still scored with red weals from Miss Morley's ruler, and her eyes were red too, because she'd cried bitterly the entire time I'd been incarcerated.

We tried to concoct a sensible plan of action. We fancied ourselves the cleverest girls but we lacked inventive ideas. We knew so little of the world outside the hospital. We only knew our foster homes – and so we thought of our lost foster mothers.

'If Miss Morrison knew the way we are treated here, I'm sure she'd take me back into her care. She'd take you too, Hetty, because you are so bright and clever.'

'If Mother knew they'd kept me locked up in an attic all night, she'd *definitely* take me back – and my goodness, Jem would rise up and seize Matron Bottomly and kick her up her stinking bottom,'

I declared. 'And of course you could stay with *us*, Polly. You might care for my brother Nat, who is almost as dear as Jem, and then you can marry him when we are older and we can live in adjoining cottages.'

We alternated futures, flying between one household and another, the way we'd pictured our pretend visits as little children. It had been so easy when we were small girls, but now it seemed incredibly difficult. We could fly there in an instant in our imagination, but it was a far harder task working out each step in reality. We had no clear idea how to get to our foster homes. I knew we had to go on a long journey by train, but I did not even know the names of the stations – and though I had a little money (Jem's sixpence and my Christmas pennies), I knew they would not be nearly enough to pay the fare.

'How will we actually get out of the hospital?' said Polly.

We rarely set foot outside the grounds. We had been taken to tea at a governor's house several times, and once some girls had been picked to go on an outing to Hampton Court – but not us. We were always carefully guarded, and the grounds were regularly patrolled by staff. Surely if we simply started running, they would seize us and bring us back? I could not stand the thought of further incarceration in the attic room.

'We have to make firm plans,' I said, though I did not have any idea how to do this. I'd lived in the hospital so long that the outside world had faded like a dream. I had pictured home often enough, but I'd added so many details that now I wasn't sure what was real.

The mother and father in my mind were now like good guardian angels. Yet contrarywise I could also remember Mother paddling me, Father shouting angrily. My brothers and sisters seemed like siblings in a storybook, not really connected to *me*. Martha was now simply the girl in spectacles who sang sweetly in the chapel on Sundays.

I even felt I'd lost contact with Gideon. I'd dared my dressing-as-a-boy trick twice more in the infants school, and last year at the boys' sports day I'd looked hard for him. He eventually spotted me and risked edging close to say hello. I did not recognize him till he did so. He was so tall now, and had filled out a little, seeming less sad and spindly.

'Hello, Hetty,' he said softly.

'Oh, Gideon, it's really you!' I said.

I did not care about hospital rules. I threw my arms around him. However, it felt odd, as if I was embracing a stranger. We asked each other politely if we were all right, but then stood smiling shyly, at a loss for further conversation. I was so glad he was still talking properly, but I did not like to point this out in case it embarrassed him. Eventually I asked him if he ever thought of Mother and home. I wished I'd held my tongue because his brown eyes grew misty. He shook his head, though I was sure he was lying. Then one of the boys' teachers looked our way and Gideon ran off hastily.

I had glimpsed him since, going in and out of the chapel, but was not even sure it was really him – there were so many tall thin boys with brown eyes.

I decided I could not include him in my escape plans. We had been parted too long. It was almost as if he wasn't my brother any more. There was only one brother I was sure of. My vision of Jem shone like a lantern in my head. I was sure I still knew every freckle on his dear face, every curl of his hair, every curve of his ear. I knew the sound of his sneeze, his yawn, his merry laughter. I felt I could instantly pick him out from fifty thousand other boys. He would be almost a man now, able to find work. He could look after me – and Polly too. She was dearer to me now than any of my sisters.

She did not give answers now in Miss Morley's class. She wrote down her sums silently from the board, and if Miss Morley made mistakes, she copied them without comment – though she bit her lip. Alone with me, she talked as usual, but she was quiet with everyone else, her head bent as if to escape notice.

But someone was quite definitely noticing her. A large woman dressed all in black, with a very pale face and dark shadows under her eyes, started coming regularly on Sundays, leaning heavily on the arm of her husband. She wore an enamelled hair locket around her neck and had a habit of rubbing it with her plump white fingers, as if it was a tiny lamp and she was trying to summon a genie.

She didn't seem interested in the tiny girls who usually attracted the most attention. She didn't glance at the capable big girls, almost ready for work. We were used to strange women eyeing them up and down, on the lookout for a useful servant. No, this large lady in black always paused at our table of ten-year-olds and hovered there, blinking her shadowed eyes and fingering her locket. She watched our every mouthful, she strained to hear our whispered remarks, she peered with her large head at an angle, as if she was Matron checking the neatness of our plaits and the cleanliness of our necks.

The large lady kept looking in our direction. Not at me, but at Polly.

'That lady in black is really starting to annoy me,' I grumbled. 'She will not stop staring. Poke your tongue out at her, Polly!'

'Don't be unkind about her, Hetty. She looks so *sad*,' said Polly. 'Who do you think she can be?'

'Maybe she's your long-lost mother, come back to claim you after all this time. She's rich and respectable now and can afford to buy you back from the governors,' I said.

'I think her husband *is* a governor,' said Polly. 'I saw him on Friday when the mothers were petitioning. I remember his whiskers and his fat watch-chain.'

'Look at the buttons on his waistcoat, all set to pop off! Have you ever seen such a stomach!' I said.

'But he looks a kindly man,' said Polly.

Perhaps he read her lips, because just then he nodded at her and smiled. Polly smiled back demurely. The lady in black gripped her husband's arm and swayed a little, as if she felt faint.

'There! She's recognizing you, her little lost Polly,' I said, carried away with my story.

I started elaborating on my romance, but Polly wasn't listening. She was looking at the couple and they were looking at her. It was almost as if they were alone in the vast dining room. The hundreds of other foundling girls did not seem to exist – even me.

I felt my stomach tighten, so much so that I could not finish my Sunday dinner. I was immensely relieved when the table was tapped and it was time to file out. I hurried Polly away from the couple, suggesting we find a quiet corner to read – but Matron Bottomly stood in the doorway.

'There you are, Polly Renfrew! Come with me to my room, child.'

Polly gasped. There was only one reason for going to Matron Bottomly's room. It meant that you were going to be severely punished.

'But Polly hasn't *done* anything,' I said, taking her hand.

'Did I ask for *your* comments, Hetty Feather?' said Matron. 'Hurry along now, if you please.'

I had to slink away while Polly marched off after Matron Bottomly. She peered back at me anxiously and I gave her a cheery wave of encouragement, though inside I was in turmoil.

I went off to the dormitory and waited by her bed. I waited and waited and waited. Normally Matron Bottomly was brisk with her punishments. She'd give you a severe talking to. If you had been exceptionally bad, you were whacked with a stick. I was the only girl so far who'd been locked up in the attic. She surely wouldn't dream of shutting *Polly* up there. Polly was so scared of the dark. If she woke in the night, she always needed to wake me up too so I could hold her hand. If she was shut up alone in the attic all night, she'd go demented. I was sure she hadn't done anything wrong at all – though we were all used to being seized indiscriminately and punished for some insignificant or imagined offence.

I cast myself down on Polly's bed, beating it with my fist in my frustration. 'I hate it here, I hate it here, I hate it here,' I muttered into Polly's pillow.

I shut my eyes tight, picturing myself marching to Matron Bottomly's room and rescuing Polly – but I so dreaded the punishment attic myself, I didn't quite have the courage. I lay there, hating myself as well as the hospital.

At long last I heard Polly's footsteps. I sat up and stared at her. She wasn't flushed and tear-stained. There were no cruel red marks on her hands. Yet she looked immeasurably different. She was walking slowly, as if treading water, and her eyes were dazed. She blinked when she saw me.

'Oh, Hetty,' she said, and her hand went to her mouth. 'Oh, Hetty, I hardly know how to tell you.'

I stood up and faced her. 'What *is* it, Polly?'

'I – I am leaving the hospital,' Polly whispered.

'What?' I said, shaking my head.

'I know. I can scarcely take it in myself, but it's true. I've to gather up my things and go now. I am to live with Mr and Mrs McCartney – she is the lady in black.'

'Oh my Lord! Is she *really* your mother?' I said.

'No, no. She had a daughter our age, Lucy, but

she died of the influenza last winter and now she wants to adopt me to take Lucy's place.'

'But people aren't allowed to adopt us! We belong to the hospital.'

'I know, but Mr McCartney is a governor and a very generous benefactor. They will do whatever he wants,' said Polly.

'And – and is it what *you* want?' I asked hoarsely.

'Oh, Hetty, I don't know!' said Polly, tears suddenly rolling down her cheeks. 'I can't bear the thought of not seeing you any more – but of course I want to leave the hospital.'

'Do you *like* them, the McCartneys?'

'I think so. They seem very kind, though still very sad. I am to have Lucy's room and all her clothes and even all her toys. She has five large china dolls, and a doll's house with an entire family of very little dolls – a mother, a father, a grandmother with little spectacles, a grandfather with a grey beard, and five children, one a tiny baby doll in a crocheted shawl. It was Mrs McCartney's when she was a child and she described it very carefully. She gave it to Lucy and now it is to be mine.'

'You are too old for dolls and doll's houses,' I said sourly.

'I know, but I don't mind,' Polly said.

'*I* mind,' I cried. 'I mind it all. Oh, Polly, don't

go and be their child. Please stay here with me. You are my only friend. I can't bear it at the hospital without you.'

'I'm so sorry,' said Polly, hugging me. 'I haven't any choice. Matron Bottomly says I have to go now. But I will beg my new mama and papa to bring me back here to visit you – and I will write to you lots and lots. Then, when we are fourteen, we can meet up properly because you will be out of the hospital too.'

'Yes, but I will be a servant then,' I said. 'You will be a lady.'

'We will still be *us*, Hetty,' said Polly.

But we knew there was already a divide between us. I could not be mean enough to rebuke Polly further. I knew I would have jumped at the chance of escaping the hospital. I would not have sacrificed that chance for anyone, not even my dearest friend. But the McCartneys had not chosen me as their new daughter. They had chosen Polly, and I could understand why.

She was fair and neat and placid, while I was small and fiery with flame-red hair. She had the table manners of her spinster schoolteacher foster mother: she cut up her food daintily, nibbled slowly and drank from her cup with her little finger stuck out at an elegant angle. I had the manners of a rough country child: I still bolted my food and talked with my mouth full and slurped my milk. Polly's voice was gentle and she enunciated every word carefully, while I spoke in a wild torrent. Of *course* they picked Polly.

I swallowed hard, trying to compose myself. I kissed her wet cheeks. 'I will miss you sorely, Polly, but I am also truly happy for you,' I said.

'I'm sorry I've been so lucky,' said Polly, still crying.

'I think those McCartneys are lucky having you for their new daughter,' I declared.

We hugged again, and then I helped her gather her few possessions. She insisted on taking every present I'd ever given her, even the little squashed heart with huge stitching. Matron Bottomly came marching into the dormitory, rubbing her hands.

'Are you ready, Polly dear?' she said, so sickly sweet now that Polly was leaving. 'Mr McCartney's carriage is waiting. *What* a fortunate girl you are!'

'I do hope you get to be fortunate too, Hetty,' said Polly earnestly, squeezing my hand.

'Ha! I doubt anyone will ever come wanting to adopt an imp of Satan like Hetty Feather,' said Matron Bottomly. 'Come along now, Polly. You have got a clean cap and tippet on? Still, you'll probably be taking them off the moment you get to your new home. Fancy!' She giggled unpleasantly, smoothing her apron. 'You'll tell them how happy you've been here in the hospital, won't you, dear?'

'Oh yes, she's been deliriously happy,' I snorted.

Matron Bottomly glared at me. 'You always have to have the last laugh, miss. But the laugh's on you this time, Hetty Feather. You'll miss your friend badly, I can tell.'

'We will stay friends, Matron Bottomly,' said Polly.

I wasn't so sure. And I was right. I waited week after week, desperately hoping that Polly and the McCartneys would attend chapel and then come to observe the grisly public Sunday dinner. But they never once put in an appearance.

I had one letter from Polly. It was formal and restrained, because she knew Matron Bottomly would have a good rummage through it before handing it over to me.

My dear Hetty,

I miss you very much, but in every other respect I am truly happy. Mama and Papa are so very kind and my new life is incredibly comfortable and luxurious. I wish you could come and visit me here. Mama does not wish me to go to the hospital to see you as she feels it will bring back too many memories. I am not even called by my own name

any more. I am Lucy now – but to you, dear Hetty, I
will always remain
 Your very affectionate friend,
 Polly

I reread her letter many times, but then one Sunday, in a fit of despair, I tore it into tiny shreds. I felt Polly might have tried just a little harder to persuade her new parents to visit the hospital. Could they not take pity on me? It was so dreadful having to live my life without Polly when she had been my dearest friend and constant companion for years.

'You must try to make a new friend, Hetty,' Ida said, patting my shoulder sympathetically as she served our dinner.

She was trying to be kind, but her advice was useless. How *could* I make a new friend? All the girls in my year were comfortably settled in their friendships. I could trail round after this group or that group but no one really *wanted* me.

Now that I was on my own, Sheila and Monica were especially tormenting. They mocked and mimicked me a dozen times a day. I affected a lofty indifference to their silliness – but I often cried bitterly into my pillow at night.

It did not help that I was at such an in-between age. I was not yet one of the big girls, with their new chests and their secrets and their infectious giggles. I was not old enough to be a maid to any of the mistresses or nurses, or given any extra responsibilities about the hospital. My life was a dreary routine of the schoolroom and repetitive domestic chores, day after day after day.

I did take my turn caring for the newly arrived foundlings, washing the hands and faces of all the little five-year-olds bawling for their mothers. You would think *I* would try to be a little mother to them, maybe making one my special baby the way Harriet had long ago cared for me. But I was in such low spirits I couldn't really feel a fig for any of these puny little girls. I washed them and carted them to the privy and lined them up two by two to walk to the infants playground without even bothering to learn their names ... until one day a brand-new foundling girl arrived. She wasn't particularly distinguishable from any of the other girls: brown eyes, shorn head, scrawny body, with a lamentable habit of bursting into floods of tears whenever she thought of home.

'Do stop crying so, Alicia,' I said, wiping her running nose.

'I cannot help it. And I'm *Eliza*, not Alicia,' she said.

I didn't react at all. My brain was sleeping. Her name meant nothing to me. But *she* was much more alert.

'Haven't you got those infants ready for bed *yet*, Hetty Feather?' Matron Pigface Peters snapped as she bustled past.

Eliza blinked. She rubbed her eyes and then stared at me, suddenly smiling, though her face was still damp with tears and snot. 'It is *you*, Hetty! I have found you!'

I stared at her blankly.

'You are my sister!' she declared.

The hospital suddenly vanished. I was back in the cottage with Jem, and Mother was there in the corner, nursing a baby in her arms – baby Eliza!

I clasped her fiercely, and she smiled and squirmed within my embrace.

'Oh, Eliza, it's so wonderful to find you!'

'Jem said I had brothers and sisters already here, but I was to look most particularly for you, Hetty,' said Eliza.

'Yes, yes, dearest Jem! We have a sister Martha – you will be so proud of her when you hear her sing in chapel, but she does not quite remember home the way we do. And we have one lovely brother here, Gideon, but sadly we will not see him often as the boys are so separate from us.'

'And Saul?' Eliza said. 'Jem taught me: *Martha who has poorly eyes, Saul who has a poorly leg, Gideon who cannot talk – and Hetty who isn't one bit poorly and talks all the time!*'

'Oh, Jem is so wonderful,' I declared fervently. 'Eliza, you must tell me every single thing you can about home, especially everything about Jem.'

'Jem *is* wonderful,' said Eliza. 'He knows everything.'

'Yes, he does – but he doesn't yet know about Saul. I'm afraid he died several years ago, Eliza. He caught the influenza.'

'Will I catch it?' Eliza asked, looking alarmed.

'Oh no, no, you seem a very strong, healthy little girl – and it's summer now, anyway.'

'Hetty Feather, get that child into bed this *instant*!' Matron Pigface bellowed.

Eliza whimpered at her harsh tone.

'Don't let her bother you – she's silly old meanie matron,' I whispered into Eliza's ear as I hurried her into bed. 'Don't cry! I'll come and find you later. I shall creep back after lights out.'

I tucked her up carefully and gave her a quick kiss on her sad little wisps of hair. The other infant foundlings stared, and Matron Peters tutted and tossed her head. I went back to my own dormitory feeling light-headed with sudden joy. I whirled round and round, dancing a little jig, flinging out my arms and stamping my boots.

'Look at Hetty Feather, she's gone totally loopy,' said Sheila, tapping her forehead significantly.

'She's *always* been loopy,' said Monica. 'My

Lord, Hetty, I hope you don't fancy you're *dancing*.'

She started up a stupid imitation. Another time I'd have slapped her, but now I couldn't be bothered. I undressed quickly and got into bed, pulling the covers over my head.

I lay in the dark, thinking of my newly-found sister. I remembered how scared and lonely I had been when I came to the hospital at her age – and how baffled to find that Martha scarcely remembered me. I would be *such* a different sister to little Eliza. I would watch out for her every day, and woe betide anyone who taunted her or stole her Sunday sweets. I would help her with her reading and writing until she was the star of the infants class. I could even help her with her darning because endless practice over the last five years had made me an accomplished needlewoman.

I would tell Ida that Eliza was my sister. I was sure Ida would give her little treats of butter and sugar too. I would make up stories to entertain her – *not* lurid adaptations from the *Police Gazette*! No, I'd tell beautiful stories of princes and palaces, tales where good fairies waved their magic wands and little foundling girls wore white silk gowns and silver slippers, and went to the ball, and lived happily ever after.

I would tell Eliza such a story tonight, I decided.

I would be her good fairy sister, waving my wand to make her warm and happy. Perhaps Eliza and I could even run away back home together? Jem had clearly remained constant. He had told Eliza to look out particularly for me. He was still my own dear Jem and I loved him with all my heart.

I had so many questions for Eliza. How tall was Jem now? How broad were his shoulders? Had his voice broken? Did he still whistle while doing his chores? Did he speak of me often? Had he told Eliza of our plans? I rather wanted him to have kept them secret, but I decided I would not mind too much if he had confided in Eliza. She was such a sweet child she could come and live with us eventually. I would be like a second mother to her.

I waited in a happy fever until all the girls in my dormitory were asleep and then crept out of bed and tiptoed along to the door. It was so black and eerie out in the corridor that I almost lost heart and scampered back to bed, but I felt ashamed of myself. Great girls of nearly eleven should not be scared of the dark.

I forced myself to picture little Eliza sobbing piteously in her infant cot, waiting in vain for me. I could not let her down. I took a deep breath, clenched my fists and stumbled on in the darkness until I reached the infant dormitory at last. I held my breath as I passed Matron Pigface Peters's room, but I could hear her ugly snorting snores through the door. I pictured her flat on her back, snout quivering, big mouth pursed, and had to clamp my hand over my mouth to stop myself laughing.

I crept past her door, down into the infants dormitory. It was still so dark I could scarcely make out the little iron beds, let alone their occupants, but I knew the newest foundlings slept nearest the door. I listened – and heard muffled sobbing.

'Eliza?' I whispered.

'Oh, Hetty, you've come at last! I'm over here!'

I felt my way towards her and then hugged her tight. 'There now! I told you I would come. Budge over and make room for me. I am freezing to death!'

I clambered in beside her. She was very cold herself, but I put my arms right round her and rubbed her little shivery shoulders and arms, and after a minute or so we both started to warm up.

'There now, is that better?' I whispered.

'Oh yes, Hetty, much!'

'Do you know something, Eliza? When I was even smaller than you, I used to jump into our brother Jem's bed and cuddle up close to get warm,' I said.

'Oh, I did too!'

I paused. I was astonished, to be truthful. Jem had never cuddled Martha or Saul or Gideon – only *me*.

'Well, Jem is very kindly,' I said, a little stiffly. 'And I'm sure he wanted to take care of you, Eliza. You must miss him dreadfully. I know I still do. Please tell me all about him, and Mother and Father, and Rosie and big Eliza and Nat.'

'Oh, they are all very well,' said Eliza. 'Mother's hands are sore with the rheumatics, and Father gets fierce sometimes, and my big sister Eliza stays at home to help Mother, and my brother Nat is courting and very silly. I saw him kissing Sally from the village and she's *horrid*, with a big fat floppy chest.'

'Ssh! *Whisper*, Eliza – we don't want the others to hear us. Now, tell about Jem.' I swallowed. 'Is *he* courting?'

'Oh no, not Jem,' said Eliza. 'He says he's waiting.'

'He's waiting, is he?' I whispered, my heart pounding under my nightgown. Oh, dear, sweet, faithful Jem, I thought. 'I wonder who he's waiting for?' I asked.

'Oh, I *know*!' said Eliza.

'Tell me then,' I said, scarcely able to speak for excitement.

Eliza took a deep breath. '*Me!*' she said, and collapsed into further giggles.

'Hush!' I said fiercely. 'Don't be so silly, Eliza. Tell me who Jem is really waiting for.'

'Me, me, me, me!' Eliza chanted.

'Yes, but you are only a little girl and Jem is nearly a man,' I said, trying to put her in her place.

'I am still his sweetheart,' Eliza declared. 'Jem says when I am quite grown up and can leave this horrid hospital, he will come and marry me.'

'*What?*'

'Yes, and I am to wear a long dress and Jem will wear a fancy gentleman's suit – and guess where we will live, Hetty!'

I did not answer her. I could not speak. I felt as if my heart was being torn in two.

'We will live in our squirrel house!' Eliza said triumphantly.

'No!' I mumbled.

'Yes yes yes! We have this squirrel house, Jem and me. It is deep in the woods. It's our secret place and we have such lovely games there.'

Eliza prattled on and on. I could scarcely bear it. I put my hands up and covered my ears, but her little mouse squeak echoed inside my head.

Jem had shared all *our* most secret special plans with this silly little child. He had repeated all his promises to her. He had duplicated everything. He had not even bothered to invent new games for her.

I bit my lip hard, but I could not stop myself sobbing.

'Are you crying, Hetty?' Eliza asked. 'Don't be

sad. We have each other now. And when we leave here I will ask Jem if he would mind very much you coming to live with us too, as you are family.'

She was doing her best to comfort me – but I had to fight hard not to push the poor little thing out of her own bed. I could not endure it. My dear Jem had betrayed me utterly. No, he wasn't *my* Jem. He had parroted all his special promises to Eliza – and she innocently triumphed in his attention. He clearly had no intention of keeping his word to her any more than he had to me. He'd just been playing with us, saying sweet things to keep us little girls happy. Oh, how it hurt now to find out he'd been mouthing meaningless nonsense.

I crept back to my own bed as soon as Eliza started dozing, but I couldn't sleep. I lay there, crying, my fists clenched. I felt so stupid. I'd believed every word Jem had said. I'd loved him with all my heart. I'd trusted him. I'd been so sure that he really would wait for me.

'Oh, Jem, how could you repeat everything to *her*?' I whispered into my pillow. 'You're wicked, wicked, wicked.'

But as the night wore on, I started to feel I was being ridiculous. Jem hadn't been *deliberately* unkind. I knew he wasn't really a wicked boy. He was a sweet, kindly soul who simply wanted to comfort his silly little sisters. I could see it was ludicrous for my five-year-old sister Eliza to talk of Jem as her sweetheart and future husband. It was equally ludicrous for me to think Jem truly wanted to marry me. We'd both been little children. Jem was telling us a fairy story to try to kid us we'd live happily ever after. Of course he wouldn't marry either of us.

He'd remember us both fondly, if a little sadly. Then, in the fullness of time, he'd fall in love with some village lass like Nat's Sally and marry her. His future was plain to me now. And my future was plain too. I was Hetty Feather, a foundling, imprisoned in the hospital. When I was fourteen, I'd leave to be a servant. That was all I had to look forward to. I would be a drudge for the rest of my days.

17

The hospital cook scalded her hands badly with boiling water, and could not work for weeks. Ida was asked to take over her duties until Cook recovered. She was allowed to choose one of us girls to help her in the kitchen. Ida selected the great fourteen-year-old girls at first, as expected – but then announced she'd like to give some of the younger girls a chance.

'I'd like to try out Hetty Feather for a day,' she said.

Matron Bottomly snorted derisively. 'You'll regret *that* decision,' she said, but she let Ida have her way.

All the other girls moaned and grumbled and said it wasn't the slightest bit fair. I said nothing at all. I stayed silent when Ida set me to peeling the vegetables, freshly picked from the hospital garden. She told me to have a little nibble at the carrots and pod a few peas for myself, but I didn't bother. I even shook my head listlessly when she offered me a spoonful of syrup from her larder.

'You're always hungry, Hetty! Aren't you feeling well?' Ida said, putting her hand to my forehead.

'I'm all right. Leave me alone,' I said, shrugging her hand away.

'Oh, Hetty, please, dear, tell me what's wrong,' said Ida.

'*Nothing!*' I snapped. 'Stop pestering me.'

If I'd spoken like that to Miss Morley or Matron Bottomly, they'd have slapped me for impertinence, but Ida just looked wounded. Her big blue eyes blinked at me reproachfully. I felt bad because she had always been so very kind to me – but I was *tired* of being kind back. I'd spent weeks making a fuss of Eliza and listening to her endless prattle about Jem when every word was a torment. I couldn't tell her to shut up and keep out of my way. She was my little sister after all. I knew just how sad and lonely she was feeling, how very bleak the hospital seemed after our cosy cottage.

When I'd first come here, it had meant so much to me that Harriet had made a special pet of me. I felt duty bound to do the same for Eliza, even though the sound of her squeaky little voice made me wince, and her habit of quoting Jem in each and every sentence drove me to distraction.

I *had* to stop myself hurting her – but I didn't

see why I had to take such care with silly old Ida. I wished she wasn't so stupidly sensitive. She had spirit enough with the others. I'd seen her put Sheila in her place often enough, and she was wonderfully sharp with the nurses, even though forced to toady to Matron Stinking Bottomly. Why did she have to care what I said?

I sighed at her set shoulders and wounded expression. She was making pastry, thumping her rolling pin with unnecessary pressure. Ida had introduced pies into our diet while Cook recovered, and they were much appreciated by everyone. I idly picked up all the cut-off ribbons of pastry. I started to fashion them into a big fat dough lady. I turned her into a matron with a silly cap and a grim expression.

Ida stopped making her endless huge pies and stared at my creation. She smiled, forgetting she was offended. 'That's so good, Hetty!'

'No, it's not,' I said, and I suddenly squashed the figure flat.

'Oh, look what you've done! I wanted to bake it to keep her. My, you're in a bad mood today, aren't you?'

I shrugged and made patterns in the spilled flour on the kitchen flags with the toe of my boot.

'Don't do that, you're just treading it in,' said Ida. She took a deep breath, still unaccountably intent on humouring me. 'How about your taking a turn with the pastry rolling?'

'I don't want to.'

'It's a skill to be proud of, making good pastry. I've picked up a lot of knowledge working in the kitchen. I could teach you all sorts, Hetty. Maybe you could eventually get a position as a cook-general if you learned a few recipes.'

'I don't *want* to be a cook-general,' I declared.

'It's far better than being a kitchen maid or a tweeny.'

'I don't want to be any kind of stupid servant,' I said. '*Especially* in a kitchen.'

This time I'd really gone too far. Ida flushed. She thumped the pastry with her rolling pin. She looked as if she'd like to give me a good thumping too.

'Oh, I'm all too well aware that you look down your nose at servants,' said Ida. 'So pray tell me, Hetty, what exactly *are* you going to do with your life?'

I could not answer her. I had clung to the idea of marrying Jem for so long. Now I could see how painfully silly I had been.

'What was it again?' said Ida angrily, putting her floury hand to her ear as if I'd spoken. 'Run away to the circus to join your real mother?'

It was my turn to flush. I'd forgotten I'd once told Ida about Madame Adeline. She was another childish dream. I remembered the roar of the crowd as we cantered around the ring, the sound of all those many pairs of hands clapping me . . .

I stuck my head in the air. 'I might just do that very thing,' I said.

'Oh, Hetty, as if that circus lady could *possibly* be your mother!'

'She could be. She practically said so,' I said fiercely. I did not really believe it now, but I could not bear to let my last dream fade away.

'You're getting a big girl now,' said Ida, shaking her head. She'd rubbed a floury sprinkle over her cheeks and her cap was awry, making her look foolish. 'You're far too old for these silly daydreams. You've got to be practical, know your place, work hard, make something of yourself.'

'Like you, you mean?' I said spitefully.

'You might not think much of my position, Miss High and Mighty, but it suits me perfectly,' said Ida. 'I work hard and I keep respectable and I save my wages.'

'Yes, but what *for*? You do the same thing day after day, week after week, year after year. You must be mad, Ida. You don't have to stay here. *You're* not a foundling. You could walk out and get a better job anywhere.'

'I've got a good job *here* and I was very lucky to get it too, coming from the workhouse,' said Ida.

'You're talking nonsense, Hetty. I know you must be missing Polly sorely but there's no need to take it out on me. I've tried my best to cheer you up.'

'I shall never be cheerful here, never never never,' I declared.

I simply could not stop myself. Ida was my only true friend left in the hospital and yet I seemed determined to alienate her. I stayed rude and sulking all day, doing the barest minimum of work.

'Judging by today, I doubt you can even be a servant when you leave here, Miss Hetty Head-in-the-Air,' Ida sniffed. 'No one in their right mind would ever take you on as a skivvy, let alone a cook. Now, are you going to snap out of it and be a good sweet girl tomorrow?'

I snapped my fingers and then presented her with my own glum face. 'Does it look like it?' I said.

'Well, go away and stew, you stupid girl. I'll pick someone else to come and help me.'

'As if I care,' I said, and marched out of the kitchen.

I cared dreadfully when Ida picked *Sheila*. I knew she'd done it deliberately to annoy me. Ida didn't like Sheila any more than I did. She just wanted to pay me back. It was bitterly painful to peep through the kitchen hatch and see Ida and Sheila stirring a vat of rice pudding together, laughing away. When Ida saw me looking, she popped a handful of raisins into Sheila's grinning mouth. She gave a little nod, as if to say, *That will show you, Hetty Feather*.

It showed me all right. It looked as if I'd lost my last friend at the hospital through my own stupid behaviour. I should have gone to Ida privately and apologized, but I was too proud. I stalked around by myself, dutifully keeping an eye on little Eliza but otherwise taking no notice of anyone.

I sat listlessly in the classroom, never bothering to answer a single question now. I felt so dull and slow I could scarcely lift my pen to write any words. I found my grades slipping. I had been first equal with Polly at everything, but now I was sliding down almost to the bottom of the class, along with Mad Jenny and Slow Freda and Stutter Mary, the three sad girls who could barely read and write.

I tried even *less* with my household tasks. Every Sunday I daydreamed in chapel and ate my dinner stony-faced, staring down all the chattering ladies and gentlemen. There seemed no point in smiling. They would never pick *me* to be their new little adopted daughter. I was small, sour, red-haired Hetty Feather.

I could not even get interested when everyone started talking about the Queen's Golden Jubilee in June. What did I care for our fat little monarch? Miss Morley's lessons became very focused on the Royal Personage. At long last she used the coloured maps on the classroom wall, showing us all the different lands the Queen ruled over.

When she told us the Queen was also Empress of India, half the class assumed she *lived* in that huge hot sub-continent. Miss Morley laughed at such ignorance. She said the Queen mostly lived here in London, at Buckingham Palace – and she would quite definitely be in London on 23 June, the day of the Golden Jubilee.

Miss Morley seemed utterly obsessed with Queen Victoria. She gave us dictation about our Loyal Sovereign, she told us the history of her fifty-year reign, she even had us calculating how many seconds would tick by during the Royal Procession if it started at eleven and ended at two. I assumed this was a specific obsession peculiar to Miss Morley – but it seemed to be shared by all the staff. Even little Eliza started babbling about our Great Queen and showed me a picture that she'd drawn in the infant class. I admired it wearily, though her Queen Victoria looked very like a fat stag beetle with a crown upon its head.

We even prayed for Queen Victoria in chapel on Sunday, which seemed to me a little bizarre. Why should all us foundlings, born in shame and destined to live our lives as servants, pray for such a fabulously rich and fortunate old woman who owned whole continents? She should surely be on her padded knees, praying for God's mercy for us.

At the end of the service Matron Bottomly marched to the front of the chapel and ascended the pulpit, her beaky nose pecking the air. She was smaller than the vicar, so only her head was in view, sticking up comically like a coconut on a shy. I had such an urge to aim my hymn book at her!

'I have a very important announcement to make, children,' she said. 'As you all know, our dear Queen has ruled over us for fifty wonderful years. Next Thursday is the day of the Golden Jubilee, when the whole country will celebrate her glorious reign. We are going to celebrate too! You have all been invited to a festive gathering at Hyde Park in London. You will be given a splendid meal at this venue and join in all kinds of fun and games, and then Her Majesty the Queen herself will come and greet you!'

There was a great '*Ooooh*' of excitement and astonishment, though perhaps we were more thrilled at the sound of the splendid meal and the fun and games than the prospect of seeing the Queen.

I was excited too, I could not help it. We were going to escape the dreary hospital for a whole day! Oh glory!

'Settle down now, children. You must be especially well behaved. Any child who is seriously surly or disobedient will *not* be included in the trip to see the Queen,' said Matron Bottomly – and her ridiculous coconut head turned so that she was looking straight at me.

Oh, I understand you very well, Matron Stinking Bottomly, I thought. *It would give you such huge delight to be able to deny me my rights. How it would please you to declare before everyone that Hetty Feather was too wicked to attend the Jubilee Celebrations.*

I smiled demurely back at Matron Bottomly. For once in my life I wasn't stupidly going to cut off my nose to spite my face. My behaviour over the next few days was exemplary. I tried hard in lessons on Monday, Tuesday and Wednesday, but not *so* hard that my knowledge irritated Miss Morley. I meekly wrote down her exact words during dictation. I figured out each silly sum, finding how many days it would take Queen Victoria to sail to India if her mighty ship steamed along at a certain terrific rate of knots. I wrote a neat, unimaginative essay on 'What I should say should I meet Her Majesty the Queen'.

I had myself performing copious curtsies, simpering 'If you please, ma'am,' repeatedly. Miss Morley gave me a big red tick and wrote *Excellent* at the bottom of my page. She actually wrote *Excellant*, but I decided not to point this out. I sewed aprons exquisitely, using tiny stitches and turning each corner with a perfectly sewn double hem, as if I was making the finest robes for the Royal Household. I dusted every corridor and corner of the hospital, my feather duster reaching *up* to the picture rails and *down* to the wainscoting. I practically lined up every infant foundling and gave them a good dusting too.

Oh, how irritated Matron Bottomly must have been when Thursday morning dawned bright and sunny, and there I was, smiling, as good as gold. She was probably tempted to give me a slap for sheer cussedness. She did not have the imagination to invent some wicked misdemeanour on the spot. She simply gave me a hard poke in the back and said, 'Mind your manners while you're out, Hetty Feather. All of London will be looking at us.'

We were all issued with clean clothes from top to bottom that Thursday, breaking with all known custom. Our caps and aprons and tippets were laundered and starched so snowy white they looked brand new. Matron had had every big girl ironing all day Wednesday, when we'd all shuffled round in our stockinged feet while every big boy polished our boots. We were given bread and butter for our breakfast because the nurses were so fearful the little ones might spill their porridge down their crisp white chests. Every child had mouth and hands dabbed at with a damp cloth after breakfast, and all the infants were forced into the privies and frightened into copious evacuation so that none would disgrace the hospital during our long outing.

We were lined up in the playground like a miniature brown army, boys one side, girls the other, in serried ranks of six, from the littlest five-year-old fresh from foster care to the biggest, blowsiest girls about to leave to go into service.

Matron Peters positioned herself at the front with the infants, Matron Bottomly brought up the rear with the big ones, while all the nurses and teachers patrolled up and down the lines.

'Right! Let us all step out and look lively. Remember, the entire reputation of the Foundling Hospital rests on *you*,' Matron Bottomly bawled.

We set off at a quick march – one two, one two, one two. It felt so extraordinary to go out of those iron gates and walk down the road. The very air smelled different, so clean and fresh and invigorating.

London would have looked wondrous to us in a thick fog, but this sparkling, sunny June morning made every great grey building gleam palatially. Every window ledge was decked with bunting, every lamppost embellished with bouquets, every flag flapping in the light breeze. We were told not to break step or loiter even for a second, though I craned my neck and stared when we were marched along Oxford Street, marvelling at the vast emporiums, their windows a wonder of patriotic red, white and blue decoration.

I couldn't get used to the crowds – such

huge numbers of people, all shouting, laughing, screaming. Some of our little children started crying in sheer shock, and even I felt frightened, especially when we had to cross a vast road. There were policemen who held up the traffic for us, but they were only puny men. I did not see how they could control so many cabs and carriages and enormous omnibuses. But somehow we all crossed safely, hanging onto each other, our palms sweating.

It was a long, long walk and the little ones in front started dragging their feet and limping in their hard boots, but our spirits picked up as we passed the great Marble Arch and entered the park.

There were ten enormous marquees and many other smaller tents as far as you could see. There were merry-go-rounds and helter-skelters and whirling chairs and swingboats. Children ran around freely everywhere, climbing on the painted horses, sliding down the helter-skelter, squealing with fearful joy in the chairs and boats high above our heads. There were thousands and thousands of children, from tiny tots in pinafores to great girls and boys much taller than me. They were all wearing such wonderful clothes! Many of the girls were dressed in white or soft flower colours, bluebell, primrose, lilac or pale rose-pink, skipping around in soft shoes. The boys wore jolly blue and white sailor suits with jaunty straw hats. They stared at all of us in our ugly brown frocks and breeches, our silly caps and aprons, our red-robin waistcoats and cumbersome jackets, our stiff stout boots. Some openly pointed and commented:

'Look, look, it's the children from the institution!'

'Are they all orphans from the workhouse?'

'No, no, they're foundlings from the hospital. Don't they look quaint!'

We stared back, still in our marching rows, red in the face from the heat and our humiliation. But then Matron Bottomly addressed us through a megaphone.

'This is a message for the senior school! You are allowed to play in the fairground for an hour, so long as you stay within close proximity. All the rides are free. But everyone must report back to marquee number ten at one o'clock sharp for our festive luncheon. Do you all understand?'

We gazed at her, barely able to take it in. Did she really mean we were free to roam as we wished? A few of the big boys made a dash for it before she could change her mind, but a lot of us wavered uncertainly. We were so used to having every minute accounted for. We did not know how to *cope* with an hour of freedom.

Well, *I* could cope. I ran to the merry-go-round,

circling it twice to select the finest horse. They all had names painted on their arched necks. I looked in vain for a Hetty, but I did find a Polly, a black-and-white stead with a red saddle. I had to lift my skirts in an unladylike fashion to clamber onto her, but I didn't care. Some of the girl riders were sitting demurely sidesaddle, but that looked so silly and lopsided. I had ridden bareback with Madame Adeline. I knew what I was doing.

The organ music struck up and the merry-go-round started turning. I clasped the gold rail and urged Polly forward. We went round and round until all the children blurred and the great green park seemed to be spinning on its axis like a giant globe.

As I stepped off dizzily, I spotted Eliza looking a little dazed amongst a cluster of infants. They were being shepherded around by dear Nurse Winnie. I dashed over to her.

'Can I take Eliza on the merry-go-round, Nurse Winterson? I promise I'll look after her most carefully,' I said.

'Yes, of course you can, Hetty,' she said. She looked longingly at it. 'For two pins I'd have a ride myself!'

I lifted Eliza onto a black horse with a white patch on his face. He was called Star. 'You shall be a little star, Eliza,' I told her.

I thought she would be in ecstasy, but she shrieked when the merry-go-round started going faster.

'Don't like it, don't like it!' she cried, squirming around. 'Let me get *off*, Hetty!'

'You can't get off, silly, you've only just got *on*. Don't be scared, Eliza, it's *lovely*.'

'No it's not!' Eliza said, shutting her eyes tight and clinging to me like a little monkey.

When at last the merry-go-round slowed down, Eliza shot off to Nurse Winterson without a backward glance. I shrugged my shoulders, telling myself I was glad to be free of her. I saw my other sister, Martha, near the helter-skelter and I went rushing over to her, worried that she'd fall trying to get up the steep steps inside. However, she had her two friends, Elizabeth and Marjorie, with her, and they elbowed me out of the way impatiently.

'Martha's got *us*, Hetty,' said Elizabeth.

'She doesn't need *you* to help her. She says you fuss far too much,' said Marjorie.

Martha herself simply smiled at all of us, blinking behind her thick glasses.

'Very well, suit yourselves. That's perfectly fine with me,' I said, sticking my nose in the air. I pretended to recognize someone in the great crowd and waved heartily. 'There's my friend! I must go,' I said, running off.

I ran and ran, circling round all the fairground rides, not quite sure which to select. It felt so odd being all by myself when everyone else seemed to be surrounded by friends.

'Oh, Polly, if only you were here,' I whispered.

I knuckled my eyes because they were unaccountably wet – and then opened them wide, because right in front of me was a tall dark boy in foundling uniform, nodding at me shyly.

'Gideon!' I said.

'I came looking for you, Hetty,' he said.

I was overwhelmed that he had taken the trouble to seek me out. In the past I had always been the one to run after him.

'How are you, Gideon?'

'I suppose I am very well,' he said solemnly. He spoke perfectly clearly and coherently, but with a hesitant, mannered air, as if he rarely opened his mouth.

'Oh, Gideon, do you hate it at the hospital too?' I asked, clutching his arm.

He blinked in alarm at my forward gesture, but nodded at me. 'I dislike it very much, but I dread leaving it too. I do not want to be a soldier.'

'It's much, much better than being a servant, you silly boy! Think of the excitement and foreign lands and great battles!'

'Think of the fear and the blood and the

hardship,' said Gideon, shuddering. 'I dream about it sometimes. I know I will not be able to bear it. I do not want to live my days in barracks and army camps. The other boys torment me here, but I'm sure it will be far worse living amongst men.'

'Then let us run away together, Gideon, and escape our fate!'

'You're still dreaming, Hetty. Don't tell me you're still planning to run back home to live with Jem so that he can take care of you!'

'No,' I said shortly. 'Not now. I will make my own way.'

'Well, that is good,' he said, clearly humouring me.

'We will make our way together. We are still special sister and brother,' I declared. I spun him round and then focused on the fair. 'Oh, Gideon, come on the swingboats with me!'

'They're swinging so rapidly. I think I shall be sick,' said Gideon, but he came with me obligingly.

We crouched on either side of the boat, tugging hard on the ropes so that we swung up and then sharply down, as if we were riding a stormy sea. I pictured the waves and the screaming seagulls and the wild wind as we tossed our way over the ocean to a distant promised land, gabbling this breathlessly to Gideon while he laughed at me.

'You're still the same old Hetty,' he said. 'Oh, stop pulling so – we're going too high!'

'Let's go higher and higher and higher!' I said, tugging with all my might.

Gideon groaned and shut his eyes as the whole park heaved this way and that beneath us, but I stared out, seeing right over the huge marquees and the milling throng of children. Way over to the south of the park, beside the silver stream of the Serpentine, I saw another big striped tent, a cluster of wagons – and a great grey creature with a long waving trunk.

'Oh my Lord! It's Elijah! It's the circus! Oh, Gideon, stop pulling, we must slow *down*.'

'Don't fret, I *want* to slow down,' said Gideon weakly, his face greenish-white.

'It's so wonderful! The circus!' I babbled, clutching the edges of the swingboat to try to make it stop.

'Hetty, you'll tip us both out,' Gideon groaned.

'Oh, stop your moaning, boy! Come on, we can jump out now. *Wheee!*' I made a leap for the ground and landed lightly. Gideon jumped after me and landed on his hands and knees.

'Ouch! Oh goodness, have I torn my breeches?'

'Of course you haven't,' I lied, pulling him up by the hands. 'Come on, Gideon. I'm going to the circus, and *this* time I'm taking you with me!'

'We *can't* go to the circus, Hetty!' said Gideon. 'It's not within close proximity! It couldn't possibly be further away.'

'Oh, for Heaven's sake, who cares!' I said gaily.

'But it's nearly one o'clock. We have to be back at marquee number ten. Didn't you listen to what the matron said?'

'As if I care what Matron Stinking Bottomly says!' I said. 'Come on, Gideon! Here's your chance to see the circus for yourself at long last. Don't you want to see Elijah close up – and wondrous Madame Adeline and her horses? And remember the boy acrobats in their sparkly silver clothes, don't you want to see *them*?'

Gideon did waver then, looking longingly in the direction of the circus, though we couldn't even see the tip of the tent or the top of Elijah's trunk now that we were down on the ground.

'And it won't cost a penny this time. Everything is free today because of the Jubilee. Come *on*, Gideon.'

'We will miss our meal in the tent,' said Gideon.

'Never mind. Maybe we'll be back in time to snatch at something.'

'But we'll get into such trouble.'

'There are so many of us I don't think anyone will notice there are two foundlings too few. And even if they do find out, what will we care? We will have seen the circus!'

'You would care if you were a boy, Hetty. If we are very bad, we get whipped.'

'Listen, I have been so fearfully bad I got locked up without food or water in a bleak attic for days and days,' I said, exaggerating slightly. 'I'm going to go to the circus now even if they lock me in the attic for the rest of my life. And so are you, Gideon.'

I tugged at his arm but he pulled away.

'I *can't*, Hetty. I simply daren't. You go, if you must, but I do so hope you won't get into trouble.'

I stared at his pale, obstinate face and knew there was no way I could persuade him.

'All right, I shall go by myself,' I said. I gave him a kiss on his white cheek. 'You will kick yourself for not coming with me!'

I ran off in what I hoped was the right direction. I looked over my shoulder to see if Gideon might just be wavering, but he'd already been swallowed up by the crowd.

'Oh, Gid,' I said, and even though I was sure he couldn't see me, I waved to him.

Then I ran off to find the circus by myself, though it was hard to work out which way to go. The crowd was so thick. I had to dodge and weave and dart between folk wherever I could. Troops of children were gathering and marching towards the marquees for their festive meal. My stomach was rumbling. I couldn't help wondering just how festive the meal would be. Perhaps cake? Jellies? But I couldn't lose my huge chance out of sheer greed!

People were peering at me strangely, laughing at my bizarre uniform. I quickly took my cap off and stuffed it down my tippet, but I had no way of hiding the rest of my clothes.

A formidable woman with an official badge pinned to her bosom seized hold of me. 'Aren't you one of the foundlings from the hospital? No, no, my child, you're going entirely the wrong way.' She consulted a list. 'You're due in marquee number ten – *that* way!'

'Yes, ma'am,' I said, spinning round and walking the way she pointed – but within seconds she was out of sight, so I could turn and fight my way back in the direction of the circus.

It took me a good half-hour before I was even near. I was so hot my frock was sticking to my back and some small child had smeared his hokey-pokey ice all over my skirts. My cap had edged its way out of my tippet and was now lost, ground underheel by hundreds of feet. But when I spied the red and purple tip of the striped circus tent, I forgot all about my bedraggled appearance. I pushed forward determinedly, so eager now I was nearly running.

I saw Elijah, standing tethered to a pole, wearing a head-dress of gold in honour of the Queen. He was smaller than I remembered, but of course *I'd* been much smaller when I last saw him.

The crowd was even thicker now that I was near the circus, and many small boys pushed and shoved. When I pushed and shoved back, one little monster kicked me hard on the shins. I kicked back harder though, for once in my life thankful for my stout institution boots, though my feet were hot as Hell inside them.

I got nearer and saw a tower of acrobats standing on each other's heads, but they weren't dressed in silver, they were all in red. Of course those tumbling boys in silver spangles would have new costumes now, and perhaps their younger brothers had joined their act. I pushed my way through the entrance, into the tent. It was boiling like a cauldron, packed with children keen to see the free show. I barged my way along the front row to claim the only empty seat.

There were clowns running backwards and forwards throwing buckets of water around. It all seemed a familiar routine and I laughed hysterically even though I did not really find them funny.

Then I heard a neigh and a thud of hooves, and I tingled all over and cried out in joy. But where was Pirate, the pale grey with the black patch? These horses were all a glossy chestnut brown, with purple plumes in their manes. And who was this? *Two* women, with big chests and fat thighs, in tight violet spangled dresses, with huge floppy purple bows stuck in their hair, one blonde, one dark.

Where was Madame Adeline? These two dumpy imposters rode round and round the ring. Their act was a travesty compared to Madame Adeline's. Surely they could not have taken her place? I knew every turn she'd taken, every trick, every toss of her beautiful red hair. I had pictured it so many hundreds of times inside my head. These two purple fools galloped round monotonously, waving their hands for applause. I could not bear to clap them. I clasped my hands in agony. When they cantered out of the ring at last, I pushed my way back along the row and elbowed my way to the entrance, taking no notice of the mutters in my wake.

I clutched hold of a circus hand giving out flyers for the circus.

'Where is Madame Adeline?' I demanded. 'When will she be performing?'

'Madame who?' said the man. 'Never heard of her.'

'Madame Adeline and her troupe of horses,' I said. 'She's the star of this circus!'

'No she ain't! The only horse act we've got is Miss Molly and Miss Polly, the Equestrian Twins. You've just missed them,' he said impatiently. 'Now leave me alone, girlie, I've got a job to do.'

He gave me one of his flyers and turned away from me. I stared down at the strip of paper in my hand.

Mr Geoffrey's Wondrous Whirligig Circus it said in big bold italics at the top of the page.

I blinked at it, even rubbing the words with my finger as if I could reassemble them into any order that made sense. Who was this Mr Geoffrey? This was Tanglefield's Travelling Circus! I was sure that was the right name. But I wavered as I slid my eyes down the list of performers. Miss Lizzie's troupe of *baboons*? Mr Lionel Luck, contortionist? The Zebidee Family of Tumblers? I had not heard of any of them. And then, in bold lettering: *Archibald, the Infant Elephant!* What were they talking about? I *knew* the elephant was called Elijah. I could not have remembered it *all* so inaccurately.

'Why has the circus changed so?' I asked the

circus hand desperately, shaking his striped sleeve. 'Why isn't it called Tanglefield's Travelling Circus any more? Why are there all these new people? Why has Elijah's name been changed? And *where* is Madame Adeline? You *must* have heard of her!'

'Will you stop pestering me? I've got a job to do. Can't you read, child?' He tapped his wad of flyers impatiently. 'It's there, plain as the nose on your face. Does it say Tanglefield's Travelling Circus? No, it does not. This is Mr Geoffrey's gaff – and he'll have my guts for garters if he catches me chatting. He's a sharp man, Mr Geoffrey, never one to miss an opportunity. This is better than a ten-foot advertisement on a hoarding. Now, on your way. Ain't all you kids meant to be having a free nosh? Little girlie . . .? Oh my Lord, don't start crying on me. I can't abide it when kiddies cry.'

I was weeping in sheer frustration, still too stunned to understand.

The circus hand sighed. 'I reckon Tanglefield's will be up on the heath. I hear they've got all the rag-tag-and-bobtail circuses up there.'

I stared at him. 'You mean there are *different* circuses?'

'There must be thousands, if you count all over Europe – and America too. I was once part of the Great Fernando's Travelling Circus in the States. Now *that* was a gaff and a half. We'd start our procession with twenty elephants – *twenty*, I tell you – and two miles later you'd come to the very last animal wagon, how about that? I'll wager this Tanglefield's Travelling Circus you hold so dear couldn't hold a candle to *that*.'

'Do you really think they'll be on this heath?' I asked.

'Without a doubt,' he said. 'Hampstead Heath, that's the one.'

'Where is that, sir?'

'Oh, for goodness' sake, what do you want of me now – a map? You hop off home and get your pa to take you.'

I hopped off. I didn't have a home and I didn't have a pa. I would have to find Hampstead Heath by myself. I'd never have another chance to find Madame Adeline.

It took me a very long time to fight my way out of the heaving park. I didn't battle back towards the big marquees just in case someone from the hospital spotted my brown dress amid the froth of fancy frocks. I followed the shimmer of the Serpentine instead. I marvelled at all the boats on the water, longing to have a go at rowing myself up and down, but I had a more pressing purpose.

I caught hold of a kindly-looking lady in charge of a bunch of small children. 'If you please, ma'am, can you tell me the way to Hampstead Heath?'

'Well, let me see now. I believe it's over in that direction.' She gestured vaguely. 'But it's a very long way off, too far for a little girl. Where is your school party, child? Are you lost?'

'Oh no, ma'am, they're over there,' I said quickly, and edged away before she could question me further.

My heart sank a little at her words. *A very long way off.* I was so very hot and starving hungry now, and my boots were pinching dreadfully – but I was still resolved. I would get to Tanglefield's Travelling Circus and find Madame Adeline even if I had to crawl there on my knees.

It was scarcely any easier making my way when I was out of the park gates. The streets were so crowded that I had to scurry along in the gutter, though I trembled every time a cab or carriage drove close, terrified of the iron-shod hooves of the horses.

I walked along the wide, grand road of Piccadilly. The crowds were thicker than ever. Then there was a clamour and a cheer, and everyone surged forward, teetering at the edge of the pavement, nearly tumbling on top of me.

'Up you come, little 'un!' said a perfectly strange man, picking me up before I could protest and perching me on his shoulder. 'There now, you're safe with me. See them coming? My, you'll be able to tell your grandchildren one day that you had a grand view of Queen Victoria's Golden Jubilee Procession!'

I saw many red-coated soldiers with white-plumed helmets riding horses – and then a black open carriage drawn by six grey horses – very fine, but not a patch on Madame Adeline's. A small fat woman sat in the carriage looking dazed, waving her plump little hand mechanically.

'There now, you've seen the Queen!' said the gentleman.

'Thank you very much, sir,' I said – though I wanted to see Madame Adeline so much more! 'Would you say I am nearly at Hampstead Heath now?'

'What's that? You're nowhere near, silly child. There now, don't look so disappointed. You've seen the Queen, God bless her!'

'Yes, sir, thank you, sir, could you set me down now, please, sir?' I said.

I started walking as soon as he put me down. It was hard to progress with the crowd thick as treacle, still cheering, chanting, singing songs, some of the younger ladies even lifting their skirts and dancing. I struggled on, asking every kind face if I was going the right way to the heath, but they either did not know or told me it was too far a journey for a little girl like me.

I was so tired and out of breath I could barely speak, but when I tugged the sleeve of maybe the fiftieth lady and asked if she could tell me the way to Hampstead Heath, she smiled at me merrily.

'Yes indeed, dearie. Don't she look like a sparrow in her brown stuff frock, Desmond?' She nudged her companion, a red-faced young man with ridiculous whiskers. 'Yes, little sparrow, Desmond and I are going there too. There's a big funfair and a circus.'

'Oh! Pray tell me, is it Tanglefield's Travelling Circus?' I asked desperately.

'I don't rightly know, my dear. I fancy there are all sorts up on the heath. You're a quaintly spoken child. Isn't she sweet, Desmond?' The lady nudged him and he nodded obligingly.

'She's a dear little thing, Rebecca. Though you are even dearer,' said Desmond.

Rebecca nudged him and laughed again. They seemed so taken with me that I dared ask: 'If you are going to Hampstead Heath, might I possibly walk with you?'

'We're not *walking*, child!' she said, bursting into peals of laughter. 'Especially not when I'm wearing these heels! We're taking the omnibus at Tottenham Court Road. You can come with us by all means.'

I went with them, though I thought Rebecca very silly and simpering, and I did not care for whiskery

Desmond either. I knew omnibuses cost money and I had none, but as I'd hoped, Desmond paid the pennies for my fare, scarcely seeming to give it a thought.

'Thank you kindly, sir,' I said. 'Do you think we might go upstairs?'

'Of course we can, little sparrow,' said Rebecca. 'Desmond, get them to make way for us.'

The omnibus was already so crowded we were all squashed hip to hip, but Rebecca managed to manoeuvre me right to the front so that I could peer out. It was wondrous to have a bird's-eye view of everything, almost as if I truly *was* a sparrow. I stared down at all the hats and bonnets below me, and then in the distance saw a long line of little white caps.

Oh my lord, surely it couldn't be the foundlings on their long march back to the hospital? I asked Rebecca the time and she got Desmond to produce his big gold watch from his waistcoat pocket. A quarter to four! I felt faint. I had lost all sense of time. I had thought I might somehow manage to rush back to Hyde Park and join up with all the others for the march back. But now it was clearly much too late. Had they counted every foundling at marquee number ten? Did Matron Bottomly realize I was missing? She would be so angry. I thought of the punishment attic

318

and shuddered. I could not go back to the hospital now. Without quite meaning to, I had run away at last!

The omnibus took us northwards, and I clutched the rail of the bus, my heart beating hard. Rebecca addressed me every now and then, and I said, 'Yes, ma'am,' and 'No, ma'am,' scarcely taking in what she was saying. My eyes were open but I'd stopped focusing on the sights of London. I was praying fervently inside my head: *Please let me find Tanglefield's Travelling Circus. Please let me find Madame Adeline. Oh, please please please let her somehow really be my mother so that I can live with her.*

The air grew fresher and the streets less crowded. I glimpsed green fields and many trees. I was reminded of the only real home I had ever known. 'Is this the countryside?' I said wonderingly.

'This is the start of the heath, little sparrow. And look, there's the funfair, right over there!'

I saw it spread out across the heath, more merry-go-rounds and helter-skelters, coconut shies and shooting games and all kinds of swings, but I scarcely gave them a glance. I saw several big striped circus tents!

'Thank you so much,' I said as we all tumbled down off the omnibus.

'Don't you want to come on the rides with us,

319

little sparrow? You shouldn't wander around by yourself, there's all sorts here today,' said Rebecca.

'Oh no, thank you. I'll be all right. I'm meeting someone here,' I said. 'Someone very special.'

'Ah, isn't she lovely, Desmond? Who is it, little sparrow? You're surely too young to have a sweetheart already?'

'It's my mother,' I blurted out – and then I rushed away from them.

I ran towards the nearest tent, so agitated that I tripped and nearly went sprawling.

Please please please let it be Tanglefield's – and please please please let me find her!

I gabbled it out loud this time, not caring if folk stared at me. I saw some words on a big placard:

THIS WAY TO THE GREAT
TANGLEFIELD'S TRAVELLING CIRCUS!

Perhaps I was imagining the words because I wanted to see them so badly. I knew all along that there was only a *chance* that Tanglefield's would be here on the heath. They could be at any town or village in the whole of Britain.

I blinked to get the words properly in focus. Oh glory, it really *did* say Tanglefield!

'Oh thank you, thank you, thank you,' I gabbled, nearly sick with excitement.

I ran nearer. I saw Elijah tethered behind the tent, the real Elijah, truly vast and more weirdly wrinkled than ever, his great ears in the air, trunk waving. I had found my circus! And now I just had to find Madame Adeline and all my dreams would come true.

The flap on the circus tent was closed. A notice declared: *Next performance at five thirty*.

I couldn't wait that long. I dodged round the tent, nervously skirted Elijah, and timidly knocked on the nearest wagon. An old man came to the door in just his undershirt and trousers, his braces flapping.

'What do you want, missy?' he said, frowning at me. There were traces of red on his nose and around his mouth.

'You're Chino the clown!' I said.

'No I'm not, not when I'm taking my break! Now be off with you. I need my forty winks.'

'I'm sorry to disturb you, Mr Chino. It's just I must see Madame Adeline. It's very urgent. Oh, please tell me she's still with the circus, Madame Adeline and her six ponies?'

'Well, she can barely run to two now. She's a bit down on her luck, our Addie. Past it, if you ask me. But the circus is in her blood, you know how it is.'

'The circus is in my blood too,' I said grandly. 'I'll thank you not to talk disparagingly of Madame Adeline. I am related to her.'

'*Are* you now?' he said, peering at me doubtfully. 'Well, she's over in the wagon at the end, the green one with the stars on the door. But she'll likely be taking a nap and won't be too happy to be disturbed.'

'She'll want to see me,' I said.

I had to believe it. I had no other dreams left. I said it so passionately that the clown believed me too.

'Go and knock at her door then,' he said, squinting at me. 'Mm, maybe I *can* see a likeness.'

I walked over to the green wagon, trembling now. I reached up and knocked timidly on the door. It was painted all over with silver stars. *My Little Star!* I waited. Perhaps I'd been *too* timid? I knocked harder, *rat-tat-tat*. I heard a murmur inside. Someone shouted crossly, 'For pity's sake, who *is* it?'

My throat was so dry I could barely call out. 'It's me, Hetty Feather,' I mumbled.

The door opened and an old lady with sparse grey hair peered out at me. She was wearing a pale-green silk dressing gown, rather grubby and stained, and scuffed slippers on her splayed feet. Oh dear Lord, I'd gone to the wrong wagon!

'Who did you say? Hetty Feather? What do you want, child?' she asked, rubbing her eyes irritably. Her hair was all awry at the back, and she combed it with her fingers when she saw me looking.

'I'm so sorry, ma'am. I did not mean to disturb you. I'm looking for Madame Adeline,' I whispered.

'And why is that?' she demanded. She held the door, looking as if she might slam it in my face.

It was time to be blunt. 'Because I think I might be her daughter,' I said.

The old woman blinked at me. *What?*

I licked my lips and repeated it. She stood staring at me, shaking her head in astonishment.

'Well, you'd better come inside,' she said at last, beckoning to me.

I climbed the steps to her wagon and walked in through the starry door. It was like a real little room inside. There was a green velvet upholstered chair with a lace antimacassar and a little table covered with a fringed chenille cloth. A cabinet crammed with china ornaments stood in a corner, though she must have had to wrap and store every one of her treasures while travelling. I spotted a little bed with rumpled covers let down like a shelf from the wagon wall. I peered at it, thinking Madame Adeline must indeed be taking a nap – but there was no head on the pillow, no body beneath the sheets.

'Sit down child,' said the old woman, indicating a padded footstool beside the chair. She set a silver kettle on top of a spirit stove and fetched two willow-pattern china cups and saucers. She then produced a slab of cake, checkered pink and yellow sponge coated with thick marzipan. My mouth watered. I had had no lunch at all and I was starving hungry. The old woman looked at my face and cut a large slice of cake.

'You look as if you need it!' she said.

'Oh, I do, and it's such lovely cake too! But mayn't I meet Madame Adeline first?'

The old woman smiled strangely. There was something familiar about her smile. Could she be Madame Adeline's mother – and therefore my very own grandmother?

'Are you perhaps recognizing me now?' she said.

I shifted uncertainly.

'Maybe this will help you?' she said, shuffling in her down-at-heel slippers over to a wooden cabinet. She opened the doors to display a little dressing table with a large mirror. There was also a bright-red head of hair balanced on a stand.

'My wig,' she said, and she picked it up and carefully positioned it over her own grey locks. '*Tra-la!*' she said, raising her arms in an ironic flourish. 'Madame Adeline herself!'

I stared at her. She still looked like an old woman in spite of her bright hair.

'You will have to imagine the greasepaint and the costume for now. I'm not getting ready for the show just yet,' she said.

'You are really Madame Adeline?' I gasped.

'Your obvious astonishment is not very flattering, child,' she said, yawning. 'Strange that you didn't recognize your own mother!' She laughed a little.

I felt my face flaming. She bent down beside me, suddenly gentle.

'Whatever put such a strange fancy into your head?' she asked.

'You said I was your Little Star,' I said.

'Did I?'

'You came to our village and picked me out from all the other children and I rode on Pirate with you,' I whispered.

'Oh, my dear Pirate,' she said, sighing. 'He broke his leg three years ago. He had to be destroyed and it nearly broke my heart. I've never had another horse like him. So I came to your village long ago?'

'Five years.'

'You must have been very young then, and yet you remember it so vividly. How old are you now, about eight?'

'I'm nearly eleven, ma'am.'

'So why did you fancy I was your mother? Don't you have a mother of your own?'

'No I don't. I'm a foundling. I've never known who she is. But I just thought, as you were so kind to me, and we look a little alike, and we both have such red hair . . . well, so I thought . . . I just so *hoped* . . .' I was crying now, gulping with great ugly sobs.

'Oh dear, Hetty, you poor little creature!' She bent down and put her arms round me. I smelled her own sweet powdery smell and howled. She held me close, rocking me as if I was a baby – her baby. I cried all over her green silk dressing gown, but she didn't seem to mind.

'There now, you poor love,' she said when at last my sobs slowed.

She lifted me up and sat me in her own armchair, then poured me a cup of tea and gave me the big slab of cake. I ate and drank with gusto in spite of my sadness. As I munched my excellent cake (she cut me another slice as soon as the first vanished), she coaxed me to tell my story. She laughed with me when I described my antics with Jem back in the village; she looked as if she might cry herself when I told her about the miseries and humiliations at the hospital.

'You poor little pet, no wonder you had such a strange fancy! But I'm still bewildered that I made such a strong impression on you that you remembered me all this time.'

'Of course I remember!' I looked at her imploringly. 'Don't you remember me, your Little Star?'

I saw her hesitate. I realized in that moment that I must have been one of many many many 'Little

Stars'. Perhaps she picked a likely child for every performance. How could she possibly remember me among so many?

'Of course I remember you,' she said quickly, but I knew she was lying to save my feelings. 'The very little girl with the flame-red hair. Yes, you were indeed a Little Star. And yes, in the ring, we must have looked like a real mother and daughter.'

'But – but you're absolutely certain that I'm *not* your daughter?' I blurted out.

'Oh dear, Hetty! I wish I could pretend, but no, I am absolutely certain you are not my daughter. Though rest assured, if you *were*, I should never have given you to this Foundling Hospital, no matter what my circumstances. I would have dearly loved a baby.' She bent her head, biting her thin lips. 'I cannot have children. There was an accident when I was a child myself. I fell while training one day, and one of the horses galloped over me and kicked me violently in the stomach. I was told it was my own fault – I should have remembered to curl up to protect myself. My womb was ruptured and I could not ride again for more than a year.' She held her stomach now as if it still hurt her.

'Can't we pretend, Madame Adeline? Can't we make out to everyone that I really *am* your daughter? Chino the clown believed me, I'm certain. You could train me up and I could ride with you and – and I'd take care of the horses and look after you – I could sew your costumes – *anything*.'

'Dear Hetty, I've never had such a dear, kind, tempting offer! But the circus is no life for a child. There's such hardship, such struggle, such pain. I've seen tiny children of three and four screaming as they're bent in two, their limbs twisted this way and that by their own parents to crick them into the right kind of bendiness for an acrobat act. It's especially no life for girls, with all the men leering at their brief costumes in the ring. Terrible things happen, Hetty, terrible things. No, you must go back to your hospital and try to be a good girl so you don't get punished any more!'

'I *can't* go back! Oh, please, please let me stay with you!'

'Dear child, I wouldn't be allowed to keep you. Folk would say I had abducted you. They would fear for your moral welfare here in the circus – and rightly so. No, after the show I will accompany you back to the hospital myself.' She looked at a brass clock ticking on a shelf. 'I must start getting ready now. Do you want to watch me one more time?'

'Yes, of course!'

I thought she might send me out of the wagon while she got ready, but she let me stay to watch her transforming herself. She sat before her mirror, placed the great red wig back on its stand, and tied her own ruffled wisps back under a kerchief. Then she applied greasepaint to her pale face, a thick white, with bright pink on her cheeks. She put blue on her lids and outlined her eyes with black kohl, and then set her lips in a strange thin smile so she could fill them in with carmine paint.

She went behind a screen, took off her dressing gown and put on her pink spangled dress and white tights. I heard her sighing and groaning as she struggled into the tight costume and squeezed her swollen feet into little pink ballet shoes. Then she emerged self-consciously and carefully put the red wig back on her head.

She stood before me, my Madame Adeline, ready to pass muster in the circus ring, though now, close up, I could still see the lines on her face under the thick make-up, the sadness of her eyes beneath her blue lids, the sag of her ageing body in the unforgiving costume. I felt a fierce protective love for her, as if she was truly my mother.

'You look beautiful, Madame Adeline,' I lied.

She gave me a kiss on the cheek and then went to wipe the smudge of carmine away, but I protected it with my hand, wanting to wear the marks of my kiss with pride. She slipped her green dressing gown round her shoulders and took me to the entrance of the tent, open now, with people pouring in to see the show.

'Make sure this child gets a good seat,' she said to one of the circus hands. 'I will come and collect her after the show to take her back home.'

She went off with one last wave to me. I sat in the front, waiting tensely, while the audience chatted and chewed food and started calling out impatiently for the show to start.

Then Chino came capering into the ring, followed by his clown friend, Beppo. Everyone laughed at their foolish antics, but now that I knew Chino was just a sad old man doing his job I could not find him funny. I did not even enjoy it when he ran rings round Elijah the elephant and performed the clockwork-mouse trick. I could not marvel at Elijah either as he wearily performed each plodding trick, his skin sagging, his tiny eyes half blinded by the bright flare of gaslight.

I watched the lady walking the tightrope, grown very plump, though she was still as nimble dancing up in the air. I saw the silver-suited tumbling boys, three of them now, one as small as me. I wished Gideon was with me to see them leap and cartwheel. I saw the gentleman throwing daggers at the lady, the seals clapping their flippers, the man eating fire. It was as if they were all phantoms in a dream. I had pictured them vividly so many times, glorifying everything, so that now their real acts seemed a dull disappointment.

'Now, ladies and gentlemen, girls and boys, Tanglewood's Travelling Circus is proud to present Madame Adeline and her rosin-backed performing horses!'

I sat up straight, fists clenched, scarcely able to bear the tension. Madame Adeline came cantering in on a piebald pony, another following close behind. The two horses stepped in time to the music, sometimes hesitating and missing the beat. They were old now, their manes yellow-grey, their flanks sunken.

Madame Adeline stood up on the back of the lead horse, straight and proud as ever, smiling with her carmine lips. I watched her perform every trick, leaping precariously from one horse to another, swinging her legs, standing on her hands, jumping through hoops – my heart in my mouth in case she slipped.

'Hello, children,' she called. 'Who would like to come and ride with me?'

She looked straight at me and beckoned. I had to go to her. I felt foolishly conspicuous in my ugly brown frock. Small though I was, I was clearly the eldest child scrambling into the ring.

Madame Adeline smiled at me and helped me up onto the first piebald horse, swinging herself up after me. We trotted round the ring while everyone clapped.

'Shall we perform properly for them, Hetty?' Madame Adeline murmured into my hair.

'Yes, yes!'

Madame Adeline clucked and our horse gathered speed, galloping round and round the ring while I grabbed his mane and dug my knees in hard to keep my balance.

'Your star turn now!' said Madame Adeline. 'Time to stand up.'

It was much harder now that I was taller and Madame Adeline not so strong. I wobbled precariously, trying desperately to keep my boots connected with the horse's back. I could only manage a split second before I collapsed back onto the horse with a bump – though everyone still clapped.

We slowed down and I scrambled off inelegantly, terrified that folk would see I wore no drawers. Madame Adeline held my hand and we took our bow together.

'Well done, dear Hetty,' she whispered. 'Watch the rest of the show and then I will come for you to take you back.'

I smiled and nodded at her – but after she'd left the ring I stood up and sidled my way along the row to the end. I slipped out of the tent.

'Goodbye, dear Madame Adeline!' I whispered, blowing a kiss in the direction of her wagon.

I could not return to the hospital and the terrible punishment attic. I had run away for ever. I had to fend for myself now.

19

I stepped out purposefully, though I had no idea where in the world I was going. The fairground smell of onions and fried potatoes made my mouth water. I had no money – but I watched a finicky lady nibble at a cone of fried potatoes, pull a face and toss them to the ground. I darted forward and snatched them up. I wolfed them down hurriedly. That was supper taken care of.

It was starting to get dark, so now I needed a bed for the night. I wandered past the noise and glare of the fairground onto the wild heath. At first there were still couples all around me, strolling through the trees, rustling and giggling in the bushes, but after five or ten minutes' walking I seemed to be all alone. I knew the heath wasn't proper countryside, but it had the same good fresh earthy smell.

I stared up at the stars and moon, marvelling in spite of my desolation. I had not seen the night sky properly since I was five. I held my arms up as if I was trying to embrace the constellations. I remembered

Jem naming some of the stars for me, and my eyes filled with tears. I knuckled them fiercely. I had done enough crying for today. I had to be practical and find a safe place to sleep.

In the dark I could not find a hollow tree to turn into a squirrel house, so I found a large bush instead. The ground felt dry and sandy underneath. I crawled under the thick branches and curled up in a ball, cradling my head with my hands.

'This is *better* than a squirrel house,' I told myself. 'This is a cosy little burrow, and if I shut my eyes I shall picture it properly.'

I pictured a sweet bedchamber with a patchwork quilt of buttercups and daisies and clover. It was very similar to the illustration of the field-mouse's burrow beneath the cornfield in my *Thumbelina* storybook. Oh, how I wished I had my precious gift from Ida with me now. However, I'd read it so many times I knew the story almost by heart. I repeated it to myself – and by the time Thumbelina flew off with her swallow I was fast asleep.

I woke with a start in the middle of the night, cold and stiff and terrified. I could not make my picturing work now. I felt utterly alone, like the last child left on earth. I could not stop myself weeping then. I went back to sleep wondering if I might not even be better incarcerated in the punishment attic of the hospital.

I felt more cheerful when I woke in the soft summer daylight. I rolled out from under my bush, stretched heartily and strolled about. I had no privy but it was easy enough to squat behind a tree. Now I needed a washroom. To my delight I found a series of ponds, gleaming silver-grey in the early sunshine. I had no idea how to swim, but I took off my boots and stockings and dress and had a quick splash in the shallows.

I had no towel to dry myself so I ran madly all the way round the pond, and when I came back to my clothes I was nearly dry. I smoothed the creases from my dress as best I could, and polished the dust from my boots with a clump of leaves. I let my hair loose, combed it with my fingers, and then replaited it as neatly as I could.

Now I needed breakfast! This was more of a problem. I wandered around looking for nuts or berries but I could not find any at all. Perhaps if I found my way back to the fair I'd be able to forage for thrown-away scraps? But I'd wandered so far now I had no sense of direction. I simply walked *on*, not sure whether I was heading north or south, or simply going round in circles.

I saw a blue wisp of smoke coming from a small copse, and as I drew nearer I smelled a wonderful savoury cooking smell. I crept closer and came upon a group of dark gypsies in strange bright clothes frying some kind of meat. I wondered if they might share their meal with me. For a few seconds I even had a fantasy of becoming a gypsy girl and travelling in their caravan and selling clothes pegs and telling fortunes, but their dog barked at me furiously and a ragged child started hurling stones at me.

They were clearly not making me welcome so I wandered on, hungrier than ever. I reached the edge of the heath at last and walked out onto the pavement, feeling strangely disorientated to be back in the town so rapidly. I kept my eyes peeled for dainty ladies throwing away half-eaten food, but there were mostly gentlemen in the streets, walking quickly, glancing at their watches, running to catch omnibuses, obviously off to work.

I walked on and on, peering in at the windows of all the big grand houses. I could sometimes see right down into the basement kitchens, with servants scurrying around.

'I am *never* going to be a servant,' I said to myself, trying to lift my spirits. 'I am Hetty Feather and I am not taking orders from anyone. I am as free as the air. I can go anywhere. I can do anything. I can totally please myself.'

But my spirits still seeped right down into my hard boots, and I was snivelling as I walked, unable to control myself. I was so tired and light-headed I sank to the ground, leaning against someone's wall. I covered my face with my hands so that folk passing by would not see I was crying. Then footsteps paused in front of me. Something landed in my lap. Oh Lord, was this another child throwing stones? I took my hands away from my eyes – and stared at a big bright penny shining on the brown stuff of my dress. I looked up and a kindly-looking lady nodded at me.

'There, dearie,' she said, and went on her way.

She thought I was a beggar child! My face flamed red – but my hand grasped the penny.

'Thank you so much, ma'am,' I called after her.

Perhaps her gesture inspired the other passers-by. Maybe they hadn't even noticed me before. But now my tear-stained face attracted attention, and another penny soon landed in my lap, a farthing, and then a halfpenny, soon a whole jingle of copper coins.

Oh my Lord, this was easy! I could sit here at my leisure and look mournful and folk would pay me! But then I saw a dark-uniformed man in the distance, a helmet on his head. I was pretty sure he was a policeman. I was also pretty sure that begging was against the law.

I gathered my coins into my fist, scrambled up and ran off as fast as I could. I careered down long, long roads of houses, my throat aching, my heart jumping in my chest, not even daring to look round in case he caught me. I feared the police had prisons and I did not want to end up in a cell.

Then I came to a parade of shops and dared to pause at last. The policeman was nowhere in sight. I loitered in front of every shop window, and then came to a stop outside a baker's shop. The smell of freshly baked bread brought a flood of water to my mouth and I felt faint.

I stared at the cakes and buns on display in the window. There were slabs of the pink and yellow cake, Madame Adeline's favourite, and white-iced fancy cakes, and red and green and yellow jam tarts, and all manner of golden latticed pies and glazed buns, shiny and soft and curranty.

I had no idea how much such wonders would cost. They could be sixpence each, even a sovereign for all I knew. Perhaps the woman in the white apron inside the shop would scoff at my impertinence if I proffered my small handful of coins. But I was so hungry I decided to risk it.

I opened the door and stepped inside. 'If you please, ma'am . . .' I started shyly.

'Yes?'

'I – I'd like to purchase a little cake – or maybe a bun?'

'Well, make your mind up, dear,' she said, but she didn't sound too impatient.

'Perhaps a cake, the pink and yellow one – *and* a

bun?' I suggested, and then I anxiously showed her my coins. 'Do I have enough money?'

'More than enough, dear.'

She put my cake and bun into a white paper bag, twirled it round so that the corners were twisted fast, took twopence halfpenny from my hand, and gave the bag to me.

'Thank you kindly, ma'am,' I said.

She laughed a little then. 'You've got the best manners of any street child I've ever come across before!' she said. 'Goodbye, dear. Take care of yourself.'

I *could* take care of myself! I had found a place to sleep, a place to wash, I had earned lots of money, and now I could breakfast like a queen! I ate my cake and bun, and when I came to a tea stall I bought myself a large mugful for another penny. Then I went marching on, refreshed and renewed, peering all about me.

I found myself wandering in more huge parkland. For a moment I thought I was back in Hyde Park because I heard an elephant trumpeting – but I discovered I was near the Zoological Gardens. I peered through the railings and saw an elephant even larger than Elijah with a curved seat on his back. Ten or twelve children were strapped onto the seat, while another boy rode bareback on his neck, his boots nudging the beast's great ears.

341

I had a desperate desire to ride an elephant too! I paid sixpence to get into the zoo, and another twopence for a ride. This was the last of my money so I very much hoped the ride would be worth it. I queued impatiently at the landing stage amongst a great crowd of girls and boys, waiting until at last it was my turn to be hoisted onto the great grey creature.

'I am very good at riding. Please may I sit on the elephant's neck?' I begged the keeper.

'Don't be silly, missy – you're a young lady,' said the keeper, and he put one of the boys on the elephant's neck.

The boy nodded at me triumphantly, pulling a silly face. Other boys shrieked and squirmed beside me, jostling for the best position on the seat – but I was adept at elbowing my way when I wanted. One of the other girls was hopelessly squashed, however, with two rude boys practically sitting on top of her.

'Move next to me,' I said.

She smiled at me timidly. She was beautiful, just like a fairy-tale princess, with big blue eyes, rosy cheeks and long golden curls. She wore a cream silk hat and a matching silk dress, with white stockings and white kid boots with tiny blue buttons.

'Come on, wriggle past those silly boys,' I said, reaching out and grabbing her.

She squeezed past them and I pulled her

safely down next to me. I could feel her trembling violently.

'What's the matter?' I asked in astonishment.

'I'm frightened!' she said.

I didn't know if she was frightened of the elephant, frightened of heights, frightened of the rude boys, or simply frightened of getting her pretty pale clothes dirty. I reached out and held her hand.

'There now, no need to be frightened. I will look after you,' I said. 'My name's Hetty. What's yours?'

'I'm Rosabel,' she said.

I sighed. Trust her to have a beautiful name too!

The elephant was fully loaded now, so the keeper gave him a little tap and we set off, plodding down the path. The boys shrieked loudly and Rosabel clutched me as if she would never let me go.

'Oh dear, it's so scary! I wish the beast wouldn't *roll* so,' she gasped. She peered down desperately. 'I've lost sight of my mama and papa. Can you see yours?'

I would have a hard job seeing either!

'I am here on my own,' I said proudly.

'Without even your nurse?' said Rosabel.

'I don't have a nurse any more,' I said. 'I am too big.'

'No you're not, you're little, much smaller than me,' said Rosabel. 'Oh, *there* is Mama. I see her

343

lilac parasol!' She risked letting go for a second, attempting a little wave.

I stared at her mother. 'She is very young and beautiful,' I said wistfully.

Her papa was waving too. He looked a kindly, jolly man, with a pink face.

'Papa is pleased with me for taking the elephant ride. He feels I am too timid,' said Rosabel. 'But Mama says all girls are naturally timid.'

'I'm a girl and I'm not the *slightest* bit timid,' I said.

'Perhaps we could be friends and then you could teach me how to be bold and independent,' said Rosabel.

My heart leaped. Maybe Rosabel's family would take me under their wing? I could be a devoted companion to their little daughter! They might even adopt me like Polly. I wasn't sure I should be happy wearing cream silk dresses and fancy hats and white boots. I knew how dirty they would be by the end of the day. Maybe they would let me choose a darker colour for my clothes, red or blue or purple – *any* colour so long as it wasn't sludge-brown. I didn't hunger after dolls and toys but I was sure a cosseted child like Rosabel would have a whole shelf of storybooks – and I could share them.

I was still eagerly picturing my future with Rosabel as the elephant plodded back up the path to the landing stage. I kept hold of Rosabel's hand and helped her down carefully.

'Rosabel! Over here, my dear!' both parents called.

I trotted over with her, but the mama suddenly looked horrified and even the papa appeared grave.

'Say goodbye to the little girl, dearest,' said the mama, very firmly.

'She is my new friend Hetty,' said Rosabel.

'Don't be ridiculous, Rosabel. She is just a dirty street child. Leave go of her hand. You should never have let her get so near to you!' said the mama.

The papa turned on me. 'Be off with you,' he said, swotting at me.

If they thought I was a street child, I would act like one. I stuck out my tongue and waggled it hard before running away. My feelings were hurt nevertheless, but I diverted myself by inspecting all the creatures in their cages: the scampering monkeys, the pacing lions, the savage bear in his pit. I felt sorry for all these poor caged animals. I wanted to set them free so that the monkeys could snatch up all the flimsy parasols, the lions could leap at all the scornful parents and the bear maul them to pieces.

I was starting to feel sorry for myself too, walking around alone in my hideous brown frock and boots, while all the well-dressed families stared and sniggered at me. Even the rude boys were here with mamas and papas, big happy families, many of them picnicking on the grass. I stared at their checked tablecloths spread with pork pies and whole chickens and egg-and-bacon tarts, and wondered about darting in like a dog and snatching something. But then what would the woman in the baker's shop say about my manners! I might be a beggar now but I was *not* going to be a thief.

I sat myself down on the grass and looked mournful, hoping that strangers would start flinging pennies at me again, but it seemed to be the wrong sort of place. People had come to the Zoological Gardens to observe the animals, not a small stray child. Folk passed me by without giving me a second glance.

I decided I'd have to move further afield if I wanted to earn enough for my supper. Most of my generous donors had been gentlemen. I needed to get away from this family environment. I figured that there would be more gentlemen in the centre of town, so I left the gardens, walked out of the park and continued on my way.

I wandered back towards Oxford Street and Regent Street, my empty stomach clamouring now, and both boots rubbing my feet sore and bloody. Finally I had to stop and take my boots off altogether. I was sitting on the kerb airing my dirty toes, my boots neatly beside me, stockings tucked inside, when two boys came dashing up. One hollered something unintelligible right in my face. I shouted back furiously. He punched me in the chest and I aimed a kick at him with my bare foot. He pushed me hard so that I fell – and he and his friend scurried off. I sat up gingerly, cursing them. I cursed even more when I went to put on my boots again. They had vanished, stolen by the two scheming boys!

I cried a little then, because I knew how much I needed those boots even though they hurt me. My genuine tears brought me a little consolation – two more gentlemen gave me pennies – but when I got to my feet to look for another baker's shop I realized I was in trouble. The pavements were hard, with sharp stones, whereas my feet were soft and blistered raw. I could not walk far now.

I bought myself a meat pie from a street stall and wolfed it down, though the meat was all fat and gristle and the pastry limp. I thought of Ida and her delicious pies. She had been such a true friend to me yet I'd been so very unkind to her. She would hate me now – if she ever thought of me. She'd have Sheila for her pet. She'd give her tiny culinary treats and save up to buy her a special Christmas present . . .

I felt miserably sick at the thought (or perhaps it was the meat pie). My bladder was also bursting. I wandered up a dark alley off Regent Street to find somewhere private so I could relieve myself.

I found myself in a wide square with a garden full of city men, smoking and larking and taking the air. There were girls too, some ragged and barefoot like me, offering posies to the gentlemen, begging them to buy their flowers. There were a couple of older girls too, their lips painted carmine like Madame Adeline's, wearing lurid dresses and showing a lot of petticoat. They kept approaching the gentlemen, seeming to be begging too.

I hesitated, wondering if I should try too.

'Clear off, you, ginger nob. This is *our* patch!' one girl yelled at me.

Another girl gave me a hard push. 'You're too young! Give way for your elders and betters!' she said, cackling with laughter.

These weren't girls I dared tangle with. They were bigger and rougher than the street boys who had stolen my boots. There was a sharpness about their pinched, painted faces that frightened me. I ran away, up another darker alley, then lifted my skirts and used the gutter, jumping when a rat leaped out at me.

A girl and a gentleman came blundering down the alleyway, arm in arm, whispering together. Their words made me feel sicker than ever. I dodged round them and scurried back to the square, desperate to reach the wide public street once more.

'Are you all right, little 'un?' said one of the

flower-sellers, a softer-looking girl in a shabby blue print dress, carrying a big basket of flowers.

'Yes, thank you, I am perfectly fine,' I said, though I knew I must look wretched and tear-stained.

'You don't *look* fine. I wouldn't stay round here. It's not a good place for a little girl like you,' she said. 'Here, do you want a posy?'

She picked out a tiny bunch of three rosebuds, their stems carefully wrapped round with ribbon so that their thorns were covered.

'It's beautiful, but I'm afraid I have no pennies,' I said.

'I don't want no pennies! It's a gift to cheer you up,' she said.

'Thank you very much! You're very kind,' I said, sniffing the sweet roses.

'Off you hop,' she said. 'I wouldn't even loiter round here. Go straight home. You're too little to be out on the streets.'

I nodded and smiled at her and turned on my way, comforted. I went back down the alley towards Regent Street, but a gentleman stepped out of the shadows right in front of me, making me jump. He was a very grand gentleman, with a fine hat and coat and a fancy silver brocade waistcoat. He could surely mean me no harm . . .

'Hello, my dear,' he said softly. 'What a lovely nosegay! May I buy it?'

'If you please, sir, it's not really for sale,' I said.

'No? But I will pay you a lot of money. A shilling? Two? Maybe half a crown?'

I stared at him. He did not seem a foolish man at all, quite the opposite, so why was he willing to pay a fortune for three little wilting roses? I wanted to keep them for myself because the flower-seller was so kind to me – but I could feed myself for days and days on half a crown.

He saw me hesitating. 'You're clearly very fond of your flowers, child. Never mind, you keep them. I'll tell you what. I have a house nearby with a very pretty garden. I will take you there and you can pick a whole armful of roses.'

'It's very kind of you, sir, but—'

'No buts, my dear. You must come with me. You're trembling! I had better find you a soft shawl to keep you warm – and stockings and shoes for those poor little bare feet. Oh dear, they do look sore.'

He bent down and stroked my feet, fondling my toes. I did not like this one jot and stepped backwards, but he had hold of my ankle. I stumbled and he caught me, lifting me right up in his arms.

'No, please! Put me down, sir!' I said, struggling, but his arms were strong and his hand clamped over my mouth.

'Ssh now, little girl. No crying. You will be fine with me,' he said, walking rapidly.

I tried to bite the hand over my mouth but he held me so tight I couldn't move my teeth, I couldn't even draw breath to scream. But then something went *bang* right on his head, someone kicked him hard between his legs, and he groaned and dropped me. A hand snatched mine.

'Quick, run!'

I ran for my life, hanging onto her hand. It was my kind flower-seller! She had hammered the man with her basket and then kicked him with swift expertise. She tugged me up even darker alleys, and then pushed me into a shadowy doorway. We flattened ourselves in the recess, listening hard – but could hear no footsteps.

'There! I didn't think he'd follow us, but you never know,' she said. 'What was you *doing*, going off with the likes of him? Couldn't you tell he was up to no good?'

'Yes, but I didn't know how to get away.'

'Yell out and give them a good kicking, that's what you do. You don't want to go *near* gentlemen like that.'

'It was so kind of you to rescue me – and you've dropped half your flowers!'

'We'll retrace our steps in a little while and see if we can find any. Don't you worry. What's your name, little 'un?'

'Hetty Feather.'

'I'm Sissy, dear. I'm fourteen.' She said it as if she was quite grown up. She did indeed look years older than the big girls at the hospital, with their prim frocks and plaits. 'How old are you, Hetty?'

'Ten, nearly eleven.'

She didn't seem surprised. 'Our Lil's ten too. She's about your size, bless her. She usually sells flowers along with me, but she's poorly just now. She's got a way of looking all big-eyed so that the gentlemen melt.'

'Can *I* help you sell flowers today?'

Sissy looked me up and down. 'I don't see why not. You need someone to look after you. There's gentlemen and gentlemen. You need to work out which is which. Not that *I* can always tell.' She sniffed. 'Still, I might work on the street, but I like to think me and Lil keep ourselves respectable. If ever I'm tempted otherwise, I just think of Mother.'

'Is your mother . . .?' I hesitated delicately.

'She died two years ago, and the last baby died with her. She were wore out, poor love.'

'Do you have a father?'

'Yes, we do, but we'd be better off without him,' Sissy said bitterly. 'What about you, Hetty?'

I shook my head. 'I haven't got a father or a mother,' I said.

Sissy plucked at the stuff of my dress. 'So is this some kind of orphan uniform?'

I felt I could trust her. 'I used to live at the Foundling Hospital, but I've run away.'

'Ah!' said Sissy, nodding. 'Were they cruel to you there?'

'Ever so cruel,' I said firmly.

'Well, you stick with me, girl, and I'll learn you some tricks. Let's have a look at you now.' She scrutinized me carefully, then wet her finger, rubbed it across the grimy wall, and marked under my eyes with soot. 'That's better. If you look really ill, the gentlemen will feel sorry for you. Can you look really sad, Hetty?'

'I'm brilliant at it,' I said, lowering my head and letting my mouth droop.

'Yes, you're a natural, almost as good as our Lil.'

'I can cry too if you like.'

'No, no, you'll smudge the soot and end up looking like a chimney sweep. Right, my dear, let us see if we can gather up those posies.' She held my hand tight. 'Don't worry about that gentleman, Hetty, or any others of that ilk. I'll be looking out for you now.'

We found the spot where Sissy had valiantly attacked the vile foot-stroker, and gathered up as many fallen flowers as we could, though some had already been trampled underfoot.

'We'll soon sort them out,' said Sissy, kneeling down and arranging them deftly. 'Lovely moss roses, these are, and gentlemen will pay a penny for a little posy. They make a sweet little surprise for a lady, my posies do. That's how me and our Lil do better than most of the other girls. We don't just sell flowers, we make 'em look special. When we sell our violets in the spring, we bind them with green leaves and a tiny piece of lace or ribbon. We beg them from this milliner who used to know our mother. Then we make such a pretty nosegay, some gentlemen might even pay threepence to show their ladies it's spring at last.'

'How pretty,' I said, trying to copy Sissy, prinking the drooping little roses and arranging them just so.

'That's right, Hetty, you're getting the hang of it already. Come with me then, girl. We'll go down St Martin's way. The gentlemen won't pay so much but it's safer there. Don't want no nasty men making off with you again, do we, Hetty?'

I trotted along beside Sissy and sat with her on the steps of a great church by a huge square with fountains and vast lion statues. It was so crowded I wondered if the Queen was returning on another Jubilee procession, but Sissy said it was simply folk coming out to go to the theatre and the halls. Most of them ignored us, though I looked extra mournful and Sissy accosted them energetically.

'Come on, sir, buy a lovely posy for the missus. Beautiful moss roses freshly picked! Make a girl happy, sir. Only tuppence – what a bargain!'

It was a novelty at first and I enjoyed myself, but then it started raining and everyone hurried by under umbrellas, not even glancing in our direction. I hoped Sissy might give up, but she sorted the few coins in her pocket anxiously and said we had to stay.

'We need at least another shilling, Hetty, hopefully twice that,' she said worriedly.

'But you could buy a big meat pie and buns for you and your Lil with the money you've got,' I said, hoping she'd share a few pennies with me too.

'Bless you, Hetty, it's not just a question of money for our food. I have to make the wherewithal tonight to buy fresh flowers from the market in the morning – these will all be withered by then. And then there's Father to consider. He'll start fretting for his drinking money. If I don't get home with enough for his beer, he'll take it out on me *and* our Lil.' She took a deep breath. 'Maybe I'd be better going back to where I was. I reckon I could earn a couple of quick sixpences there. You could stay here, Hetty, and I'll come and collect you, I promise.'

I wasn't quite sure what she meant, but I clung to her nevertheless. 'No, Sissy, stay. We'll get the money here.' I cast my eyes around. I was used to weighing up the hospital visitors on Sunday, working out who might be generous with sweets. I saw a portly middle-aged couple and took a chance.

I snatched a posy and ran up to them in the pouring rain. 'Oh please, ma'am, sir, would you care to buy one of my pretty posies?'

They seemed taken aback.

'What are you doing in the rain, child? And barefoot too! Why don't you run along home?' said the lady.

'Oh, I daren't, ma'am, for my father will beat me viciously if I don't take him money for his drink. And then there's our Lil too, she's poorly.' I decided to embellish things a little. 'And then there's my sister Sheila, she's got the smallpox and is hideously disfigured, and my sister Monica, who's been kicked by a horse and is very dim-witted now.' I started going through half the dormitory at the hospital, inventing ailments and misfortunes galore. I took care to keep my tone tragic and my face a mask of mournfulness – but to my astonishment the lady and gentleman started *laughing*.

'Be off with you, you naughty minx. You should not tell such stories!' said the lady.

'Yes, it's very bad of you to try and con us – but here's a little something for your cheek,' said the gentleman. He fished in his pocket and handed me a couple of coins.

'Oh thank you kindly, sir,' I said, bobbing him a curtsy.

I thought he'd handed me a couple of pennies, but when I opened my fist I saw it was *two shillings*!

'Oh, Hetty, you're a marvel!' said Sissy, giving me a hug. 'There, you've brought us luck! We can indeed go home now.'

I stood still. 'But . . . I have no home,' I said.

'You come along with me,' said Sissy. 'You can stay with Lil and me for now.'

'Won't your father mind?' I asked anxiously.

'So long as he's got enough to drink he don't mind anything,' said Sissy. 'Come on, little Hetty. Come home and meet our Lil. She'll take a shine to you, I'm sure.'

20

Sissy led me through a maze of dark alleyways to her home. They were so dark that I kept stumbling on the uneven cobblestones, and when I tried walking in the gutter I stepped in something unspeakable in my bare feet. I hoped I might be able to have a proper wash at Sissy's house – but when we got there at last, it came as a rude shock.

I was not a fool. I knew Sissy was very poor. I hadn't pictured her in a palace. I'd thought she would live in a very modest house, rather like the country cottage where I'd lived with my foster family.

But Sissy's family didn't have their own house. They had one room in a large, bleak, five-storey tenement building, the bricks black with grime, the window glass mostly missing, the roof partly collapsed.

I stared up at it in horror. 'Is it falling down?' I asked.

'It soon will. It's been condemned a while now so the rent's cheap. Do you want to pee first? We're up four flights of stairs, so it's a good idea to go now if you want to.'

There was no proper privy, just a stinking hole in a tumbledown shed in the back yard. Judging from the smell and the slime on the walls, folk simply tipped their chamber pots out of the window. There was a tap over a drain. Sissy turned it on for me so I could sluice my feet – but only a dribble of water came out.

'That tap's no use. Never mind,' said Sissy. 'I'll go up to the pump at the end of the street later on and bring a jug back.'

There were cockroaches crawling along the dark corridor of the fourth floor. Sissy stamped on them with her boots, while I walked on tiptoe, agonized. She opened the door of the room right at the end. It was very dark, but I could see it was pitifully small and barely furnished. There were two thin mattresses on the floor, and a rickety chair and a stool. Someone had hung sacking curtains at the narrow window and worked a rag rug for the floor, but these were the only homely touches. A big slovenly man sprawled on one mattress while a little girl huddled on the other, coughing and coughing.

'Lil? Oh, dearie, ssh now. Here, darling, take a drink,' said Sissy, hurrying to her side.

She helped Lil sit up and held an old tin cup

to her lips. 'There now, my lovey, this will help,' she said.

'Cough, cough, cough! It drives me mad,' said the father, scratching his head. 'She only does it to annoy, I'm sure. A man can't even have a little nap for that cough, cough, cough. Clear your throat, Lil, and then shut up.'

He rubbed his eyes and then blinked at me. 'Who's this? Clear off out of here, this ain't your room!'

'Hush, Father, this is my new little friend Hetty. She's brought me luck. She's a dab hand at flower-selling, almost as good as our Lil. Look what she's earned for us!' She held out one of the silver shillings.

He snatched it, bit it hard and then shoved it in his pocket. 'Well, I'll be off for a little constitutional,' he said, not giving me a second glance now. 'I'll just stretch my legs and maybe take a drink to ease my parched throat. I'll be back within the hour.'

He stuck his feet in his old broken boots, clapped a greasy bowler hat on his tousled hair and made his way over to the door.

'Within the hour!' Sissy muttered. 'We won't see him till midnight – and good riddance. There now, Lil, take another sip, that's my good girl. Give Hetty a smile, dearie, and show her that *someone* in our family has good manners.'

Lil tried valiantly to master her cough. She was a tiny scrap of a girl, her eyes very large in her peaky face. Her hair was limp and bedraggled, but tied up jauntily with a bright red ribbon, which sadly emphasized her eerie pallor. Her eyes popped as she coughed, her whole face contorting alarmingly – but as soon as she could draw breath she grinned at me.

'Hello, Hetty! Oh my Lord, look at your red hair! That's a queer dress – do you like it? How old are you? Do you have a mother? How much did you get for one posy? I got threepence one day 'cos the gentleman took a shine to me!'

'Now, Lil, give Hetty a chance to answer!' said Sissy, laughing. 'She don't see many folk now, Hetty, so that's why she's so excited to see you. You have a little chat with her while I run out for more water and some supper.' She jingled the coins in her pocket. 'We'll have a treat tonight, girls!'

I sat on the edge of Lil's mattress and let her question me relentlessly. I told her all about the Golden Jubilee, and Madame Adeline at the circus, and my night on Hampstead Heath, and the Zoological Gardens, and the horrid gentleman who seized me before Sissy rescued me.

Lil listened, wide-eyed. 'Dear Sissy! She's always looked out for me and she'll look out for you too,

Hetty,' she said. 'When I die, perhaps you can be a comfort to her.'

Her words came as a total shock. I blinked at her anxiously, not knowing what to say. 'I'm sure you'll get better, Lil,' I mumbled.

'No, no, I'm coughing blood. That means you're dying. Can't fool me!' said Lil. 'I'll miss Sissy so when I'm dead.'

'And she will miss you too, Lil, terribly. But at least you'll be with your mother then,' I said, trying to be comforting.

'I'll be with Mother?' Lil echoed. 'Oh, I should like that very much! Are you sure, Hetty?'

'Certain,' I said, trying to sound convincing. 'Your mother is up in Heaven, and when you die you will be an angel with her.'

'An angel with wings? Will I be able to fly?' Lil asked.

'Oh yes, you'll have great white feathery wings and be able to fly all over Heaven. Sometimes you might swoop down to earth and see Sissy and make sure she's all right,' I said, warming to this theme.

'Oh, I'd love that! Will she be able to see me or are angels invisible?'

'She might just catch a glimpse of you, or hear you whispering her name,' I said.

I'd never glimpsed my brother Saul or heard him

calling me – but I *had* sometimes felt a poke in my ribs, as if he'd prodded me with his old crutch.

Lil spread her arms and flapped them like wings, but the effort made her start coughing again.

'Oh, Lil, don't cough so,' I begged, frightened that she might die then and there in front of me.

I tried to give her the murky water in her cup, but she just choked and spluttered. I patted her helplessly on her back, feeling her sharp little shoulder blades under the thin stuff of her nightgown – almost as if she was already sprouting small wings.

'There now,' said Sissy, bursting into the room, bringing with her a warm savoury smell. 'Oh dear, Lil! Here's some fresh water. Clever girl, Hetty, it helps to rub her back. Now, Lil, see what a feast I've got – *and* some more of that nice medicine. Oh, how it will soothe your poor chest. We're going to get you better and running about in no time.'

It was clear that Sissy wouldn't have any truck with talk of dying and angels. She held the medicine bottle to Lil's lips and made her swig a mouthful between coughs – and it did seem to help a little. Then Sissy unwrapped a waxed-paper parcel to show us three large potatoes and a quantity of fried onions. We seized a potato each and munched ravenously.

They tasted very good, though they were not quite the great treat I had expected.

'What did they feed you at this hospital place, bread and water?' asked Sissy.

'Yes, they did give me bread and water,' I said, remembering my night in the punishment attic.

'Was they really cruel to you, Hetty?' asked Lil.

'Really, really cruel,' I said.

'Did they beat you with a big stick?'

'Well . . . they had whips,' I said.

'Whips!' said Lil, her eyes round. 'Did they whip you till you bled?'

'They were always *threatening* to whip me,' I said. It sounded a little lame. 'They once locked me up in a little attic room all day and all night, and that was far worse than being whipped. Imagine, Lil, being shut up in a tiny room, a total prisoner . . .' My voice trailed away, because Lil could imagine it all too well.

'Did they go out and get sodden drunk and then come back and beat you in a fearsome rage?' asked Lil.

I pictured Matron Bottomly and Matron Peters glugging from a gin bottle. It was such a bizarre idea I couldn't help laughing – and dear Lil laughed too.

'No, they didn't drink, but they frequently got into fearsome rages, especially with me.'

'Did they all hate you, Hetty?'

'Yes! Well, both matrons did. Some of the nurses were all right. Nurse Winnie was very kind, but the teachers were very cruel. Miss Morley once beat my friend Polly with a ruler and I snatched it away and beat her back,' I said, getting a little carried away.

'You had *teachers*?' said Sissy. 'Did they learn you to read and write, Hetty? Could you teach our Lil? She's very bright, I know she is. If she could only read, it would pass the day for her.'

They had no books or paper but I improvised, 'writing' on the bare floorboards with a sooty stick. Sissy squashed up beside us on the mattress. I taught them *a* and *b* and *c*, making them sound out each letter. When Lil succeeded in spelling out *cab*, we clapped her. She got so excited she jumped about, and that started her coughing again, very badly this time, as if she would never stop. Sissy held her close and gently laid her down when she stopped at last.

'There now, my little Lil. No more excitement for today. You go to sleep, dearie. You should try and sleep too, Hetty.'

I lay down beside Lil on the mattress, fully clothed. I had no nightgown and I could not take off my frock as I would reveal I had no underwear.

'Have you read lots of books, Hetty?' said Sissy. 'How about telling Lil one of the stories to help her get off to sleep?'

'Once upon a time there was a very little girl no bigger than my thumb,' I started. 'She was so tiny she curled up every night in a walnut shell . . .'

We all curled up too and went sound asleep until the girls' father came stumbling into the dark room. I felt Sissy tense and Lil gave a little frightened whimper as he staggered over to our mattress. He bent over us, smelling horribly of beer.

'All tucked up like birds in a nest,' he mumbled, slurring his words. 'Goodnight, my chicks. Cheep-cheep!' He laughed at his own joke and then crawled on his hands and knees to his own mattress. He fell on top of it and was snoring heavily in seconds.

'Thank the Lord he's happy-drunk rather than roaring for a fight,' Sissy whispered. 'We never know how it will take him.'

'Does he get drunk *every* night?' I said.

'If he has the money. He's been so much worse since Mother died,' said Sissy. She sounded much younger now – and despairing. 'He used to work at the docks, but he can't hold down a job, the state he's in. I have to earn to keep us all. I never make quite *enough*.'

'I'll help you, Sissy. I'll look proper mournful tomorrow and we'll make a fortune, you'll see,' I said.

Sissy got up before dawn, moving slowly and softly so as not to wake Lil.

'Sissy?' I whispered.

'I'm off to market to buy my flowers,' she murmured.

'I'll come with you,' I said, though I was dizzy from lack of sleep.

I was already dressed and I seemed to have given up on washing, so I was ready in an instant. It was raining, which made my lack of boots particularly uncomfortable. My feet were numb from walking across the slippery cobblestones. It was a struggle keeping up with Sissy.

We walked to the huge market at Covent Garden, abuzz with activity though it was still dark. Even though I was exhausted, I paused to marvel at all the wagon-loads of peas and potatoes, the barrows and carts piled high with tomatoes and lettuces, the great baskets scarlet with cherries and strawberries.

There were people fresh from the country, tall men in smocks like Father, round red-faced women like Mother, reminding me painfully of long-ago times. Sissy tapped me gently and we walked on to the flower market. Again I was dazzled, my eyes stinging with the shock of such bright colours, sunny yellow asters, hot orange pokers, fat pink peonies, blue and deep-purple lupins, my nose wrinkling with the overpowering smell of roses and great white lilies.

Sissy sprang into action, bargaining with last night's money until she had a huge basketful of flowers. Then we sat beneath the big arcade, fashioning the flowers into bright bouquets and tiny posies. I tried to help her, though I still felt lightheaded and my hands were clumsy. When at last we were done, she spent her last penny at the coffee stall, sharing the hot drink with me. We had no more money for buns or rolls, but Sissy kept a sharp eye on the floor of the fruit market and snatched up a discarded withered apple and a bruised pear, providing us with a meagre breakfast.

We went to the steps of St Martin's, but another older flower-seller was there already, and she wouldn't let us stay too. Sissy tried Charing Cross Station, but again we were too late. We had to go to the square off Regent Street, though Sissy made me sit close beside her, and whenever any weird-seeming gentleman paused, she put her arm round me protectively. There weren't too many gentlemen, weird or otherwise, because the rain was relentless. I wasn't really *cold* because it was summer, but I felt chilled right to the bone, and by afternoon my stomach was rumbling pathetically.

'Aren't you hungry, Sissy?' I asked.

'I'm always hungry,' she said. 'But you get used to it.'

I wasn't sure I would ever get used to this. Selling flowers had been a novelty yesterday, but now it was so tiring and tedious.

369

'Buy my sweet flowers, sir. A posy for your lady, only a penny. Go on, sir, there's a gent,' I'd gabble, but nearly always they walked straight past, ignoring me. I didn't have to rub soot under my eyes or adopt a mournful expression – I am sure I looked genuinely ill and exhausted.

'Please, oh, please buy my flowers,' I begged, but I could have been a sparrow cheeping for all the attention I attracted. Then a plain lady in charcoal grey paused nearby. She watched while Sissy and I accosted each passing gentleman. I wondered why she was lingering. Did she want a nosegay to brighten her severe outfit? I smiled in her direction.

'Would you care to buy a posy, ma'am?' I asked.

She shook her head and I drooped a little more.

'Are you a regular flower-seller, child? I do not recollect seeing you here before.' She was looking at me strangely. 'What are you doing here?'

'She's with me, missus. She's all right,' said Sissy protectively.

'She looks a little tired,' said the lady.

'I am, ma'am,' I said. 'If you buy some flowers, we will be able to buy a bite to eat. We have had no breakfast today, nor dinner.'

'Are you both very hungry?' she said. 'I have an idea. Perhaps you would like to accompany me to a nearby teashop?'

My heart jumped. A teashop! Oh, how I longed for

a cup of tea and a bite to eat! But Sissy was looking dubious.

'We ain't got the wherewithal to go in no teashop,' she said.

'I will happily pay for you,' said the lady.

'Oh, Sissy, please, do say yes!' I begged.

She still seemed reluctant. 'What's the catch, eh?' she asked.

The lady smiled. 'Yes, you're right, Sissy, there *is* a catch. I would like to ask you a few questions.'

'What about?' Sissy looked alarmed. 'Look, missus, we bought our flowers fair and square from Covent Garden Market. I've got a regular pitch. We don't get no hassle from no one, not even the police. We're totally honest and respectable. We never go off with no gentlemen.'

'I'm sure you're right. I'm not here on any official business, I promise you. I'll be frank. I'm a writer. My books are published by the Religious Tract Society. They are stories of street children very much like you.'

'What's your name then?'

'Sarah Smith.'

Sissy looked at me. 'You read books, Hetty. Have you ever heard of her?'

The only children's writers I knew of were Mr Andersen and the two Mr Grimms. I'd had no idea that ladies could write storybooks. I looked at

Sarah Smith with great interest. She was staring back at me.

'So you can read, Hetty?' she said. 'Who taught you?'

Ah. I had to be a little careful now. I could not breathe a word about the hospital or she'd act like Madame Adeline, and want to take me straight back.

'My brother Jem taught me, ma'am,' I said, truthfully enough.

'And where is he now?'

'I lost him long ago,' I said sadly.

'So what is your name, child?'

'Hetty Feather, ma'am.'

She nodded as if she approved of my name. 'Then do please come with me, Hetty. And you too, Sissy. I simply wish to ask you a few questions to use as background for a new story of mine. I'm thinking of calling it *A Penny for a Posy*. Do you like the title? It will be all about little flower-sellers like you.'

'Could you put us *in* your story, ma'am?' I asked excitedly. 'Could you use our names? Oh, I should so like to be in a real storybook.'

'I don't want *my* name in no storybook,' said Sissy.

She made it clear she was only accompanying me on sufferance. We made our way out to the busy thoroughfare of Regent Street. I thought we would go to a humble teashop full of working folk, but Miss Smith made for the door of a grand restaurant, all great glass windows and gilt decoration.

'We can't go in there. We'll get chased away,' said Sissy. 'It's much too grand for the likes of us.'

Certainly the waiter at the door was looking us up and down and glaring. Sissy was neat enough in her print dress, but her hair was straggly and she wore men's boots with their soles flapping. I looked even worse by now, my hair a-tangle, my brown dress dirty and crumpled, my bare feet filthy.

'We are too shabby, miss,' I said.

'Nonsense,' said Miss Smith, taking our hands. She led us into the restaurant, giving the waiter haughty directions. 'We would like a table for three, please. Could we have the menu brought straight away? My companions are very hungry.'

The waiter bowed reluctantly and ushered us to a table right in the corner. He held the chair out for Miss Smith and then hesitated. Miss Smith coughed reprovingly. The waiter sat Sissy and me down too, though he grimaced, as if he'd been asked to seat two monkeys at the zoo.

He made a particular to-do over Sissy's flower basket, trying to take it from her. Sissy hung onto it determinedly.

'I'll put these in the cloakroom for you, miss,' he said.

'No, you don't! I want them where I can see them. Anyone could help themselves in the cloakroom,' said Sissy.

'Yes, that basket will be fine at our feet, under the table. The flowers smell heavenly,' said Miss Smith.

The waiter did as he was told, though he raised his eyebrows and sighed. Sissy jutted her chin out and glared back at him, but she was biting her lip and fiddling with a lock of her lank hair. She stared at the gleaming knives and forks on the white tablecloth before us, clearly unused to copious cutlery.

The waiter handed us three large menus. Sissy stared at hers, blinking rapidly.

'What would you like?' said Miss Smith. 'You can have anything on the menu. What's your favourite food, Sissy?'

Sissy shrugged her shoulders, seeming ungracious because she simply did not know what to say. I glanced down the long list of items, utterly astonished at the choice. I'd had no idea you could select whatever you wanted in a restaurant. I would have liked to linger over my choices, picturing each dish, but I knew I had to help Sissy as tactfully as possible. The words on the menu were just elegant squiggles to her.

'If you please, I would like the steak-and-kidney pudding,' I said. 'Would you like that too, Sissy?'

Sissy nodded dumbly.

Miss Smith summoned the waiter back and ordered two meat puddings for us, and a little fish for herself. Then she poured us a glass of water each from a crystal carafe. Sissy and I drank thirstily while Miss Smith sipped. She started asking Sissy questions, perhaps trying to put her at her ease.

'How long have you been selling flowers, Sissy?'

'Since I was little.'

'And what do you do in winter, when fresh flowers are in short supply?'

'Sell oranges.'

'Is your mother a flower-seller too?'

'No, miss, she sewed stuff.'

'What sort of a seamstress was she?'

'I dunno.'

'And what about your father?'

Sissy sniffed, not bothering to reply. Miss Smith persisted gently, but Sissy's answers became more and more monosyllabic.

Then our dinners arrived and all our attention was taken by the steak-and-kidney pudding, a great soft suet mound stuffed with choice meat and oozing with gravy. There were potatoes too, and carrots and peas, a big plateful.

I waited cautiously in case Miss Smith wanted to say grace, but Sissy simply sat, stunned.

'You may begin, girls,' said Miss Smith.

I picked up my knife and fork and Sissy copied me, though she held the knife in her left hand and the fork in her right. I did not like to tell her in case I embarrassed her. She struggled with her cutlery but still managed to eat with gusto. I was surprised to see the inroads she'd made on her pudding almost immediately. Then I realized she'd transferred half of it to the napkin on her lap. I guessed she wanted to take it home for Lil. I hoped it wouldn't ooze gravy too soggily.

'Now, Hetty, it's your turn to sing for your supper,' said Miss Smith. 'Tell me about your life. How did you come to be a flower-seller? What did you do before that? Start right from the beginning.'

Sissy looked anxious, but I smiled serenely. I felt Miss Smith had been short-changed by Sissy, who hadn't provided her with any telling details for her *Penny for a Posy* story. I decided to do my best. I could not tell the truth of course, and relate my *own* story. I could picture a much more colourful tale.

'I was born in the country, but my dear mother died when I was born,' I began. 'Father went to pieces and started drinking. It wasn't so bad when he came home merry, but he could get into fearsome tempers sometimes and we all trembled in our beds.'

Sissy stared at me, astonished that I was appropriating *her* father. I carried on determinedly, picturing for all I was worth, inventing a cruel stepmother who sent me off to work in a loathsome factory when I was only eight, and a grasping landlord who cast us out into the streets. I told of two evil women, Miss Peters and Miss Bottomly, gin-soaked old harridans, who harassed us most dreadfully. To give my story a little variety I had a magical episode when I joined a circus and performed nightly in a magnificent equestrian act.

I continued this alternative life history throughout my steak-and-kidney pudding, and talked non-stop through a plum tart and custard, and then a cup of real coffee and a little dish of chocolates.

Sissy stayed silent and open-mouthed, only fidgeting when I told Miss Smith the prices of flowers and my favourite Covent Garden supplier, because I was clearly getting a few of my facts wrong. I was not deterred, however. So long as I spoke fluently, filling in many little details, I was absolutely certain I was convincing.

Miss Smith seemed to think so anyway. She took copious notes in her black notebook.

'There!' I said eventually, feeling that I had certainly earned our splendid dinner. 'Will you put some of my story in your book, Miss Smith?'

'I am very tempted,' she said, closing her notebook

and smiling at me. 'However, I think *you* should write your story, Hetty. You are far more inventive than I am. I rather suspect your story is pure fiction from beginning to end, but twice as interesting for that very reason.'

I blinked at her. 'What – what do you mean?' I said.

'She means she knows you're telling whopping great lies, Hetty,' said Sissy, standing up. She had her napkin of suet pudding carefully tucked under her shawl. She reached for her flower basket. 'Come on, little 'un. Time to scarper.'

'No, wait, Sissy! I haven't paid you for your time,' said Miss Smith. She fumbled in her reticule and brought out two silver half-crowns and a little card.

'This card has my name and an address on it. It is an office off The Strand where we are setting up a rescue society for young girls on the street. If you show anyone the address, they will be able to direct you there. You will always be sure of a warm welcome – and if you ever find yourself in need of new accommodation or an alternative occupation, we will do our best to help you. Now off you go, my dear. Thank you so very much for taking care of Hetty, but she is in my charge now. I will take her back to the Foundling Hospital.'

I stared at her. How did she *know*? I hadn't

breathed a word to her about the hospital. I looked at Sissy. 'You didn't tell her, did you?'

'Of course I didn't,' said Sissy. She looked at Miss Smith. 'She can't go back there, miss. They're dreadful cruel to her there – they whip her and lock her up in attics.'

'Do they, Hetty?' said Miss Smith. 'Answer truthfully now.'

'They will quite *definitely* lock me up if you take me back there now!' I said.

'We will see about that,' said Miss Smith. 'Don't worry about Hetty, Sissy. I promise I will make sure she's all right. You have clearly been very kind to her and looked after her well, but I don't think she could survive on the streets without you.'

'I'll say!' said Sissy. She pocketed Miss Smith's coins, eyes gleaming at the thought of what they could buy in the way of treats for Lil.

'Take the card too, please. And do not hesitate to use it,' said Miss Smith.

'Thank you kindly, miss.' Sissy took the card and then lugged her flower basket off the floor. 'Have a posy, do. And you truly won't be too hard on Hetty? She was only romancing. She tells lovely stories – she can't seem to help it.'

She handed Miss Smith her biggest bunch of roses, gave me a quick peck on the cheek, and then lumbered out of the restaurant with her basket, taking care to bump into the supercilious waiter on her way out.

I could not bear to see her go. I got up to run after her, but Miss Smith had hold of me.

'No, Hetty.'

I started crying. 'Poor Sissy truly does have a dreadful father, and they don't have enough food, and there's a little sister, Lil, but she is very ill and I think she is dying,' I wept. 'I swear I'm not picturing now, Miss Smith.'

'I know. Sissy seems a brave, resilient girl, but she certainly has a very hard life. But tell me, Hetty, do you really want that life for yourself? You know you don't belong on the streets.'

'Perhaps that's true – but I *don't* want to belong to the hospital,' I said. 'I still don't understand how you knew I came from there.'

'Your distinctive name has been on many people's lips since your disappearance on the trip to Hyde Park. You have even been mentioned in the newspapers,' said Miss Smith.

'Really!' I said, rather thrilled. 'But how did you know *I* was Hetty the foundling when you saw me selling flowers?'

'Oh, come now! The foundling uniform is very distinctive, even without your cap and tippet. And, oh dear, what happened to your boots?'

'Two horrid boys stole them.'

'There, you see, you're not safe to be on the streets. You need to be properly cared for in the hospital.'

'They *don't* care for me there,' I sniffed. 'You don't know what it's *like*, Miss Smith.'

'Yes I do. At least, I have an outsider's view. I used to visit on Sundays with my brother, Peter, though I always felt uncomfortable staring at all of you while you ate your Sunday dinners.'

I stared at her: her pale, serious face, her plain charcoal-grey dress. I remembered Harriet's beloved, the man with the tie-pin in the shape of a P . . .

'Oh, I remember you now!'

'Yes, and I remember you, the cross little red-haired girl with the big friend who fluttered her eyelashes at my foolish fop of a brother,' said Miss Smith, laughing. 'Don't look abashed, Hetty. I think you had every right to be sulky in those particular circumstances. But I *am* concerned that you hate the hospital so. I have recently been invited onto the board of governors because of my rescue work with children and my books for the Religious Tract society. I thought the Foundling Hospital an excellent institution in most respects. The children all seem well-nourished and healthy, their food is fresh and simple, and I'm particularly impressed that everyone receives a decent education and proper training.'

'But all the girls are trained to be *servants*,' I said.

'There is nothing wrong with being a skilled servant, Hetty,' said Miss Smith, shaking her head at me.

I sniffed again, lolling back in my chair. '*You* wouldn't care to be a servant, Miss Smith,' I said impatiently.

'I agree I would sooner be a writer,' she said. 'But I wasn't joking when I said that *you* could be a writer too, Hetty Feather. You have a very vivid imagination and a gift with words. Your invented life history was immensely entertaining.'

'But you didn't believe me.'

'I think if your story was down on paper, you might write with true conviction.'

'Do you think I could really have one of my stories published in a *book*?'

'Not yet a while. I can't quite promise you that, Hetty. We will have to see. You will have to work hard, practising your art. Try writing for at least half an hour each day. I *can* promise I will keep in touch with you and do my best to help you.'

'But I have to go back to the hospital?'

'You do indeed.'

'Matron Bottomly will be so very angry with me,' I said.

'I dare say – but I will do my best to protect you.'

382

Miss Smith gave me a most unladylike wink. 'I am a governor now, Hetty. Your Matron Bottomly has to answer to me.'

Miss Smith gave the money for our sumptuous meal to the waiter, who had been hovering for quite a while. I saw how much money it was.

'My goodness, writers must earn a great deal, Miss Smith!' I said with keen interest.

'Do not get too excited, Hetty. Many writers earn a pittance, or cannot sell their work at all. You might well have to earn your keep as a servant while you hone your craft.'

'I shall start honing for all I am worth,' I said. 'If Ida is still talking to me, I shall beg her for a whole stack of kitchen paper and start writing my story straight away.'

'Ida?'

'She works in the kitchen and has been my dear friend ever since I arrived at the hospital. But I have *not* been a dear friend to her. I don't think she will like me any more now.'

'I am sure she will, Hetty, but just in case, it might be prudent to make a little purchase before we take you back to the hospital,' said Miss Smith.

She took me by the hand and let me up Regent Street and along a little arcade. She stopped outside a stationer's shop. There were wondrous marbled notebooks in the window, patterned with swirling combinations of colour, some sky-blue and purple and pearly pink; some silver and emerald and jade; some scarlet and vivid orange and gold.

'Oh!' I exclaimed, looking at them in awe. I ran my finger over the glass window, following the flow of the design. 'I know the pattern is abstract, but does that swirling shape remind you of anything?'

'It looks like feathers, Hetty,' said Miss Smith. 'How felicitous! You must select one of the notebooks – and perhaps you need a pen?'

'I have an excellent quill pen given to me by my long-lost friend, Polly. Oh, Miss Smith, might I have my very own bottle of ink?' I asked.

We went inside the stationer's and I deliberated deliciously over each and every notebook. Perhaps the purple was the prettiest, the shades of green the most pleasing to the eye – but I chose the notebook with scarlet and orange swirls picked out in gold, because it was as bright as the hair on my head.

The stationer parcelled it up in a special canvas satchel, with a bottle of black ink in its own little leather pouch for safe-keeping. Miss Smith and I had only been acquainted for a matter of hours, but I threw my arms about her and kissed her pale cheek.

She hailed a hansom cab and asked the driver to take us to the Foundling Hospital. I clutched my wondrous present and tried to feel brave – but when we drew up outside the great gates of the hospital, I was trembling.

'Courage, Hetty,' said Miss Smith.

The gatekeeper boggled as we climbed out of the cab. 'Oh my Lord, it's the missing child!' he exclaimed.

'Indeed it is,' said Miss Smith. 'Come along, Hetty dear. Let us seek out Matron Bottomly and tell her your sad tale. Now, Hetty, quick, give me a very brief and *truthful* resumé of the last two days.'

I told her about going to see the wrong circus in Hyde Park, and my omnibus journey to Hampstead Heath, and my encounter with Madame Adeline, and my night under the bush, and my begging in the street, and my ride on the elephant in the Zoological Gardens, and my alarming encounter with the weird gentleman, and my rescue by dear Sissy and subsequent night in her room in the condemned house. I kept it utterly concise, with no picturing whatsoever, but we had to take three turns of the grounds before my tale was fully told.

'My goodness, Hetty, you've certainly had your fair share of adventures. My poor fictional heroines lead very dull lives by comparison!' said Miss Smith.

'Matron Bottomly will be so angry. She will lock me up in the punishment attic for a week,' I said fearfully.

'Wait and see, child,' said Miss Smith. 'Come now, let us confront her.'

We went in through the girls' entrance. The infant foundlings were all filing off to the privies after their darning session. They stopped and stared at me, clutching each other.

'Oh, wonders!' Nurse Winnie cried, dashing up to us. 'It's Hetty Feather back from the dead! Oh, Hetty, God be praised, you're safe!' She seized hold of me and whirled me round, then gave me a kiss on both cheeks.

'There, Hetty! Now tell me, is she one of the cruel nurses who beat you?' said Miss Smith as we proceeded along the corridor towards Matron Bottomly's room.

'Nurse Winnie is a darling,' I admitted. 'But wait till you meet Matron. *She* will not be thankful I am back from the dead. She will very likely *wish* me dead. And buried. And burning to a crisp in H-e-l-l.'

Miss Smith knocked on Matron Bottomly's door and pulled me inside. Matron Bottomly's head jerked up at the sight of me. Her mouth opened comically. She took in my ragged, unkempt state, my missing cap and tippet and apron, my filthy bare feet. She took a deep breath.

'Hetty Feather!' she said. 'I knew *you* would be the child to bring disgrace to the Foundling Hospital!

If you only knew the trouble you've caused! We have never had a child run away before.'

'Oh no, you are very much mistaken!' said Miss Smith quickly. 'Do let me introduce myself, Matron. I am Sarah Smith, newly elected to your board of governors – and very happily I rescued Hetty myself. She did *not* run away, I assure you. She was captured by a band of brigands at the funfair at Hyde Park. They chloroformed the poor child and kept her trussed up in an attic, ready to be shipped overseas.'

Miss Smith leaned forward and hissed dramatically, 'The white slave trade! But I happened to be in the area reporting on slum dwellings and I heard her desperate screams. I rescued her and she begged me to take her back to the hospital. I hope no long-term harm has been done to her – but I fear her confinement will prey on her mind. She must never be confined in a locked room again, her nerves would never stand it.'

It was my turn to marvel at Miss Smith's picturing. I practically applauded when she insisted I must not be locked up! I'm not sure how much Matron Bottomly truly believed – but Miss Smith was a governor and she could not accuse her of lying.

'I feel Hetty Feather is a child of enormous creative potential. I have given her a notebook in which to write. I shall come and visit her regularly and examine her work,' said Miss Smith. 'I am sure I can rely on you, Matron Bottomly, to make sure Hetty is not parted from her notebook. I know you have her welfare at heart.'

Oh, glorious and devious Miss Smith! Matron Bottomly still hates the very sight of me, but she allows me to write write write in this notebook! She has *not* locked me in the punishment attic – though I'm sure she was sorely tempted when Madame Adeline paid a visit to the Foundling Hospital to make sure I'd returned safely!

I have been writing my own story this past year. Miss Smith has been writing too. *A Penny for a Posy* has already been published. I have my own copy, dedicated thus: *To Hetty and Sissy – and in memory of Lil*. Miss Smith tracked them down and paid for a doctor to attend poor little Lil, but sadly he could not help her. However, Miss Smith's rescue organization has found Sissy decent lodgings away from her father, and she is now being trained as a milliner, making neat nosegays for bonnets, so her story ends happily too.

This is *my* story and I promise it is not a work of fiction. I have tried hard not to exaggerate or embroider too much. Miss Smith says very complimentary things about my writing, but says

I have a tendency to be too fanciful. But sometimes the truth is stranger and more wondrous than fiction. I have kept the very best part till last. *I have found my mother!*

I wonder if you have guessed who she is?

I had a very thorough bath the day I returned to the hospital and was given a brand-new uniform and new boots too. I walked into the dining room for supper and a general hubbub broke out, with girls clapping and crying, because everyone had been convinced I'd disappeared for ever. Even Sheila and Monica clasped me close! Little Eliza was beside herself, leaping up at me like a little monkey, her arms about my neck.

However, it was Ida who reacted most dramatically. She took one look at me, turned white as a sheet, and fainted dead away. She had to be carried bodily out of the dining room by two nurses and taken to her room. Her shoe fell off as she was dragged away. I snatched it up and cradled the ugly black brogue as if it was Cinderella's glass slipper.

'I must return Ida's shoe,' I mumbled to a nurse, and fled from the dining room, even though I had not had my supper.

I followed the nurses and poor Ida through the kitchens and down a long corridor to the cramped servants' quarters. Ida's room was as small as the punishment attic and almost as bare. The nurses laid her down on her truckle bed. Ida murmured my name.

'Yes, yes, Hetty Feather's here. She has scared us all but she has turned up like a bad penny,' said one nurse.

'Fancy you taking on so, Ida! You've a kind heart,' said the other nurse. 'There now, you'd better rest. Come along, Hetty, leave Ida to recover.'

'Mayn't I stay for five minutes, just to make sure she doesn't swoon again,' I begged. 'I was so very mean to Ida and I feel so bad about it now. *Please* let me tell her how sorry I am.'

The nurses laughed at me, but let me stay.

'Oh, dear Ida, please be all right,' I whispered.

I smoothed the hair off her forehead and stroked her temple. Her eyes opened. They looked very raw and bloodshot.

'Oh, Ida, your eyes look so sore,' I said, concerned. 'Have you been crying?'

'Of course I've been crying!' Ida said. 'I've been fair demented these last two days. I've been out searching the streets both nights trying to find you. I thought I'd truly lost you and I couldn't bear it. I feared you'd run away because you thought I favoured Sheila, when I was simply making a fuss of her to spite you.'

'And no wonder! I was so horrid to you. Please

390

forgive me, dearest Ida. You mean the whole world to me,' I declared.

Fresh tears welled in her poor eyes.

'Oh, Ida, don't!' I said, and I hugged her hard, burying my head in her bony shoulder.

Her hands reached up and she wound her fingers in my red hair. 'My little Hetty – my own child,' she murmured.

I raised my head. 'What did you say?' I whispered.

Ida wiped her tears with her fingers, keeping her face covered with her hands. 'Nothing, nothing,' she said.

I took hold of her hands and gently pulled them away so I could see her properly. I looked deep into her eyes and saw the truth. 'You are my *mother*?' I whispered.

'Hush, Hetty, hush! No one must ever know!'

'But . . . but . . .' I saw the strands of our hair side by side on the pillow, Ida's light-brown locks and my fiery red ones.

'Your father has red hair,' Ida whispered.

I clasped her hands. 'Tell me!' I begged.

'His name's Robert – but everyone always called him Bobbie. He was the brightest boy in our village and I loved him with all my heart, though he did not truly care for me. He left to go to sea and voyage round the world.'

'And where is he now, my father?'

'I truly do not know, Hetty. He never came back. He swore he'd write to me but he never did. I waited and waited for him to return – because I realized I was having his baby.'

'Me!'

'Yes, you, Hetty!' Her arms went round me, holding me tightly. 'I did not know what to do. I didn't tell a soul but soon I became so big that people started to notice. My parents could not stand the shame and turned me out.'

'Oh, Ida!'

'I was so lonely, so frightened. I didn't know what to do,' she said, clinging to me. 'I gave birth to you all alone, and you were so terrifyingly tiny, but, oh, so precious. I held you close in my arms all day long and felt I could never ever let you go. But I had no way of supporting us. I did not dare farm you out to some woman while I worked. You were so small and sickly, I knew you would not thrive unless you were cared for most particularly. So I decided it would be best if I took you to the Foundling Hospital.'

'I *wish* you could have kept me, Ida.'

'I wished it too. It was an agony to give you up. I missed you so badly. I nearly lost my mind with wretchedness. I ended up in the workhouse, changing my name so that no one should ever know. It was very hard there, but I did my best to bear it.

Eventually the mistress helped me find a position as a kitchen maid. I worked in that post for a year, but when I knew you were due back from your foster home I applied for work at the hospital. It was my only way of being near you, Hetty. I could never earn enough to buy you back, and the governors would not deem me a fit mother anyway.'

'You are the most fit mother in the world, and the only one I could ever want,' I said fervently.

'It's been such a secret joy these past five years watching you grow, but a torment too, unable to give you a true mother's love. I resolved never to tell you. If anyone found out, I would be sent away in disgrace.'

'Oh, Ida, I will keep our secret, I swear,' I promised. 'But could you tell me just one thing more. Did you give me a name when I was born?'

'I called you a fancy pet name, Sapphire, because your eyes were so blue.'

'Oh my Lord, I pictured that! I *knew* my real mother would have chosen a beautiful name for me! Listen, Ida, I hope to be a writer one day and have my stories published – and then I shall use Sapphire as my pen name. You're not laughing at me, are you?'

'No, my darling, I'm crying because I'm so happy.'

'We will leave the hospital together when I'm

old enough, and my stories will earn lots of money, and I'll find us a fine house, and we will live there together, mother and daughter, just you wait and see.'

'Happily ever after, like the fairy stories,' said Ida, still weeping.

'Happily ever after,' I declared. 'I am absolutely certain!'

Many real children experienced childhoods similar to Hetty's, growing up in the Foundling Hospital. Thomas Coram started this 'Hospital for the Maintenance and Education of Exposed and Deserted Children' in 1739.

This was the first special children's charity in the UK, and over two and a half centuries it rescued more than 27,000 abandoned babies. It continues today simply known as Coram, helping children who are alone or at risk, marginalized at school or without a real home. You can find out more about Coram by visiting **www.coram.org.uk** or see for yourself what life was like for children like Hetty by visiting its Foundling Museum in London and at **www.foundlingmuseum.org.uk**.

Turn over for an exclusive extract from
Jacqueline Wilson's wonderful new novel,
SAPPHIRE BATTERSEA,
out now!

My name is Sapphire Battersea. Doesn't that sound beautiful? I write it over and over again on the covers of this private notebook. I stitch a secret S.B. inside the neck of my uniform. I stir a swirly S.B. into the soup when I am helping the cook. I scrub a soapy S.B. when I am cleaning the floor. I whisper my own name in bed at night in the freezing dormitory, and my breath rises and forms the letters in the dark.

I am Sapphire Battersea, but nobody calls me by my real name, not even my dear mother. Mama chose to call me Sapphire because my eyes were so blue when I was born. But even she calls me Hetty now.

'I'm *not* Hetty. It's such a stupid name. It's just a hateful foundling label. I *hate* the way

1

they change all our names, making them up randomly. They don't sound like real names. Hetty Feather! It's ridiculous.'

'You could have had worse,' said Mama. 'Just think, you could have been Grizel Grump.'

Poor Grizel is a girl in little Eliza's year at the Foundling Hospital. Everyone calls her Gristle, and consequently she is always a grump, like her name.

'Sapphire is so elegant, so romantic. It's a perfect name for a writer,' I said, signing it in the air with a flourish.

'Let us hope you become one, then,' said Mama, a little tartly.

'You wait and see. I will publish my memoirs and make our fortune. Miss Smith will help me. My story will be turned into a proper book with gold lettering and a fancy picture on the front, just like all her own Sarah Smith stories published by the Religious Tract.'

'I'm not sure *your* stories would be suitable for a religious press, Hetty,' said Mama, laughing.

2

'*Sapphire!* Why won't you call me by my true name – the one you chose for me?"

'I suppose Hetty has become a habit, dearie,' said Mama, tweaking my red plait.

'I always call you Mama when we're alone,' I said, a little hurt.

'Yes, but I wish you wouldn't. It's tempting fate. One slip in front of the others and we're done for,' said Mama, and she pulled me close.

'I will never slip, Mama,' I swore fervently. 'No one will ever find out that you are my real mother.'

I hadn't known myself for the first ten long years of my life. Poor Mama had been forced to give me to the Foundling Hospital when I was a little baby because she had no means of supporting me. I was soon fostered out to the country. I lived with a kind family. I loved my foster mother and father and all my foster siblings. I especially adored my foster brother Jem.

I had hero-worshipped him. I treasured the silver sixpence he'd given me when I was taken off to the Foundling Hospital at five.

3

He promised he'd wait for me and marry me one day. I was so little and stupid I actually believed him – until young Eliza arrived at the hospital from the same foster home five years later. She prattled away about *her* dear Jem. I found out that he'd made exactly the same empty promises to her. I couldn't forgive him. I decided to put him out of my mind for ever.

I had found the rigid life of the hospital horribly hard. Some of the nurses were kind, but the two matrons were excessively cruel. I suffered from the attentions of Matron Pigface Peters when I was small, and of Matron Stinking Bottomly when I went into the Seniors. They each went out of their way to punish and humiliate me. I hated them both.

I found it difficult to make friends with the other girls too. I made downright enemies of Sheila and Monica. When Polly came to the hospital, we were like soul mates, but she was adopted by rich folk and we never saw each other again.

My only true friend was Ida, the kitchen

maid. I ran away from the hospital on Queen Victoria's Golden Jubilee – and when I came back, Ida was so overwhelmed that she called me her own child when she hugged me. I could scarcely believe it! Ida was my true birth mother. She had skivvied and slaved at the Foundling Hospital for years just so that she could get a glimpse of me every day. She'd slip me an extra potato at dinner, or sprinkle secret sugar on my breakfast porridge. She'd always had a smile or a kind word, and helped me to blossom in that bleak institutional world.

When I became aware of the wondrous truth of our relationship, my whole life changed. I cannot say I became an exemplary foundling. Whether I am Sapphire or Hetty, I still have a temper that lives up to my flaming red hair. But whenever Matron Stinking Bottomly slapped me for impertinence and forced me to scrub the whole length of the hall, I knew Mama was nearby, watching and waiting, burning with sympathy. She'd catch my eye across the crowded dining room at mealtimes, and I'd feel calmed.

Sometimes, when everyone slept in the dormitories, I dared creep right out of the door, along the shadowy landing, down, down, down the great stairs, through kitchens that still smelled of stewed mutton and rice pudding, along the winding corridor to Mama's own tiny bedroom. I'd push open the door and she'd leap up from her bed and hug me hard. We'd sit together and whisper well into the night. Sometimes we'd lie close together on Mama's narrow bed, clasping each other close. I'd trace her dear face in the dark and she'd wind my long plaits around her own neck. We'd feel utterly united, making up for all those many years we'd lived apart.

But then – oh, I can hardly bear to write it. It was all because of Sheila. She was always a light sleeper. She must have woken when I crept through the long dormitory. She didn't call out. She lay there, waiting, and then slid stealthily out of her bed, intent on following me, the sly cat. She was so furtive and silent on her bare feet that I didn't hear her padding behind me. I didn't notice the creak of the stairs as she followed me down to the ground floor.

She stole along behind me all the way to Mama's room. I wonder how long she waited outside, her ear to the door? She suddenly burst in upon us, as Mama and I cuddled close in a fond embrace, clearly visible in the flickering candlelight.

'Whatever are you *doing*, Hetty Feather!' she exclaimed. 'Why are you lying there with *Ida*?'

'Go away! Get out! Get out of Mama's room!' I cried in a furious passion.

'*Mama's* room?' said Sheila.

'It is just Hetty's little game,' Mama said quickly, giving me a shake.

But Sheila was no fool. 'You are Hetty's *mother*?' she said.

'No! Like Ida said, it's just my silly game,' I declared, springing off the bed.

Sheila was still staring, open-mouthed. 'Yes, now I see it!' She darted between us, staring rudely. 'You two *are* alike. You're both so small and slight – and you both have blue eyes. Oh my goodness, how extraordinary!

Have you known all this time, Hetty? I'd never have thought you could keep such a secret so long,' she said.

It was no use denying it further.

'It's the most private, precious secret! If you dare breathe a word of this to anyone, I'll tear out your tattle-tale tongue and feed it to the pigs,' I said.

'Temper temper!' said Sheila, eyes gleaming. 'So, what will you do for me to keep me sweet and silent?'

'This isn't a schoolgirl game, Sheila,' said Mama, getting out of bed and gripping her by the shoulders. 'I haven't lived this life year after year to have it carelessly destroyed by a spiteful girl. You *mustn't* tell a soul. If those matrons find out, then we're done for. Swear that you'll keep silent!'

'I won't say a word to anyone, I promise,' said Sheila, but her eyes were still bright. I feared she'd tell Monica the moment she was back in the dormitory.

I'll never know how much she'd have told and whether she'd have deliberately betrayed Mama and me. We were discovered anyway. Mama and I were used to whispering, but Sheila had a high clear voice that travelled far. By terrible chance Matron Pigface Peters had shuffled down to the kitchen, seeking out a midnight snack from the pantry. She heard Sheila repeating, 'Just fancy Ida being your real mother, Hetty!'

Matron Pigface barged her way into Mama's crowded bedroom, a hideous sight in her nightcap and ruffled gown, her greasy hair coiling in true pigs' tails about her cheeks. She stared at Mama, at Sheila, at me.

'Repeat what you said just now, Sheila Mayhew!' she commanded.

'I – I don't remember what I said,' Sheila stammered.

'The girls were playing a silly game, Matron. I was about to scold them and send them back to their dormitory,' Mama said.

'Don't lie to me, Ida Battersea!' She was squinting at her now, then peering at me. 'Can this really be *true*? Are you Hetty Feather's mother?'

'How could I be?' said Mama. 'It's a game, I told you, an idle fancy, because the girls all long for their mothers.'

Matron Pigface Peters dragged me over to the candle, clutching my chin, turning my face this way and that. Then she went to grab hold of Mama.

'Don't you dare touch me! And take your hands off that child too – look, you're hurting her!'

'It's the truth that hurts, Ida Battersea! I see the likeness now! How could you have been so devious? You've been deceiving us for years and years! You were supposed to give up your ill-gotten child for ever – not work here with her, glorying in your disgraceful situation. Have you two been secretly communing all this time? It beggars belief! How *dare* you both deceive us like this!'

'It wasn't Hetty's fault, Matron. She didn't know – not for ever so long. I meant no harm. I just wanted a glimpse of her every day – that was enough,' said Mama, starting to sob. 'When she disappeared on the day of the Jubilee, I could hardly contain myself. I worried fit to burst. When she came back at last, I was so relieved I fainted dead away.'

'Oh yes, I remember that!' said Sheila. 'We all thought you'd died on the spot! So did you tell Hetty then?"

'Hold your tongue, Sheila Mayhew! This is nothing to do with you. Go back to the dormitory this instant. You are to keep utterly silent on this shameful matter,' said Matron Pigface.

'It's not shameful to love your own child!' I said furiously. 'Mama's done nothing wrong.'

'We'll see if the Board of Governors agrees with you! It's my opinion they'll take a very grave view of this deception. I would prepare yourself for instant dismissal, Ida Battersea – with no character reference, so don't expect to get another job in any decent God-fearing establishment. You're morally corrupt and an evil influence on all our girls.'

'How dare you threaten Mama like that!' I cried. 'You wait, Matron Peters! My friend and benefactress Miss Sarah Smith is on the Board of Governors. She will never send my own mama away. *You* will be the one who's sent away, because you're cruel and wicked, and you have no heart at all inside your big fat chest!'

She dragged me away, shouting and screaming. I did not even have time to kiss Mama and say goodbye. I struggled hard, but Matron Pigface slapped me about the head and picked me up bodily. Half the girls from the dormitory were clustered on the stairs, gawping at me.

'Go back to your beds this instant!' Matron Pigface shrieked, and they scuttled away.

She carried on dragging me up another flight of stairs.

'No! No, please don't put me in the punishment room!' I screamed. 'I can't stand it there, you know I can't!'

'You deserve to stay locked up in there for ever!' said Matron Pigface, thrusting me into the terrifying dark cupboard.

'No, please, I beg you! Don't lock me in! Please, I haven't done anything *wrong*!'

'You're the most evil child I've ever come across. You have no shame, show no respect! You act as if you're as good as anyone else.

Just remember you're a common foundling, born in sin, without a father. I wouldn't be surprised if you were the spawn of the Devil himself,' she panted, and she locked the door on me.

It was the longest, most agonizing night of my life. I hit the door and walls until my knuckles were bloody – and then I cast myself down on the floor and wept. I called again and again for Mama, but she didn't come. I was frightened they'd locked her up too.

When one of the nurses let me out in the morning, I pushed right past her and ran all the way downstairs to Mama's room . . . but she wasn't there! Her cap and apron and print dresses were gone from the pegs on her wall, her brush and comb and her cake of soap and her flannel were gone from her washstand, her little violet-patterned vase and her lavender heart were gone from her chest. The very pillowcase and sheets had been stripped from her bed, leaving a bare black-and-white striped mattress. There was no trace left of Mama. It was as if she had never existed.

ABOUT THE ILLUSTRATOR

NICK SHARRATT has written and illustrated
many books for children and won numerous awards
for his picture books, including the Children's
Book Award and the Educational Writers' Award.
He has also enjoyed great success illustrating
Jacqueline Wilson's books.

CHECK OUT JACQUELINE WILSON'S BRILLIANT WEBSITE!

Did you know there's a whole Jacqueline Wilson town to explore? There's lots of fun stuff, including games, amazing competitions and exclusive news. You can generate a special username, customize your online bedroom, test your knowledge of Jacqueline's books with exciting quizzes and upload book reviews! And if you like writing, make sure you visit the special storytelling area.

Plus, you can find out about the latest news from Jacqueline in her monthly diary, chat to other fans on the message boards and find out whether she's doing an event near you!

Join in today at
www.jacquelinewilson.co.uk

Jacqueline has written many wonderful
stories inspired by the Victorian era –
have you read them all?

HAVE YOU READ THEM ALL?

LAUGH OUT LOUD
THE STORY OF TRACY BEAKER
I DARE YOU, TRACY BEAKER
STARRING TRACY BEAKER
THE WORST THING ABOUT MY SISTER
DOUBLE ACT
FOUR CHILDREN AND IT
THE BED AND BREAKFAST STAR

HISTORICAL HEROES
HETTY FEATHER
HETTY FEATHER'S CHRISTMAS
SAPPHIRE BATTERSEA
EMERALD STAR
DIAMOND
LITTLE STARS
CLOVER MOON
ROSE RIVERS
WAVE ME GOODBYE
OPAL PLUMSTEAD
QUEENIE

LIFE LESSONS
THE BUTTERFLY CLUB
THE SUITCASE KID
KATY
BAD GIRLS
LITTLE DARLINGS
CLEAN BREAK
RENT A BRIDESMAID
CANDYFLOSS
THE LOTTIE PROJECT